THE RETURN OF DR. FU-MANCHU

By
Sax Rohmer

The Return Of Dr. Fu-Manchu
by Sax Rohmer

Copyright © 2022

All Rights reserved.
No part of this publication may be reproduced, stored in a retrieval system, or transmitted in any form or by any means, electronic, mechanical, photocopying or Otherwise, without the written permission of the publisher.

The author/editor asserts the moral right to be identified as the author/editor of this work.

ISBN: 978-93-56566-34-7

Published by
DOUBLE 9 BOOKS
2/13-B, Ansari Road
Daryaganj, New Delhi – 110002
info@double9books.com
www.double9books.com
Tel. 011-40042856

This book is under public domain

Printed in India.

ABOUT THE AUTHOR

Sax Rohmer was born on Feb. 15, 1883, in Birmingham, England, to William Ward and Margaret Mary. He was an internationally famous British writer who created the evil Chinese criminal Fu Manchu, the hero-villain of various books. The character Fu Manchu later appeared in films, radio, and TV. From childhood, Rohmer was fascinated by ancient Egypt, the Middle East, and witchcraft. Later on, working in brief in the financial district of London and as a Journalist, his developing interest in East Asia creates him more into fiction writing. He started using the middle name Sarsfield as a teenager and published his first stories under the name A. Sarsfield Ward. He began to publish only as Sax Rohmer in 1912, and he in the end utilised this name professionally.

CONTENTS

CHAPTER I.
A MIDNIGHT SUMMONS 7

CHAPTER II.
ELTHAM VANISHES 15

CHAPTER III.
THE WIRE JACKET..20

CHAPTER IV.
THE CRY OF A NIGHTHAWK..29

CHAPTER V.
THE NET..34

CHAPTER VI.
UNDER THE ELMS 45

CHAPTER VII.
ENTER MR. ABEL SLATTIN 51

CHAPTER VIII.
DR. FU-MANCHU STRIKES 55

CHAPTER IX.
THE CLIMBER..65

CHAPTER X.
THE CLIMBER RETURNS...69

CHAPTER XI.
THE WHITE PEACOCK..75

CHAPTER XII.
DARK EYES LOOKED INTO MINE..83

CHAPTER XIII.
THE SACRED ORDER 90

CHAPTER XIV.
THE COUGHING HORROR...99

CHAPTER XV.
BEWITCHMENT.. 107

CHAPTER XVI.
THE QUESTING HANDS.. 114

CHAPTER XVII.
ONE DAY IN RANGOON 120
CHAPTER XVIII.
THE SILVER BUDDHA 126
CHAPTER XIX.
DR. FU-MANCHU'S LABORATORY 129
CHAPTER XX.
THE CROSS BAR 134
CHAPTER XXI.
CRAGMIRE TOWER 144
CHAPTER XXII.
THE MULATTO 150
CHAPTER XXIII.
A CRY ON THE MOOR 161
CHAPTER XXIV.
STORY OF THE GABLES 168
CHAPTER XXV.
THE BELLS 175
CHAPTER XXVI.
THE FIERY HAND 180
CHAPTER XXVII.
THE NIGHT OF THE RAID 188
CHAPTER XXVIII.
THE SAMURAI'S SWORD 193
CHAPTER XXIX.
THE SIX GATES 202
CHAPTER XXX.
THE CALL OF THE EAST 206
CHAPTER XXXI.
"MY SHADOW LIES UPON YOU" 209
CHAPTER XXXII.
THE TRAGEDY 215
CHAPTER XXXIII.
THE MUMMY 221

CHAPTER I.

A MIDNIGHT SUMMONS

"When did you last hear from Nayland Smith?" asked my visitor.

I paused, my hand on the syphon, reflecting for a moment.

"Two months ago," I said; "he's a poor correspondent and rather soured, I fancy."

"What—a woman or something?"

"Some affair of that sort. He's such a reticent beggar, I really know very little about it."

I placed a whisky and soda before the Rev. J. D. Eltham, also sliding the tobacco jar nearer to his hand. The refined and sensitive face of the clergy-man offered no indication of the truculent character of the man. His scanty fair hair, already gray over the temples, was silken and soft-looking; in appearance he was indeed a typical English churchman; but in China he had been known as "the fighting missionary," and had fully deserved the title. In fact, this peaceful-looking gentleman had directly brought about the Boxer Risings!

"You know," he said, in his clerical voice, but meanwhile stuffing tobacco into an old pipe with fierce energy, "I have often wondered, Petrie—I have never left off wondering—"

"What?"

"That accursed Chinaman! Since the cellar place beneath the site of the burnt-out cottage in Dulwich Village—I have wondered more than ever."

He lighted his pipe and walked to the hearth to throw the match in the grate.

"You see," he continued, peering across at me in his oddly nervous way, "one never knows, does one? If I thought that Dr. Fu-Manchu lived; if I seriously suspected that that stupendous intellect, that wonderful genius, Petrie, er—" he hesitated characteristically—"survived, I should feel it my duty—"

"Well?" I said, leaning my elbows on the table and smiling slightly.

"If that Satanic genius were not indeed destroyed, then the peace of the world, may be threatened anew at any moment!"

He was becoming excited, shooting out his jaw in the truculent manner I knew, and snapping his fingers to emphasize his words; a man composed of the oddest complexities that ever dwelt beneath a clerical frock.

"He may have got back to China, Doctor!" he cried, and his eyes had the fighting glint in them. "Could you rest in peace if you thought that he lived? Should you not fear for your life every time that a night-call took you out alone? Why, man alive, it is only two years since he was here among us, since we were searching every shadow for those awful green eyes! What became of his band of assassins—his stranglers, his dacoits, his damnable poisons and insects and what-not—the army of creatures—"

He paused, taking a drink.

"You—" he hesitated diffidently—"searched in Egypt with Nayland Smith, did you not?"

I nodded.

"Contradict me if I am wrong," he continued; "but my impression is that you were searching for the girl—the girl—Karamaneh, I think she was called?"

"Yes," I replied shortly; "but we could find no trace—no trace."

"You—er—were interested?"

"More than I knew," I replied, "until I realized that I had—lost her."

"I never met Karamaneh, but from your account, and from others, she was quite unusually—"

"She was very beautiful," I said, and stood up, for I was anxious to terminate that phase of the conversation.

Eltham regarded me sympathetically; he knew something of my search with Nayland Smith for the dark-eyed, Eastern girl who had brought romance into my drab life; he knew that I treasured my memories of her as I loathed and abhorred those of the fiendish, brilliant Chinese doctor who had been her master.

Eltham began to pace up and down the rug, his pipe bubbling furiously; and something in the way he carried his head reminded me momentarily of Nayland Smith. Certainly, between this pink-faced clergyman, with his deceptively mild appearance, and the gaunt, bronzed, and steely-eyed Burmese commissioner, there was externally little in common; but it was some little nervous trick in his carriage that conjured up through the smoky haze one distant summer evening when Smith had paced that very room as Eltham paced it now, when before my startled eyes he had rung up the curtain upon the savage drama in which, though I little suspected it then, Fate had cast me for a leading role.

I wondered if Eltham's thoughts ran parallel with mine. My own were centered upon the unforgettable figure of the murderous Chinaman. These words, exactly as Smith had used them, seemed once again to sound in my ears: "Imagine a person tall, lean, and feline, high shouldered, with a brow like Shakespeare and a face like Satan, a close-shaven skull, and long magnetic eyes of the true cat green. Invest him with all the cruel cunning of an entire Eastern race accumulated in one giant intellect, with all the resources of science, past and present, and you have a mental picture of Dr. Fu-Manchu, the 'Yellow Peril' incarnate in one man."

This visit of Eltham's no doubt was responsible for my mood; for this singular clergyman had played his part in the drama of two years ago.

"I should like to see Smith again," he said suddenly; "it seems a pity that a man like that should be buried in Burma. Burma makes a mess of the best of men, Doctor. You said he was not married?"

"No," I replied shortly, "and is never likely to be, now."

"Ah, you hinted at something of the kind."

"I know very little of it. Nayland Smith is not the kind of man to talk much."

"Quite so—quite so! And, you know, Doctor, neither am I; but"—he was growing painfully embarrassed—"it may be your due—I—er—I have a correspondent, in the interior of China—"

"Well?" I said, watching him in sudden eagerness.

"Well, I would not desire to raise—vain hopes—nor to occasion, shall I say, empty fears; but—er... no, Doctor!" He flushed like a girl—"It was wrong of me to open this conversation. Perhaps, when I know more—will you forget my words, for the time?"

The telephone bell rang.

"Hullo!" cried Eltham—"hard luck, Doctor!"—but I could see that he welcomed the interruption. "Why!" he added, "it is one o'clock!"

I went to the telephone.

"Is that Dr. Petrie?" inquired a woman's voice.

"Yes; who is speaking?"

"Mrs. Hewett has been taken more seriously ill. Could you come at once?"

"Certainly," I replied, for Mrs. Hewett was not only a profitable patient but an estimable lady—"I shall be with you in a quarter of an hour."

I hung up the receiver.

"Something urgent?" asked Eltham, emptying his pipe.

"Sounds like it. You had better turn in."

"I should much prefer to walk over with you, if it would not be intruding. Our conversation has ill prepared me for sleep."

"Right!" I said; for I welcomed his company; and three minutes later we were striding across the deserted common.

A sort of mist floated amongst the trees, seeming in the moonlight like a veil draped from trunk to trunk, as in silence we passed the Mound pond, and struck out for the north side of the common.

I suppose the presence of Eltham and the irritating recollection of his half-confidence were the responsible factors, but my mind persistently dwelt upon the subject of Fu-Manchu and the atrocities which he had committed during his sojourn in England. So actively was my imagination at work that I felt again the menace which so long had hung over me; I felt as though that murderous yellow cloud still cast its shadow upon England. And I found myself longing for the company of Nayland Smith. I cannot state what was the nature of Eltham's reflections, but I can guess; for he was as silent as I.

It was with a conscious effort that I shook myself out of this morbidly reflective mood, on finding that we had crossed the common and were come to the abode of my patient.

"I shall take a little walk," announced Eltham; "for I gather that you don't expect to be detained long? I shall never be out of sight of the door, of course."

"Very well," I replied, and ran up the steps.

There were no lights to be seen in any of the windows, which circumstance rather surprised me, as my patient occupied, or had occupied when last I had visited her, a first-floor bedroom in the front of the house. My knocking and ringing produced no response for three or four minutes; then, as I persisted, a scantily clothed and half awake maid servant unbarred the door and stared at me stupidly in the moonlight.

"Mrs. Hewett requires me?" I asked abruptly.

The girl stared more stupidly than ever.

"No, sir," she said, "she don't, sir; she's fast asleep!"

"But some one 'phoned me!" I insisted, rather irritably, I fear.

"Not from here, sir," declared the now wide-eyed girl. "We haven't got a telephone, sir."

For a few moments I stood there, staring as foolishly as she; then abruptly I turned and descended the steps. At the gate I stood looking up and down the road. The houses were all in darkness. What could be the meaning of the mysterious summons? I had made no mistake respecting the name of my patient; it had been twice repeated over the telephone; yet that the call had not emanated from Mrs. Hewett's house was now palpably evident. Days had been when I should have regarded the episode as preluding some outrage, but to-night I felt more disposed to ascribe it to a silly practical joke.

Eltham walked up briskly.

"You're in demand to-night, Doctor," he said. "A young person called for you almost directly you had left your house, and, learning where you were gone, followed you."

"Indeed!" I said, a trifle incredulously. "There are plenty of other doctors if the case is an urgent one."

"She may have thought it would save time as you were actually up and dressed," explained Eltham; "and the house is quite near to here, I understand."

I looked at him a little blankly. Was this another effort of the unknown jester?

"I have been fooled once," I said. "That 'phone call was a hoax—"

"But I feel certain," declared Eltham, earnestly, "that this is genuine! The poor girl was dreadfully agitated; her master has broken his leg and is lying helpless: number 280, Rectory Grove."

"Where is the girl?" I asked, sharply.

"She ran back directly she had given me her message."

"Was she a servant?"

"I should imagine so: French, I think. But she was so wrapped up I had little more than a glimpse of her. I am sorry to hear that some one has played a silly joke on you, but believe me—" he was very earnest—"this is no jest. The poor girl could scarcely speak for sobs. She mistook me for you, of course."

"Oh!" said I grimly, "well, I suppose I must go. Broken leg, you said?—and my surgical bag, splints and so forth, are at home!"

"My dear Petrie!" cried Eltham, in his enthusiastic way—"you no doubt can do something to alleviate the poor man's suffering immediately. I will run back to your rooms for the bag and rejoin you at 280, Rectory Grove."

"It's awfully good of you, Eltham—"

He held up his hand.

"The call of suffering humanity, Petrie, is one which I may no more refuse to hear than you."

I made no further protest after that, for his point of view was evident and his determination adamant, but told him where he would find the bag and once more set out across the moonbright common, he pursuing a westerly direction and I going east.

Some three hundred yards I had gone, I suppose, and my brain had been very active the while, when something occurred to me which placed a new complexion upon this second summons. I thought of the falsity of the first, of the improbability of even the most hardened practical joker practising his wiles at one o'clock in the morning. I thought of our recent conversation; above all I thought of the girl who had delivered the message to Eltham, the girl whom he had described as a French maid—whose personal charm had so completely enlisted his sympathies. Now, to this train of thought came a new one, and, adding it, my suspicion became almost a certainty.

I remembered (as, knowing the district, I should have remembered before) that there was no number 280 in Rectory Grove.

Pulling up sharply I stood looking about me. Not a living soul was in sight; not even a policeman. Where the lamps marked the main paths across the common nothing moved; in the shadows about me nothing stirred. But something stirred within me—a warning voice which for long had lain dormant.

What was afoot?

A breeze caressed the leaves overhead, breaking the silence with mysterious whisperings. Some portentous truth was seeking for admittance to my brain. I strove to reassure myself, but the sense of impending evil and of mystery became heavier. At last I could combat my strange fears no longer. I turned and began to run toward the south side of the common—toward my rooms—and after Eltham.

I had hoped to head him off, but came upon no sign of him. An all-night tramcar passed at the moment that I reached the high road, and as I ran around behind it I saw that my windows were lighted and that there was a light in the hall.

My key was yet in the lock when my housekeeper opened the door.

"There's a gentleman just come, Doctor," she began—

I thrust past her and raced up the stairs into my study.

Standing by the writing-table was a tall, thin man, his gaunt face brown as a coffee-berry and his steely gray eyes fixed upon me. My heart gave a great leap—and seemed to stand still.

It was Nayland Smith!

"Smith," I cried. "Smith, old man, by God, I'm glad to see you!"

He wrung my hand hard, looking at me with his searching eyes; but there was little enough of gladness in his face. He was altogether grayer than when last I had seen him—grayer and sterner.

"Where is Eltham?" I asked.

Smith started back as though I had struck him.

"Eltham!" he whispered—"Eltham! is Eltham here?"

"I left him ten minutes ago on the common—"

Smith dashed his right fist into the palm of his left hand and his eyes gleamed almost wildly.

"My God, Petrie!" he said, "am I fated always to come too late?"

My dreadful fears in that instant were confirmed. I seemed to feel my legs totter beneath me.

"Smith, you don't mean—"

"I do, Petrie!" His voice sounded very far away. "Fu-Manchu is here; and Eltham, God help him... is his first victim!"

•••◆•••

CHAPTER II.

ELTHAM VANISHES

Smith went racing down the stairs like a man possessed. Heavy with such a foreboding of calamity as I had not known for two years, I followed him—along the hall and out into the road. The very peace and beauty of the night in some way increased my mental agitation. The sky was lighted almost tropically with such a blaze of stars as I could not recall to have seen since, my futile search concluded, I had left Egypt. The glory of the moonlight yellowed the lamps speckled across the expanse of the common. The night was as still as night can ever be in London. The dimming pulse of a cab or car alone disturbed the stillness.

With a quick glance to right and left, Smith ran across on to the common, and, leaving the door wide open behind me, I followed. The path which Eltham had pursued terminated almost opposite to my house. One's gaze might follow it, white and empty, for several hundred yards past the pond, and further, until it became overshadowed and was lost amid a clump of trees.

I came up with Smith, and side by side we ran on, whilst pantingly, I told my tale.

"It was a trick to get you away from him!" cried Smith. "They meant no doubt to make some attempt at your house, but as he came out with you, an alternative plan—"

Abreast of the pond, my companion slowed down, and finally stopped.

"Where did you last see Eltham?" he asked rapidly.

I took his arm, turning him slightly to the right, and pointed across the moonbathed common.

"You see that clump of bushes on the other side of the road?" I said. "There's a path to the left of it. I took that path and he took this. We parted at the point where they meet—"

Smith walked right down to the edge of the water and peered about over the surface.

What he hoped to find there I could not imagine. Whatever it had been he was disappointed, and he turned to me again, frowning perplexedly, and tugging at the lobe of his left ear, an old trick which reminded me of gruesome things we had lived through in the past.

"Come on," he jerked. "It may be amongst the trees."

From the tone of his voice I knew that he was tensed up nervously, and his mood but added to the apprehension of my own.

"What may be amongst the trees, Smith?" I asked.

He walked on.

"God knows, Petrie; but I fear—"

Behind us, along the highroad, a tramcar went rocking by, doubtless bearing a few belated workers homeward. The stark incongruity of the thing was appalling. How little those weary toilers, hemmed about with the commonplace, suspected that almost within sight from the car windows, in a place of prosy benches, iron railings, and unromantic, flickering lamps, two fellow men moved upon the border of a horror-land!

Beneath the trees a shadow carpet lay, its edges tropically sharp; and fully ten yards from the first of the group, we two, hatless both, and sharing a common dread, paused for a moment and listened.

The car had stopped at the further extremity of the common, and now with a moan that grew to a shriek was rolling on its way again. We stood and listened until silence reclaimed the night. Not a footstep could be heard. Then slowly we walked on. At the edge of the little coppice we stopped again abruptly.

Smith turned and thrust his pistol into my hand. A white ray of light pierced the shadows; my companion carried an electric torch. But no trace of Eltham was discoverable.

There had been a heavy shower of rain during the evening just before sunset, and although the open paths were dry again, under the trees the ground was still moist. Ten yards within the coppice we came upon tracks—the tracks of one running, as the deep imprints of the toes indicated.

Abruptly the tracks terminated; others, softer, joined them, two sets converging from left and right. There was a confused patch, trailing off to the west; then this became indistinct, and was finally lost upon the hard ground outside the group.

For perhaps a minute, or more, we ran about from tree to tree, and from bush to bush, searching like hounds for a scent, and fearful of what we might find. We found nothing; and fully in the moonlight we stood facing one another. The night was profoundly still.

Nayland Smith stepped back into the shadows, and began slowly to turn his head from left to right, taking in the entire visible expanse of the common. Toward a point where the road bisected it he stared intently. Then, with a bound, he set off.

"Come on, Petrie!" he cried. "There they are!"

Vaulting a railing he went away over a field like a madman. Recovering from the shock of surprise, I followed him, but he was well ahead of me, and making for some vaguely seen object moving against the lights of the roadway.

Another railing was vaulted, and the corner of a second, triangular grass patch crossed at a hot sprint. We were twenty yards from the road when the sound of a starting motor broke the silence. We gained the graveled footpath only to see the taillight of the car dwindling to the north!

Smith leaned dizzily against a tree.

"Eltham is in that car!" he gasped. "Just God! are we to stand here and see him taken away to—"

He beat his fist upon the tree, in a sort of tragic despair. The nearest cab-rank was no great distance away, but, excluding the possibility of no cab being there, it might, for all practical purposes, as well have been a mile off.

The beat of the retreating motor was scarcely audible; the lights might but just be distinguished. Then, coming in an opposite direction, appeared the headlamp of another car, of a car that raced nearer and nearer to us, so that, within a few seconds of its first appearance, we found ourselves bathed in the beam of its headlights.

Smith bounded out into the road, and stood, a weird silhouette, with upraised arms, fully in its course!

The brakes were applied hurriedly. It was a big limousine, and its driver swerved perilously in avoiding Smith and nearly ran into me. But, the breathless moment past, the car was pulled up, head on to the railings; and a man in evening clothes was demanding excitedly what had happened. Smith, a hatless, disheveled figure, stepped up to the door.

"My name is Nayland Smith," he said rapidly—"Burmese Commissioner." He snatched a letter from his pocket and thrust it into the hands of the bewildered man. "Read that. It is signed by another Commissioner—the Commissioner of Police."

With amazement written all over him, the other obeyed.

"You see," continued my friend, tersely—"it is carte blanche. I wish to commandeer your car, sir, on a matter of life and death!".

The other returned the letter.

"Allow me to offer it!" he said, descending. "My man will take your orders. I can finish my journey by cab. I am—"

But Smith did not wait to learn whom he might be.

"Quick!" he cried to the stupefied chauffeur—"You passed a car a minute ago—yonder. Can you overtake it?"

"I can try, sir, if I don't lose her track."

Smith leaped in, pulling me after him.

"Do it!" he snapped. "There are no speed limits for me. Thanks! Goodnight, sir!"

We were off! The car swung around and the chase commenced.

One last glimpse I had of the man we had dispossessed, standing alone by the roadside, and at ever increasing speed, we leaped away in the track of Eltham's captors.

Smith was too highly excited for ordinary conversation, but he threw out short, staccato remarks.

"I have followed Fu-Manchu from Hongkong," he jerked. "Lost him at Suez. He got here a boat ahead of me. Eltham has been corresponding with some mandarin up-country. Knew that. Came straight to you. Only got in this evening. He—Fu-Manchu—has been sent here to get Eltham. My God! and he has him! He will question him! The interior of China—a seething pot, Petrie! They had to stop the leakage of information. He is here for that."

The car pulled up with a jerk that pitched me out of my seat, and the chauffeur leaped to the road and ran ahead. Smith was out in a trice, as the man, who had run up to a constable, came racing back.

"Jump in, sir—jump in!" he cried, his eyes bright with the lust of the chase; "they are making for Battersea!"

And we were off again.

Through the empty streets we roared on. A place of gasometers and desolate waste lots slipped behind and we were in a narrow way where gates of yards and a few lowly houses faced upon a prospect of high blank wall.

"Thames on our right," said Smith, peering ahead. "His rathole is by the river as usual. Hi!"—he grabbed up the speaking-tube—"Stop! Stop!"

The limousine swung in to the narrow sidewalk, and pulled up close by a yard gate. I, too, had seen our quarry—a long, low bodied car, showing no inside lights. It had turned the next corner, where a street lamp shone greenly, not a hundred yards ahead.

Smith leaped out, and I followed him.

"That must be a cul de sac," he said, and turned to the eager-eyed chauffeur. "Run back to that last turning," he ordered, "and wait there, out of sight. Bring the car up when you hear a police-whistle."

The man looked disappointed, but did not question the order. As he began to back away, Smith grasped me by the arm and drew me forward.

"We must get to that corner," he said, "and see where the car stands, without showing ourselves."

◆

CHAPTER III.

THE WIRE JACKET

I suppose we were not more than a dozen paces from the lamp when we heard the thudding of the motor. The car was backing out!

It was a desperate moment, for it seemed that we could not fail to be discovered. Nayland Smith began to look about him, feverishly, for a hiding-place, a quest in which I seconded with equal anxiety. And Fate was kind to us—doubly kind as after events revealed. A wooden gate broke the expanse of wall hard by upon the right, and, as the result of some recent accident, a ragged gap had been torn in the panels close to the top.

The chain of the padlock hung loosely; and in a second Smith was up, with his foot in this as in a stirrup. He threw his arm over the top and drew himself upright. A second later he was astride the broken gate.

"Up you come, Petrie!" he said, and reached down his hand to aid me.

I got my foot into the loop of chain, grasped at a projection in the gatepost and found myself up.

"There is a crossbar on this side to stand on," said Smith.

He climbed over and vanished in the darkness. I was still astride the broken gate when the car turned the corner, slowly, for there was scanty room; but I was standing upon the bar on the inside and had my head below the gap ere the driver could possibly have seen me.

"Stay where you are until he passes," hissed my companion, below. "There is a row of kegs under you."

The sound of the motor passing outside grew loud—louder—then began to die away. I felt about with my left foot; discerned the top of a keg, and dropped, panting, beside Smith.

"Phew!" I said—"that was a close thing! Smith—how do we know—"

"That we have followed the right car?" he interrupted. "Ask yourself the question: what would any ordinary man be doing motoring in a place like this at two o'clock in the morning?"

"You are right, Smith," I agreed. "Shall we get out again?"

"Not yet. I have an idea. Look yonder."

He grasped my arm, turning me in the desired direction.

Beyond a great expanse of unbroken darkness a ray of moonlight slanted into the place wherein we stood, spilling its cold radiance upon rows of kegs.

"That's another door," continued my friend—I now began dimly to perceive him beside me. "If my calculations are not entirely wrong, it opens on a wharf gate—"

A steam siren hooted dismally, apparently from quite close at hand.

"I'm right!" snapped Smith. "That turning leads down to the gate. Come on, Petrie!"

He directed the light of the electric torch upon a narrow path through the ranks of casks, and led the way to the further door. A good two feet of moonlight showed along the top. I heard Smith straining; then—

"These kegs are all loaded with grease!" he said, "and I want to reconnoiter over that door."

"I am leaning on a crate which seems easy to move," I reported. "Yes, it's empty. Lend a hand."

We grasped the empty crate, and between us, set it up on a solid pedestal of casks. Then Smith mounted to this observation platform and I scrambled up beside him, and looked down upon the lane outside.

THE RETURN OF DR. FU-MANCHU

It terminated as Smith had foreseen at a wharf gate some six feet to the right of our post. Piled up in the lane beneath us, against the warehouse door, was a stack of empty casks. Beyond, over the way, was a kind of ramshackle building that had possibly been a dwelling-house at some time. Bills were stuck in the ground-floor window indicating that the three floors were to let as offices; so much was discernible in that reflected moonlight.

I could hear the tide, lapping upon the wharf, could feel the chill from the river and hear the vague noises which, night nor day, never cease upon the great commercial waterway.

"Down!" whispered Smith. "Make no noise! I suspected it. They heard the car following!"

I obeyed, clutching at him for support; for I was suddenly dizzy, and my heart was leaping wildly—furiously.

"You saw her?" he whispered.

Saw her! yes, I had seen her! And my poor dream-world was toppling about me, its cities, ashes and its fairness, dust.

Peering from the window, her great eyes wondrous in the moonlight and her red lips parted, hair gleaming like burnished foam and her anxious gaze set upon the corner of the lane—was Karamaneh... Karamaneh whom once we had rescued from the house of this fiendish Chinese doctor; Karamaneh who had been our ally; in fruitless quest of whom,—when, too late, I realized how empty my life was become—I had wasted what little of the world's goods I possessed;—Karamaneh!

"Poor old Petrie," murmured Smith—"I knew, but I hadn't the heart—He has her again—God knows by what chains he holds her. But she's only a woman, old boy, and women are very much alike—very much alike from Charing Cross to Pagoda Road."

He rested his hand on my shoulder for a moment; I am ashamed to confess that I was trembling; then, clenching my teeth with that mechanical physical effort which often accompanies a mental one, I swallowed the bitter draught of Nayland Smith's philosophy. He was raising himself, to peer, cautiously, over the top of the door. I did likewise.

The window from which the girl had looked was nearly on a level with our eyes, and as I raised my head above the woodwork, I quite distinctly saw her go out of the room. The door, as she opened it, admitted a dull light, against which her figure showed silhouetted for a moment. Then the door was reclosed.

"We must risk the other windows," rapped Smith.

Before I had grasped the nature of his plan he was over and had dropped almost noiselessly upon the casks outside. Again I followed his lead.

"You are not going to attempt anything, singlehanded—against him?" I asked.

"Petrie—Eltham is in that house. He has been brought here to be put to the question, in the medieval, and Chinese, sense! Is there time to summon assistance?"

I shuddered. This had been in my mind, certainly, but so expressed it was definitely horrible—revolting, yet stimulating.

"You have the pistol," added Smith—"follow closely, and quietly."

He walked across the tops of the casks and leaped down, pointing to that nearest to the closed door of the house. I helped him place it under the open window. A second we set beside it, and, not without some noise, got a third on top.

Smith mounted.

His jaw muscles were very prominent and his eyes shone like steel; but he was as cool as though he were about to enter a theater and not the den of the most stupendous genius who ever worked for evil. I would forgive any man who, knowing Dr. Fu-Manchu, feared him; I feared him myself—feared him as one fears a scorpion; but when Nayland Smith hauled himself up on the wooden ledge above the door and swung thence into the darkened room, I followed and was in close upon his heels. But I admired him, for he had every ampere of his self-possession in hand; my own case was different.

He spoke close to my ear.

"Is your hand steady? We may have to shoot."

I thought of Karamaneh, of lovely dark-eyed Karamaneh whom this wonderful, evil product of secret China had stolen from me—for so I now adjudged it.

"Rely upon me!" I said grimly. "I..."

The words ceased—frozen on my tongue.

There are things that one seeks to forget, but it is my lot often to remember the sound which at that moment literally struck me rigid with horror. Yet it was only a groan; but, merciful God! I pray that it may never be my lot to listen to such a groan again.

Smith drew a sibilant breath.

"It's Eltham!" he whispered hoarsely—"they're torturing—"

"No, no!" screamed a woman's voice—a voice that thrilled me anew, but with another emotion—

"Not that, not—"

I distinctly heard the sound of a blow. Followed a sort of vague scuffling. A door somewhere at the back of the house opened—and shut again. Some one was coming along the passage toward us!

"Stand back!" Smith's voice was low, but perfectly steady. "Leave it to me!"

Nearer came the footsteps and nearer. I could hear suppressed sobs. The door opened, admitting again the faint light—and Karamaneh came in. The place was quite unfurnished, offering no possibility of hiding; but to hide was unnecessary.

Her slim figure had not crossed the threshold ere Smith had his arm about the girl's waist and one hand clapped to her mouth. A stifled gasp she uttered, and he lifted her into the room.

I stepped forward and closed the door. A faint perfume stole to my nostrils—a vague, elusive breath of the East, reminiscent of strange days that, now, seemed to belong to a remote past. Karamaneh! that faint, indefinable perfume was part of her dainty personality; it may appear absurd—impossible—but many and many a time I had dreamt of it.

"In my breast pocket," rapped Smith; "the light."

I bent over the girl as he held her. She was quite still, but I could have wished that I had had more certain mastery of myself. I took the torch from Smith's pocket, and, mechanically, directed it upon the captive.

She was dressed very plainly, wearing a simple blue skirt, and white blouse. It was easy to divine that it was she whom Eltham had mistaken for a French maid. A brooch set with a ruby was pinned at the point where the blouse opened—gleaming fierily and harshly against the soft skin. Her face was pale and her eyes wide with fear.

"There is some cord in my right-hand pocket," said Smith; "I came provided. Tie her wrists."

I obeyed him, silently. The girl offered no resistance, but I think I never essayed a less congenial task than that of binding her white wrists. The jeweled fingers lay quite listlessly in my own.

"Make a good job of it!" rapped Smith, significantly.

A flush rose to my cheeks, for I knew well enough what he meant.

"She is fastened," I said, and I turned the ray of the torch upon her again.

Smith removed his hand from her mouth but did not relax his grip of her. She looked up at me with eyes in which I could have sworn there was no recognition. But a flush momentarily swept over her face, and left it pale again.

"We shall have to—gag her—"

"Smith, I can't do it!"

The girl's eyes filled with tears and she looked up at my companion pitifully.

"Please don't be cruel to me," she whispered, with that soft accent which always played havoc with my composure. "Every one—every one-is cruel to me. I will promise—indeed I will swear, to be quiet. Oh, believe me, if you can save him I will do nothing to hinder you." Her beautiful head drooped. "Have some pity for me as well."

"Karamaneh" I said. "We would have believed you once. We cannot, now."

She started violently.

"You know my name!" Her voice was barely audible. "Yet I have never seen you in my life—"

"See if the door locks," interrupted Smith harshly.

Dazed by the apparent sincerity in the voice of our lovely captive—vacant from wonder of it all—I opened the door, felt for, and found, a key.

We left Karamaneh crouching against the wall; her great eyes were turned towards me fascinatedly. Smith locked the door with much care. We began a tip-toed progress along the dimly lighted passage.

From beneath a door on the left, and near the end, a brighter light shone. Beyond that again was another door. A voice was speaking in the lighted room; yet I could have sworn that Karamaneh had come, not from there but from the room beyond—from the far end of the passage.

But the voice!—who, having once heard it, could ever mistake that singular voice, alternately guttural and sibilant!

Dr. Fu-Manchu was speaking!

"I have asked you," came with ever-increasing clearness (Smith had begun to turn the knob), "to reveal to me the name of your correspondent in Nan-Yang. I have suggested that he may be the Mandarin Yen-Sun-Yat, but you have declined to confirm me. Yet I know" (Smith had the door open a good three inches and was peering in) "that some official, some high official, is a traitor. Am I to resort again to the question to learn his name?"

Ice seemed to enter my veins at the unseen inquisitor's intonation of the words "the question." This was the Twentieth Century, yet there, in that damnable room...

Smith threw the door open.

Through a sort of haze, born mostly of horror, but not entirely, I saw Eltham, stripped to the waist and tied, with his arms upstretched, to a rafter in the ancient ceiling. A Chinaman who wore a slop-shop blue suit and who held an open knife in his hand, stood beside him. Eltham was ghastly white. The appearance of his chest puzzled me momentarily, then I realized that a sort of tourniquet of wire-netting was screwed so tightly about him that the flesh swelled out in knobs through the mesh. There was blood—

"God in heaven!" screamed Smith frenziedly—"they have the wire-jacket on him! Shoot down that damned Chinaman, Petrie! Shoot! Shoot!"

Lithely as a cat the man with the knife leaped around—but I raised the Browning, and deliberately—with a cool deliberation that came to me suddenly—shot him through the head. I saw his oblique eyes turn up to the whites; I saw the mark squarely between his brows; and with no word nor cry he sank to his knees and toppled forward with one yellow hand beneath him and one outstretched, clutching—clutching—convulsively. His pigtail came unfastened and began to uncoil, slowly, like a snake.

I handed the pistol to Smith; I was perfectly cool, now; and I leaped forward, took up the bloody knife from the floor and cut Eltham's lashings. He sank into my arms.

"Praise God," he murmured, weakly. "He is more merciful to me than perhaps I deserve. Unscrew... the jacket, Petrie... I think ... I was very near to.... weakening. Praise the good God, Who... gave me... fortitude..."

I got the screw of the accursed thing loosened, but the act of removing the jacket was too agonizing for Eltham—man of iron though he was. I laid him swooning on the floor.

"Where is Fu-Manchu?"

Nayland Smith, from just within the door, threw out the query in a tone of stark amaze. I stood up—I could do nothing more for the poor victim at the moment—and looked about me. The room was innocent of furniture, save for heaps of rubbish on the floor, and a tin oil-lamp hung, on the wall. The dead Chinaman lay close beside Smith. There was no second door, the one window was barred, and from this room we had heard the voice, the unmistakable, unforgettable voice, of Dr. Fu-Manchu.

But Dr. Fu-Manchu was not there!

Neither of us could accept the fact for a moment; we stood there, looking from the dead man to the tortured man who only swooned, in a state of helpless incredulity.

Then the explanation flashed upon us both, simultaneously, and with a cry of baffled rage Smith leaped along the passage to the second door. It was wide open. I stood at his elbow when he swept its emptiness with the ray of his pocket-lamp.

There was a speaking-tube fixed between the two rooms!

Smith literally ground his teeth.

"Yet, Petrie," he said, "we have learnt something. Fu-Manchu had evidently promised Eltham his life if he would divulge the name of his correspondent. He meant to keep his word; it is a sidelight on his character."

"How so?"

"Eltham has never seen Dr. Fu-Manchu, but Eltham knows certain parts of China better than you know the Strand. Probably, if he saw Fu-Manchu, he would recognize him for who he really is, and this, it seems, the Doctor is anxious to avoid."

We ran back to where we had left Karamaneh.

The room was empty!

"Defeated, Petrie!" said Smith, bitterly. "The Yellow Devil is loosed on London again!"

He leaned from the window and the skirl of a police whistle split the stillness of the night.

•••◆•••

CHAPTER IV.

THE CRY OF A NIGHTHAWK

Such were the episodes that marked the coming of Dr. Fu-Manchu to London, that awakened fears long dormant and reopened old wounds—nay, poured poison into them. I strove desperately, by close attention to my professional duties, to banish the very memory of Karamaneh from my mind; desperately, but how vainly! Peace was for me no more, joy was gone from the world, and only mockery remained as my portion.

Poor Eltham we had placed in a nursing establishment, where his indescribable hurts could be properly tended: and his uncomplaining fortitude not infrequently made me thoroughly ashamed of myself. Needless to say, Smith had made such other arrangements as were necessary to safeguard the injured man, and these proved so successful that the malignant being whose plans they thwarted abandoned his designs upon the heroic clergyman and directed his attention elsewhere, as I must now proceed to relate.

Dusk always brought with it a cloud of apprehensions, for darkness must ever be the ally of crime; and it was one night, long after the clocks had struck the mystic hour "when churchyards yawn," that the hand of Dr. Fu-Manchu again stretched out to grasp a victim. I was dismissing a chance patient.

"Good night, Dr. Petrie," he said.

"Good night, Mr. Forsyth," I replied; and, having conducted my late visitor to the door, I closed and bolted it, switched off the light and went upstairs.

My patient was chief officer of one of the P. and O. boats. He had cut his hand rather badly on the homeward run, and signs of poisoning having developed, had called to have the wound treated, apologizing for troubling me at so late an hour, but explaining that he had only just come from the docks. The hall clock announced the hour of one as I ascended the stairs. I found myself wondering what there was in Mr. Forsyth's appearance which excited some vague and elusive memory. Coming to the top floor, I opened the door of a front bedroom and was surprised to find the interior in darkness.

"Smith!" I called.

"Come here and watch!" was the terse response. Nayland Smith was sitting in the dark at the open window and peering out across the common. Even as I saw him, a dim silhouette, I could detect that tensity in his attitude which told of high-strung nerves.

I joined him.

"What is it?" I said, curiously.

"I don't know. Watch that clump of elms."

His masterful voice had the dry tone in it betokening excitement. I leaned on the ledge beside him and looked out. The blaze of stars almost compensated for the absence of the moon and the night had a quality of stillness that made for awe. This was a tropical summer, and the common, with its dancing lights dotted irregularly about it, had an unfamiliar look to-night. The clump of nine elms showed as a dense and irregular mass, lacking detail.

Such moods as that which now claimed my friend are magnetic. I had no thought of the night's beauty, for it only served to remind me that somewhere amid London's millions was lurking an uncanny being, whose life was a mystery, whose very existence was a scientific miracle.

"Where's your patient?" rapped Smith.

His abrupt query diverted my thoughts into a new channel. No footstep disturbed the silence of the highroad; where was my patient?

I craned from the window. Smith grabbed my arm.

"Don't lean out," he said.

I drew back, glancing at him surprisedly.

"For Heaven's sake, why not?"

"I'll tell you presently, Petrie. Did you see him?"

"I did, and I can't make out what he is doing. He seems to have remained standing at the gate for some reason."

"He has seen it!" snapped Smith. "Watch those elms."

His hand remained upon my arm, gripping it nervously. Shall I say that I was surprised? I can say it with truth. But I shall add that I was thrilled, eerily; for this subdued excitement and alert watching of Smith could only mean one thing:

Fu-Manchu!

And that was enough to set me watching as keenly as he; to set me listening; not only for sounds outside the house but for sounds within. Doubts, suspicions, dreads, heaped themselves up in my mind. Why was Forsyth standing there at the gate? I had never seen him before, to my knowledge, yet there was something oddly reminiscent about the man. Could it be that his visit formed part of a plot? Yet his wound had been genuine enough. Thus my mind worked, feverishly; such was the effect of an unspoken thought—Fu-Manchu.

Nayland Smith's grip tightened on my arm.

"There it is again, Petrie!" he whispered.

"Look, look!"

His words were wholly unnecessary. I, too, had seen it; a wonderful and uncanny sight. Out of the darkness under the elms, low down upon the ground, grew a vaporous blue light. It flared up, elfinish, then began to ascend. Like an igneous phantom, a witch flame, it rose, high—higher—higher, to what I adjudged to be some twelve feet or more from the ground. Then, high in the air, it died away again as it had come!

"For God's sake, Smith, what was it?"

"Don't ask me, Petrie. I have seen it twice. We—"

He paused. Rapid footsteps sounded below. Over Smith's shoulder I saw Forsyth cross the road, climb the low rail, and set out across the common.

Smith sprang impetuously to his feet.

"We must stop him!" he said hoarsely; then, clapping a hand to my mouth as I was about to call out—"Not a sound, Petrie!"

He ran out of the room and went blundering downstairs in the dark, crying:

"Out through the garden—the side entrance!"

I overtook him as he threw wide the door of my dispensing room. Through it he ran and opened the door at the other end. I followed him out, closing it behind me. The smell from some tobacco plants in a neighboring flower-bed was faintly perceptible; no breeze stirred; and in the great silence I could hear Smith, in front of me, tugging at the bolt of the gate.

Then he had it open, and I stepped out, close on his heels, and left the door ajar.

"We must not appear to have come from your house," explained Smith rapidly. "I will go along the highroad and cross to the common a hundred yards up, where there is a pathway, as though homeward bound to the north side. Give me half a minute's start, then you proceed in an opposite direction and cross from the corner of the next road. Directly you are out of the light of the street lamps, get over the rails and run for the elms!"

He thrust a pistol into my hand and was off.

While he had been with me, speaking in that incisive, impetuous way of his, with his dark face close to mine, and his eyes gleaming like steel, I had been at one with him in his feverish mood, but now, when I stood alone, in that staid and respectable byway, holding a loaded pistol in my hand, the whole thing became utterly unreal.

It was in an odd frame of mind that I walked to the next corner, as directed; for I was thinking, not of Dr. Fu-Manchu, the great and evil man who dreamed of Europe and America under Chinese rule, not of Nayland Smith, who alone stood between the Chinaman and the realization of his monstrous schemes, not even of Karamaneh the slave girl, whose glorious beauty was a weapon of might in Fu-Manchu's hand, but of what impression I must have made upon a patient had I encountered one then.

Such were my ideas up to the moment that I crossed to the common and vaulted into the field on my right. As I began to run toward the elms I found myself wondering what it was all about, and for what we were come. Fifty yards west of the trees it occurred to me that if Smith had counted on cutting Forsyth off we were too late, for it appeared to me that he must already be in the coppice.

I was right. Twenty paces more I ran, and ahead of me, from the elms, came a sound. Clearly it came through the still air—the eerie hoot of a nighthawk. I could not recall ever to have heard the cry of that bird on the common before, but oddly enough I attached little significance to it until, in the ensuing instant, a most dreadful scream—a scream in which fear, and loathing, and anger were hideously blended—thrilled me with horror.

After that I have no recollection of anything until I found myself standing by the southernmost elm.

"Smith!" I cried breathlessly. "Smith! my God! where are you?"

As if in answer to my cry came an indescribable sound, a mingled sobbing and choking. Out from the shadows staggered a ghastly figure—that of a man whose face appeared to be streaked. His eyes glared at me madly and he mowed the air with his hands like one blind and insane with fear.

I started back; words died upon my tongue. The figure reeled and the man fell babbling and sobbing at my very feet.

Inert I stood, looking down at him. He writhed a moment—and was still. The silence again became perfect. Then, from somewhere beyond the elms, Nayland Smith appeared. I did not move. Even when he stood beside me, I merely stared at him fatuously.

"I let him walk to his death, Petrie," I heard dimly. "God forgive me—God forgive me!"

The words aroused me.

"Smith"—my voice came as a whisper—"for one awful moment I thought—"

"So did some one else," he rapped. "Our poor sailor has met the end designed for me, Petrie!"

At that I realized two things: I knew why Forsyth's face had struck me as being familiar in some puzzling way, and I knew why Forsyth now lay dead upon the grass. Save that he was a fair man and wore a slight mustache, he was, in features and build, the double of Nayland Smith!

CHAPTER V.

THE NET

We raised the poor victim and turned him over on his back. I dropped upon my knees, and with unsteady fingers began to strike a match. A slight breeze was arising and sighing gently through the elms, but, screened by my hands, the flame of the match took life. It illuminated wanly the sun-baked face of Nayland Smith, his eyes gleaming with unnatural brightness. I bent forward, and the dying light of the match touched that other face.

"Oh, God!" whispered Smith.

A faint puff of wind extinguished the match.

In all my surgical experience I had never met with anything quite so horrible. Forsyth's livid face was streaked with tiny streams of blood, which proceeded from a series of irregular wounds. One group of these clustered upon his left temple, another beneath his right eye, and others extended from the chin down to the throat. They were black, almost like tattoo marks, and the entire injured surface was bloated indescribably. His fists were clenched; he was quite rigid.

Smith's piercing eyes were set upon me eloquently as I knelt on the path and made my examination—an examination which that first glimpse when Forsyth came staggering out from the trees had rendered useless—a mere matter of form.

"He's quite dead, Smith," I said huskily. "It's—unnatural—it—"

Smith began beating his fist into his left palm and taking little, short, nervous strides up and down beside the dead man. I could hear a car humming along the highroad, but I remained there on my knees staring dully at the disfigured bloody face which but a matter of minutes since had been that of a clean looking British seaman. I found myself contrasting his neat, squarely trimmed mustache with the bloated face above it, and counting the little drops of blood which trembled upon its edge. There were footsteps approaching. I stood up. The footsteps quickened; and I turned as a constable ran up.

"What's this?" he demanded gruffly, and stood with his fists clenched, looking from Smith to me and down at that which lay between us. Then his hand flew to his breast; there was a silvern gleam and—

"Drop that whistle!" snapped Smith—and struck it from the man's hand. "Where's your lantern? Don't ask questions!"

The constable started back and was evidently debating upon his chances with the two of us, when my friend pulled a letter from his pocket and thrust it under the man's nose.

"Read that!" he directed harshly, "and then listen to my orders."

There was something in his voice which changed the officer's opinion of the situation. He directed the light of his lantern upon the open letter and seemed to be stricken with wonder.

"If you have any doubts," continued Smith—"you may not be familiar with the Commissioner's signature—you have only to ring up Scotland Yard from Dr. Petrie's house, to which we shall now return, to disperse them." He pointed to Forsyth. "Help us to carry him there. We must not be seen; this must be hushed up. You understand? It must not get into the press—"

The man saluted respectfully; and the three of us addressed ourselves to the mournful task. By slow stages we bore the dead man to the edge of the common, carried him across the road and into my house, without exciting attention even on the part of those vagrants who nightly slept out in the neighborhood.

We laid our burden upon the surgery table.

"You will want to make an examination, Petrie," said Smith in his decisive way, "and the officer here might 'phone for the ambulance. I have some investigations to make also. I must have the pocket lamp."

He raced upstairs to his room, and an instant later came running down again. The front door banged.

"The telephone is in the hall," I said to the constable.

"Thank you, sir."

He went out of the surgery as I switched on the lamp over the table and began to examine the marks upon Forsyth's skin. These, as I have said, were in groups and nearly all in the form of elongated punctures; a fairly deep incision with a pear-shaped and superficial scratch beneath it. One of the tiny wounds had penetrated the right eye.

The symptoms, or those which I had been enabled to observe as Forsyth had first staggered into view from among the elms, were most puzzling. Clearly enough, the muscles of articulation and the respiratory muscles had been affected; and now the livid face, dotted over with tiny wounds (they were also on the throat), set me mentally groping for a clue to the manner of his death.

No clue presented itself; and my detailed examination of the body availed me nothing. The gray herald of dawn was come when the police arrived with the ambulance and took Forsyth away.

I was just taking my cap from the rack when Nayland Smith returned.

"Smith!" I cried—"have you found anything?"

He stood there in the gray light of the hallway, tugging at the lobe of his left ear, an old trick of his.

The bronzed face looked very gaunt, I thought, and his eyes were bright with that febrile glitter which once I had disliked, but which I had learned from experience were due to tremendous nervous excitement. At such times he could act with icy coolness and his mental faculties seemed temporarily to acquire an abnormal keenness. He made no direct reply; but—

"Have you any milk?" he jerked abruptly.

So wholly unexpected was the question, that for a moment I failed to grasp it. Then—

"Milk!" I began.

"Exactly, Petrie! If you can find me some milk, I shall be obliged."

I turned to descend to the kitchen, when—

"The remains of the turbot from dinner, Petrie, would also be welcome, and I think I should like a trowel."

I stopped at the stairhead and faced him.

"I cannot suppose that you are joking, Smith," I said, "but—"

He laughed dryly.

"Forgive me, old man," he replied. "I was so preoccupied with my own train of thought that it never occurred to me how absurd my request must have sounded. I will explain my singular tastes later; at the moment, hustle is the watchword."

Evidently he was in earnest, and I ran downstairs accordingly, returning with a garden trowel, a plate of cold fish and a glass of milk.

"Thanks, Petrie," said Smith—"If you would put the milk in a jug—"

I was past wondering, so I simply went and fetched a jug, into which he poured the milk. Then, with the trowel in his pocket, the plate of cold turbot in one hand and the milk jug in the other, he made for the door. He had it open when another idea evidently occurred to him.

"I'll trouble you for the pistol, Petrie."

I handed him the pistol without a word.

"Don't assume that I want to mystify you," he added, "but the presence of any one else might jeopardize my plan. I don't expect to be long."

The cold light of dawn flooded the hallway momentarily; then the door closed again and I went upstairs to my study, watching Nayland Smith as he strode across the common in the early morning mist. He was making for the Nine Elms, but I lost sight of him before he reached them.

I sat there for some time, watching for the first glow of sunrise. A policeman tramped past the house, and, a while later, a belated reveler in evening clothes. That sense of unreality assailed me again. Out there in the gray mists a man who was vested with powers which rendered him a law unto himself, who had the British Government behind him in all that he might choose to do, who had been summoned from Rangoon to London on singular and dangerous business, was employing himself with a plate of cold turbot, a jug of milk, and a trowel!

Away to the right, and just barely visible, a tramcar stopped by the common; then proceeded on its way, coming in a westerly direction. Its lights twinkled yellowly through the grayness, but I was less concerned with the approaching car than with the solitary traveler who had descended from it.

As the car went rocking by below me, I strained my eyes in an endeavor more clearly to discern the figure, which, leaving the highroad, had struck out across the common. It was that of a woman, who seemingly carried a bulky bag or parcel.

One must be a gross materialist to doubt that there are latent powers in man which man, in modern times, neglects, or knows not how to develop. I became suddenly conscious of a burning curiosity respecting this lonely traveler who traveled at an hour so strange. With no definite plan in mind, I went downstairs, took a cap from the rack, and walked briskly out of the house and across the common in a direction which I thought would enable me to head off the woman.

I had slightly miscalculated the distance, as Fate would have it, and with a patch of gorse effectually screening my approach, I came upon her, kneeling on the damp grass and unfastening the bundle which had attracted my attention. I stopped and watched her.

She was dressed in bedraggled fashion in rusty black, wore a common black straw hat and a thick veil; but it seemed to me that the dexterous hands at work untying the bundle were slim and white; and I perceived a pair of hideous cotton gloves lying on the turf beside her. As she threw open the wrappings and lifted out something that looked like a small shrimping net, I stepped around the bush, crossed silently the intervening patch of grass, and stood beside her.

A faint breath of perfume reached me—of a perfume which, like the secret incense of Ancient Egypt, seemed to assail my soul. The glamour of the Orient was in that subtle essence; and I only knew one woman who used it. I bent over the kneeling figure.

"Good morning," I said; "can I assist you in any way?"

She came to her feet like a startled deer, and flung away from me with the lithe movement of some Eastern dancing girl.

Now came the sun, and its heralding rays struck sparks from the jewels upon the white fingers of this woman who wore the garments of a mendicant. My heart gave a great leap. It was with difficulty that I controlled my voice.

"There is no cause for alarm," I added.

She stood watching me; even through the coarse veil I could see how her eyes glittered. I stooped and picked up the net.

"Oh!" The whispered word was scarcely audible, but it was enough; I doubted no longer.

"This is a net for bird snaring," I said. "What strange bird are you seeking—Karamaneh?"

With a passionate gesture Karamaneh snatched off the veil, and with it the ugly black hat. The cloud of wonderful, intractable hair came rumpling about her face, and her glorious eyes blazed out upon me. How beautiful they were, with the dark beauty of an Egyptian night; how often had they looked into mine in dreams!

To labor against a ceaseless yearning for a woman whom one knows, upon evidence that none but a fool might reject, to be worthless—evil; is there any torture to which the soul of man is subject, more pitiless? Yet this was my lot, for what past sins assigned to me I was unable to conjecture; and this was the woman, this lovely slave of a monster, this creature of Dr. Fu-Manchu.

"I suppose you will declare that you do not know me!" I said harshly.

Her lips trembled, but she made no reply.

"It is very convenient to forget, sometimes," I ran on bitterly, then checked myself; for I knew that my words were prompted by a feckless desire to hear her defense, by a fool's hope that it might be an acceptable one.

I looked again at the net contrivance in my hand; it had a strong spring fitted to it and a line attached. Quite obviously it was intended for snaring.

"What were you about to do?" I demanded sharply—but in my heart, poor fool that I was, I found admiration for the exquisite arch of Karamaneh's lips, and reproach because they were so tremulous.

She spoke then.

"Dr. Petrie—"

"Well?"

"You seem to be—angry with me, not so much because of what I do, as because I do not remember you. Yet—"

"Kindly do not revert to the matter," I interrupted. "You have chosen, very conveniently, to forget that once we were friends. Please yourself. But answer my question."

She clasped her hands with a sort of wild abandon.

"Why do you treat me so!" she cried; she had the most fascinating accent imaginable. "Throw me into prison, kill me if you like, for what I have done!" She stamped her foot. "For what I have done! But do not torture me, try to drive me mad with your reproaches—that I forget you! I tell you—again I tell you—that until you came one night, last week, to rescue some one from—" There was the old trick of hesitating before the name of Fu-Manchu—"from him, I had never, never seen you!"

The dark eyes looked into mine, afire with a positive hunger for belief—or so I was sorely tempted to suppose. But the facts were against her.

"Such a declaration is worthless," I said, as coldly as I could. "You are a traitress; you betray those who are mad enough to trust you—"

"I am no traitress!" she blazed at me; her eyes were magnificent.

"This is mere nonsense. You think that it will pay you better to serve Fu-Manchu than to remain true to your friends. Your 'slavery'—for I take it you are posing as a slave again—is evidently not very harsh. You serve Fu-Manchu, lure men to their destruction, and in return he loads you with jewels, lavishes gifts—"

"Ah! so!"

She sprang forward, raising flaming eyes to mine; her lips were slightly parted. With that wild abandon which betrayed the desert blood in her veins, she wrenched open the neck of her bodice and slipped a soft shoulder free of the garment. She twisted around, so that the white skin was but inches removed from me.

"These are some of the gifts that he lavishes upon me!"

I clenched my teeth. Insane thoughts flooded my mind. For that creamy skin was red with the marks of the lash!

She turned, quickly rearranging her dress, and watching me the while. I could not trust myself to speak for a moment, then:

"If I am a stranger to you, as you claim, why do you give me your confidence?" I asked.

"I have known you long enough to trust you!" she said simply, and turned her head aside.

"Then why do you serve this inhuman monster?"

She snapped her fingers oddly, and looked up at me from under her lashes. "Why do you question me if you think that everything I say is a lie?"

It was a lesson in logic—from a woman! I changed the subject.

"Tell me what you came here to do," I demanded.

She pointed to the net in my hands.

"To catch birds; you have said so yourself."

"What bird?"

She shrugged her shoulders.

And now a memory was born within my brain; it was that of the cry of the nighthawk which had harbingered the death of Forsyth! The net was a large and strong one; could it be that some horrible fowl of the air—some creature unknown to Western naturalists—had been released upon the common last night? I thought of the marks upon Forsyth's face and throat; I thought of the profound knowledge of obscure and dreadful things possessed by the Chinaman.

The wrapping, in which the net had been, lay at my feet. I stooped and took out from it a wicker basket. Karamaneh stood watching me and biting her lip, but she made no move to check me. I opened the basket. It contained a large phial, the contents of which possessed a pungent and peculiar smell.

I was utterly mystified.

"You will have to accompany me to my house," I said sternly.

Karamaneh upturned her great eyes to mine. They were wide with fear. She was on the point of speaking when I extended my hand to grasp her. At that, the look of fear was gone and one of rebellion held its place. Ere I had time to realize her purpose, she flung back from me with that wild grace which I had met with in no other woman, turned and ran!

Fatuously, net and basket in hand, I stood looking after her. The idea of pursuit came to me certainly; but I doubted if I could have outrun her. For Karamaneh ran, not like a girl used to town or even country life, but with the lightness and swiftness of a gazelle; ran like the daughter of the desert that she was.

Some two hundred yards she went, stopped, and looked back. It would seem that the sheer joy of physical effort had aroused the devil in her, the devil that must lie latent in every woman with eyes like the eyes of Karamaneh.

In the ever brightening sunlight I could see the lithe figure swaying; no rags imaginable could mask its beauty. I could see the red lips and gleaming teeth. Then—and it was music good to hear, despite its taunt—she laughed defiantly, turned, and ran again!

I resigned myself to defeat; I blush to add, gladly! Some evidences of a world awakening were perceptible about me now. Feathered choirs hailed the new day joyously. Carrying the mysterious contrivance which I had captured from the enemy, I set out in the direction of my house, my mind very busy with conjectures respecting the link between this bird snare and the cry like that of a nighthawk which we had heard at the moment of Forsyth's death.

The path that I had chosen led me around the border of the Mound Pond—a small pool having an islet in the center. Lying at the margin of the pond I was amazed to see the plate and jug which Nayland Smith had borrowed recently!

Dropping my burden, I walked down to the edge of the water. I was filled with a sudden apprehension. Then, as I bent to pick up the now empty jug, came a hail:

"All right, Petrie! Shall join you in a moment!"

I started up, looked to right and left; but, although the voice had been that of Nayland Smith, no sign could I discern of his presence!

"Smith!" I cried—"Smith!"

"Coming!"

Seriously doubting my senses, I looked in the direction from which the voice had seemed to proceed—and there was Nayland Smith.

He stood on the islet in the center of the pond, and, as I perceived him, he walked down into the shallow water and waded across to me!

"Good heavens!" I began—

One of his rare laughs interrupted me.

"You must think me mad this morning, Petrie!" he said. "But I have made several discoveries. Do you know what that islet in the pond really is?"

"Merely an islet, I suppose—"

"Nothing of the kind; it is a burial mound, Petrie! It marks the site of one of the Plague Pits where victims were buried during the Great Plague of London. You will observe that, although you have seen it every morning for some years, it remains for a British Commissioner resident in Burma to acquaint you with its history! Hullo!"—the laughter was gone from his eyes, and they were steely hard again—"what the blazes have we here!"

He picked up the net. "What! a bird trap!"

"Exactly!" I said.

Smith turned his searching gaze upon me. "Where did you find it, Petrie?"

"I did not exactly find it," I replied; and I related to him the circumstances of my meeting with Karamaneh.

He directed that cold stare upon me throughout the narrative, and when, with some embarrassment, I had told him of the girl's escape—

"Petrie," he said succinctly, "you are an imbecile!"

I flushed with anger, for not even from Nayland Smith, whom I esteemed above all other men, could I accept such words uttered as he had uttered them. We glared at one another.

"Karamaneh," he continued coldly, "is a beautiful toy, I grant you; but so is a cobra. Neither is suitable for playful purposes."

"Smith!" I cried hotly—"drop that! Adopt another tone or I cannot listen to you!"

"You must listen," he said, squaring his lean jaw truculently. "You are playing, not only with a pretty girl who is the favorite of a Chinese Nero, but with my life! And I object, Petrie, on purely personal grounds!"

I felt my anger oozing from me; for this was strictly just. I had nothing to say, and Smith continued:

"You know that she is utterly false, yet a glance or two from those dark eyes of hers can make a fool of you! A woman made a fool of me, once; but I learned my lesson; you have failed to learn yours. If you are determined to go to pieces on the rock that broke up Adam, do so! But don't involve me in the wreck, Petrie—for that might mean a yellow emperor of the world, and you know it!"

"Your words are unnecessarily brutal, Smith," I said, feeling very crestfallen, "but there—perhaps I fully deserve them all."

"You do!" he assured me, but he relaxed immediately. "A murderous attempt is made upon my life, resulting in the death of a perfectly innocent man in no way concerned. Along you come and let an accomplice, perhaps a participant, escape, merely, because she has a red mouth, or black lashes, or whatever it is that fascinates you so hopelessly!"

He opened the wicker basket, sniffing at the contents.

"Ah!" he snapped, "do you recognize this odor?"

"Certainly."

"Then you have some idea respecting Karamaneh's quarry?"

"Nothing of the kind!"

Smith shrugged his shoulders.

"Come along, Petrie," he said, linking his arm in mine.

We proceeded. Many questions there were that I wanted to put to him, but one above all.

"Smith," I said, "what, in Heaven's name, were you doing on the mound? Digging something up?"

"No," he replied, smiling dryly; "burying something!"

CHAPTER VI.

UNDER THE ELMS

Dusk found Nayland Smith and me at the top bedroom window. We knew, now that poor Forsyth's body had been properly examined, that he had died from poisoning. Smith, declaring that I did not deserve his confidence, had refused to confide in me his theory of the origin of the peculiar marks upon the body.

"On the soft ground under the trees," he said, "I found his tracks right up to the point where something happened. There were no other fresh tracks for several yards around. He was attacked as he stood close to the trunk of one of the elms. Six or seven feet away I found some other tracks, very much like this."

He marked a series of dots upon the blotting pad at his elbow.

"Claws!" I cried. "That eerie call! like the call of a nighthawk—is it some unknown species of—flying thing?"

"We shall see, shortly; possibly to-night," was his reply. "Since, probably owing to the absence of any moon, a mistake was made," his jaw hardened at the thoughts of poor Forsyth—"another attempt along the same lines will almost certainly follow—you know Fu-Manchu's system?"

So in the darkness, expectant, we sat watching the group of nine elms. To-night the moon was come, raising her Aladdin's lamp up to the star world and summoning magic shadows into being. By midnight the highroad showed deserted, the common was a place of mystery; and save for the periodical passage of an electric car, in blazing modernity, this was a fit enough stage for an eerie drama.

No notice of the tragedy had appeared in print; Nayland Smith was vested with powers to silence the press. No detectives, no special constables, were posted. My friend was of opinion that the publicity which had been given to the deeds of Dr. Fu-Manchu in the past, together with the sometimes clumsy co-operation of the police, had contributed not a little to the Chinaman's success.

"There is only one thing to fear," he jerked suddenly; "he may not be ready for another attempt to-night."

"Why?"

"Since he has only been in England for a short time, his menagerie of venomous things may be a limited one at present."

Earlier in the evening there had been a brief but violent thunderstorm, with a tropical downpour of rain, and now clouds were scudding across the blue of the sky. Through a temporary rift in the veiling the crescent of the moon looked down upon us. It had a greenish tint, and it set me thinking of the filmed, green eyes of Fu-Manchu.

The cloud passed and a lake of silver spread out to the edge of the coppice, where it terminated at a shadow bank.

"There it is, Petrie!" hissed Nayland Smith.

A lambent light was born in the darkness; it rose slowly, unsteadily, to a great height, and died.

"It's under the trees, Smith!"

But he was already making for the door. Over his shoulder:

"Bring the pistol, Petrie!" he cried; "I have another. Give me at least twenty yards' start or no attempt may be made. But the instant I'm under the trees, join me."

Out of the house we ran, and over onto the common, which latterly had been a pageant ground for phantom warring. The light did not appear again; and as Smith plunged off toward the trees, I wondered if he knew what uncanny thing was hidden there. I more than suspected that he had solved the mystery.

His instructions to keep well in the rear I understood. Fu-Manchu, or the creature of Fu-Manchu, would attempt nothing in the presence of a witness. But we knew full well that the instrument of death which was hidden in the elm coppice could do its ghastly work and leave no clue, could slay and vanish. For had not Forsyth come to a dreadful end while Smith and I were within twenty yards of him?

Not a breeze stirred, as Smith, ahead of me—for I had slowed my pace—came up level with the first tree. The moon sailed clear of the straggling cloud wisps which alone told of the recent storm; and I noted that an irregular patch of light lay silvern on the moist ground under the elms where otherwise lay shadow.

He passed on, slowly. I began to run again. Black against the silvern patch, I saw him emerge—and look up.

"Be careful, Smith!" I cried—and I was racing under the trees to join him.

Uttering a loud cry, he leaped—away from the pool of light.

"Stand back, Petrie!" he screamed—"Back! further!"

He charged into me, shoulder lowered, and sent me reeling!

Mixed up with his excited cry I had heard a loud splintering and sweeping of branches overhead; and now as we staggered into the shadows it seemed that one of the elms was reaching down to touch us! So, at least, the phenomenon presented itself to my mind in that fleeting moment while Smith, uttering his warning cry, was hurling me back.

Then the truth became apparent.

With an appalling crash, a huge bough fell from above. One piercing, awful shriek there was, a crackling of broken branches, and a choking groan...

The crack of Smith's pistol close beside me completed my confusion of mind.

"Missed!" he yelled. "Shoot it, Petrie! On your left! For God's sake don't miss it!"

I turned. A lithe black shape was streaking past me. I fired—once—twice. Another frightful cry made yet more hideous the nocturne.

Nayland Smith was directing the ray of a pocket torch upon the fallen bough.

"Have you killed it, Petrie?" he cried.

"Yes, yes!"

I stood beside him, looking down. From the tangle of leaves and twigs an evil yellow face looked up at us. The features were contorted with agony, but the malignant eyes, wherein light was dying, regarded us with inflexible hatred. The man was pinned beneath the heavy bough; his back was broken; and as we watched, he expired, frothing slightly at the mouth, and quitted his tenement of clay, leaving those glassy eyes set hideously upon us.

"The pagan gods fight upon our side," said Smith strangely. "Elms have a dangerous habit of shedding boughs in still weather—particularly after a storm. Pan, god of the woods, with this one has performed Justice's work of retribution."

"I don't understand. Where was this man—"

"Up the tree, lying along the bough which fell, Petrie! That is why he left no footmarks. Last night no doubt he made his escape by swinging from bough to bough, ape fashion, and descending to the ground somewhere at the other side of the coppice."

He glanced at me.

"You are wondering, perhaps," he suggested, "what caused the mysterious light? I could have told you this morning, but I fear I was in a bad temper, Petrie. It's very simple: a length of tape soaked in spirit or something of the kind, and sheltered from the view of any one watching from your windows, behind the trunk of the tree; then, the end ignited, lowered, still behind the tree, to the ground. The operator swinging it around, the flame ascended, of course. I found the unburned fragment of the tape last night, a few yards from here."

I was peering down at Fu-Manchu's servant, the hideous yellow man who lay dead in a bower of elm leaves.

"He has some kind of leather bag beside him," I began—

"Exactly!" rapped Smith. "In that he carried his dangerous instrument of death; from that he released it!"

"Released what?"

"What your fascinating friend came to recapture this morning."

"Don't taunt me, Smith!" I said bitterly. "Is it some species of bird?"

"You saw the marks on Forsyth's body, and I told you of those which I had traced upon the ground here. They were caused by claws, Petrie!"

"Claws! I thought so! But what claws?"

"The claws of a poisonous thing. I recaptured the one used last night, killed it—against my will—and buried it on the mound. I was afraid to throw it in the pond, lest some juvenile fisherman should pull it out and sustain a scratch. I don't know how long the claws would remain venomous."

"You are treating me like a child, Smith," I said slowly. "No doubt I am hopelessly obtuse, but perhaps you will tell me what this Chinaman carried in a leather bag and released upon Forsyth. It was something which you recaptured, apparently with the aid of a plate of cold turbot and a jug of milk! It was something, also, which Karamaneh had been sent to recapture with the aid—"

I stopped.

"Go on," said Nayland Smith, turning the ray to the left, "what did she have in the basket?"

"Valerian," I replied mechanically.

The ray rested upon the lithe creature that I had shot down.

It was a black cat!

"A cat will go through fire and water for valerian," said Smith; "but I got first innings this morning with fish and milk! I had recognized the imprints under the trees for those of a cat, and I knew, that if a cat had been released here it would still be hiding in the neighborhood, probably in the bushes. I finally located a cat, sure enough, and came for bait! I laid my trap, for the animal was too frightened to be approachable, and then shot it; I had to. That yellow fiend used the light as a decoy. The branch which killed him jutted out over the path at a spot where an opening in the foliage above allowed some moon rays to penetrate. Directly the victim stood beneath, the Chinaman uttered his bird cry; the one below looked up, and the cat, previously held silent and helpless in the leather sack, was dropped accurately upon his head!"

"But"—I was growing confused.

Smith stooped lower.

"The cat's claws are sheathed now," he said; "but if you could examine them you would find that they are coated with a shining black substance. Only Fu-Manchu knows what that substance is, Petrie, but you and I know what it can do!"

CHAPTER VII.

ENTER MR. ABEL SLATTIN

"I don't blame you!" rapped Nayland Smith. "Suppose we say, then, a thousand pounds if you show us the present hiding-place of Fu-Manchu, the payment to be in no way subject to whether we profit by your information or not?"

Abel Slattin shrugged his shoulders, racially, and returned to the armchair which he had just quitted. He reseated himself, placing his hat and cane upon my writing-table.

"A little agreement in black and white?" he suggested smoothly.

Smith raised himself up out of the white cane chair, and, bending forward over a corner of the table, scribbled busily upon a sheet of notepaper with my fountain-pen.

The while he did so, I covertly studied our visitor. He lay back in the armchair, his heavy eyelids lowered deceptively. He was a thought overdressed—a big man, dark-haired and well groomed, who toyed with a monocle most unsuitable to his type. During the preceding conversation, I had been vaguely surprised to note Mr. Abel Slattin's marked American accent.

Sometimes, when Slattin moved, a big diamond which he wore upon the third finger of his right hand glittered magnificently. There was a sort of bluish tint underlying the dusky skin, noticeable even in his hands but proclaiming itself significantly in his puffy face and especially under the eyes. I diagnosed a laboring valve somewhere in the heart system.

Nayland Smith's pen scratched on. My glance strayed from our Semitic caller to his cane, lying upon the red leather before me. It was of most unusual workmanship, apparently Indian, being made of some kind of dark brown, mottled wood, bearing a marked resemblance to a snake's skin; and the top of the cane was carved in conformity, to represent the head of what I took to be a puff-adder, fragments of stone, or beads, being inserted to represent the eyes, and the whole thing being finished with an artistic realism almost startling.

When Smith had tossed the written page to Slattin, and he, having read it with an appearance of carelessness, had folded it neatly and placed it in his pocket, I said:

"You have a curio here?"

Our visitor, whose dark eyes revealed all the satisfaction which, by his manner, he sought to conceal, nodded and took up the cane in his hand.

"It comes from Australia, Doctor," he replied; "it's aboriginal work, and was given to me by a client. You thought it was Indian? Everybody does. It's my mascot."

"Really?"

"It is indeed. Its former owner ascribed magical powers to it! In fact, I believe he thought that it was one of those staffs mentioned in biblical history—"

"Aaron's rod?" suggested Smith, glancing at the cane.

"Something of the sort," said Slattin, standing up and again preparing to depart.

"You will 'phone us, then?" asked my friend.

"You will hear from me to-morrow," was the reply.

Smith returned to the cane armchair, and Slattin, bowing to both of us, made his way to the door as I rang for the girl to show him out.

"Considering the importance of his proposal," I began, as the door closed, "you hardly received our visitor with cordiality."

"I hate to have any relations with him," answered my friend; "but we must not be squeamish respecting our instruments in dealing with Dr. Fu-Manchu. Slattin has a rotten reputation—even for a private inquiry agent. He is little better than a blackmailer—"

"How do you know?"

"Because I called on our friend Weymouth at the Yard yesterday and looked up the man's record."

"Whatever for?"

"I knew that he was concerning himself, for some reason, in the case. Beyond doubt he has established some sort of communication with the Chinese group; I am only wondering—"

"You don't mean—"

"Yes—I do, Petrie! I tell you he is unscrupulous enough to stoop even to that."

No doubt, Slattin knew that this gaunt, eager-eyed Burmese commissioner was vested with ultimate authority in his quest of the mighty Chinaman who represented things unutterable, whose potentialities for evil were boundless as his genius, who personified a secret danger, the extent and nature of which none of us truly understood. And, learning of these things, with unerring Semitic instinct he had sought an opening in this glittering Rialto. But there were two bidders!

"You think he may have sunk so low as to become a creature of Fu-Manchu?" I asked, aghast.

"Exactly! If it paid him well I do not doubt that he would serve that master as readily as any other. His record is about as black as it well could be. Slattin is of course an assumed name; he was known as Lieutenant Pepley when he belonged to the New York Police, and he was kicked out of the service for complicity in an unsavory Chinatown case."

"Chinatown!"

"Yes, Petrie, it made me wonder, too; and we must not forget that he is undeniably a clever scoundrel."

"Shall you keep any appointment which he may suggest?"

"Undoubtedly. But I shall not wait until tomorrow."

"What!"

"I propose to pay a little informal visit to Mr. Abel Slattin, to-night."

"At his office?"

"No; at his private residence. If, as I more than suspect, his object is to draw us into some trap, he will probably report his favorable progress to his employer to-night!"

"Then we should have followed him!"

Nayland Smith stood up and divested himself of the old shooting-jacket.

"He has been followed, Petrie," he replied, with one of his rare smiles. "Two C.I.D. men have been watching the house all night!"

This was entirely characteristic of my friend's farseeing methods.

"By the way," I said, "you saw Eltham this morning. He will soon be convalescent. Where, in heaven's name, can he—"

"Don't be alarmed on his behalf, Petrie," interrupted Smith. "His life is no longer in danger."

I stared, stupidly.

"No longer in danger!"

"He received, some time yesterday, a letter, written in Chinese, upon Chinese paper, and enclosed in an ordinary business envelope, having a typewritten address and bearing a London postmark."

"Well?"

"As nearly as I can render the message in English, it reads: 'Although, because you are a brave man, you would not betray your correspondent in China, he has been discovered. He was a mandarin, and as I cannot write the name of a traitor, I may not name him. He was executed four days ago. I salute you and pray for your speedy recovery. Fu-Manchu.'"

"Fu-Manchu! But it is almost certainly a trap."

"On the contrary, Petrie—Fu-Manchu would not have written in Chinese unless he were sincere; and, to clear all doubt, I received a cable this morning reporting that the Mandarin Yen-Sun-Yat was assassinated in his own garden, in Nan-Yang, one day last week."

◆

CHAPTER VIII.

DR. FU-MANCHU STRIKES

Together we marched down the slope of the quiet, suburban avenue; to take pause before a small, detached house displaying the hatchet boards of the Estate Agent. Here we found unkempt laurel bushes and acacias run riot, from which arboreal tangle protruded the notice—"To be Let or Sold."

Smith, with an alert glance to right and left, pushed open the wooden gate and drew me in upon the gravel path. Darkness mantled all; for the nearest street lamp was fully twenty yards beyond.

From the miniature jungle bordering the path, a soft whistle sounded.

"Is that Carter?" called Smith, sharply.

A shadowy figure uprose, and vaguely I made it out for that of a man in the unobtrusive blue serge which is the undress uniform of the Force.

"Well?" rapped my companion.

"Mr. Slattin returned ten minutes ago, sir," reported the constable. "He came in a cab which he dismissed—"

"He has not left again?"

"A few minutes after his return," the man continued, "another cab came up, and a lady alighted."

"A lady!"

"The same, sir, that has called upon him before."

"Smith!" I whispered, plucking at his arm—"is it—"

He half turned, nodding his head; and my heart began to throb foolishly. For now the manner of Slattin's campaign suddenly was revealed to me. In our operations against the Chinese murder-group two years before, we had had an ally in the enemy's camp—Karamaneh the beautiful slave, whose presence in those happenings of the past had colored the sometimes sordid drama with the opulence of old Arabia; who had seemed a fitting figure for the romances of Bagdad during the Caliphate—Karamaneh, whom I had thought sincere, whose inscrutable Eastern soul I had presumed, fatuously, to have laid bare and analyzed.

Now, once again she was plying her old trade of go-between; professing to reveal the secrets of Dr. Fu-Manchu, and all the time—I could not doubt it—inveigling men into the net of this awful fisher.

Yesterday, I had been her dupe; yesterday, I had rejoiced in my captivity. To-day, I was not the favored one; to-day I had not been selected recipient of her confidences—confidences sweet, seductive, deadly: but Abel Slattin, a plausible rogue, who, in justice, should be immured in Sing Sing, was chosen out, was enslaved by those lovely mysterious eyes, was taking to his soul the lies which fell from those perfect lips, triumphant in a conquest that must end in his undoing; deeming, poor fool, that for love of him this pearl of the Orient was about to betray her master, to resign herself a prize to the victor!

Companioned by these bitter reflections, I had lost the remainder of the conversation between Nayland Smith and the police officer; now, casting off the succubus memory which threatened to obsess me, I put forth a giant mental effort to purge my mind of this uncleanness, and became again an active participant in the campaign against the Master—the director of all things noxious.

Our plans being evidently complete, Smith seized my arm, and I found myself again out upon the avenue. He led me across the road and into the gate of a house almost opposite. From the fact that two upper windows were illuminated, I adduced that the servants were retiring; the other windows were in darkness, except for one on the ground floor to the extreme left of the building, through the lowered venetian blinds whereof streaks of light shone out.

"Slattin's study!" whispered Smith. "He does not anticipate surveillance, and you will note that the window is wide open!"

With that my friend crossed the strip of lawn, and careless of the fact that his silhouette must have been visible to any one passing the gate, climbed carefully up the artificial rockery intervening, and crouched upon the window-ledge peering into the room.

A moment I hesitated, fearful that if I followed, I should stumble or dislodge some of the larva blocks of which the rockery was composed.

Then I heard that which summoned me to the attempt, whatever the cost.

Through the open window came the sound of a musical voice—a voice possessing a haunting accent, possessing a quality which struck upon my heart and set it quivering as though it were a gong hung in my bosom.

Karamaneh was speaking.

Upon hands and knees, heedless of damage to my garments, I crawled up beside Smith. One of the laths was slightly displaced and over this my friend was peering in. Crouching close beside him, I peered in also.

I saw the study of a business man, with its files, neatly arranged works of reference, roll-top desk, and Milner safe. Before the desk, in a revolving chair, sat Slattin. He sat half turned toward the window, leaning back and smiling; so that I could note the gold crown which preserved the lower left molar. In an armchair by the window, close, very close, and sitting with her back to me, was Karamaneh!

She, who, in my dreams, I always saw, was ever seeing, in an Eastern dress, with gold bands about her white ankles, with jewel-laden fingers, with jewels in her hair, wore now a fashionable costume and a hat that could only have been produced in Paris. Karamaneh was the one Oriental woman I had ever known who could wear European clothes; and as I watched that exquisite profile, I thought that Delilah must have been just such another as this, that, excepting the Empress Poppaea, history has record of no woman, who, looking so innocent, was yet so utterly vile.

"Yes, my dear," Slattin was saying, and through his monocle ogling his beautiful visitor, "I shall be ready for you to-morrow night."

I felt Smith start at the words.

"There will be a sufficient number of men?"

Karamaneh put the question in a strangely listless way.

"My dear little girl," replied Slattin, rising and standing looking down at her, with his gold tooth twinkling in the lamplight, "there will be a whole division, if a whole division is necessary."

He sought to take her white gloved hand, which rested upon the chair arm; but she evaded the attempt with seeming artlessness, and stood up. Slattin fixed his bold gaze upon her.

"So now, give me my orders," he said.

"I am not prepared to do so, yet," replied the girl, composedly; "but now that I know you are ready, I can make my plans."

She glided past him to the door, avoiding his outstretched arm with an artless art which made me writhe; for once I had been the willing victim of all these wiles.

"But—" began Slattin.

"I will ring you up in less than half an hour," said Karamaneh and without further ceremony, she opened the door.

I still had my eyes glued to the aperture in the blind, when Smith began tugging at my arm.

"Down! you fool!" he hissed harshly—"if she sees us, all is lost!"

Realizing this, and none too soon, I turned, and rather clumsily followed my friend. I dislodged a piece of granite in my descent; but, fortunately, Slattin had gone out into the hall and could not well have heard it.

We were crouching around an angle of the house, when a flood of light poured down the steps, and Karamaneh rapidly descended. I had a glimpse of a dark-faced man who evidently had opened the door for her, then all my thoughts were centered upon that graceful figure receding from me in the direction of the avenue. She wore a loose cloak, and I saw this fluttering for a moment against the white gate posts; then she was gone.

Yet Smith did not move. Detaining me with his hand he crouched there against a quick-set hedge; until, from a spot lower down the hill, we heard the start of the cab which had been waiting. Twenty seconds elapsed, and from some other distant spot a second cab started.

"That's Weymouth!" snapped Smith. "With decent luck, we should know Fu-Manchu's hiding-place before Slattin tells us!"

"But—"

"Oh! as it happens, he's apparently playing the game."—In the half-light, Smith stared at me significantly—"Which makes it all the more important," he concluded, "that we should not rely upon his aid!"

Those grim words were prophetic.

My companion made no attempt to communicate with the detective (or detectives) who shared our vigil; we took up a position close under the lighted study window and waited—waited.

Once, a taxi-cab labored hideously up the steep gradient of the avenue... It was gone. The lights at the upper windows above us became extinguished. A policeman tramped past the gateway, casually flashing his lamp in at the opening. One by one the illuminated windows in other houses visible to us became dull; then lived again as mirrors for the pallid moon. In the silence, words spoken within the study were clearly audible; and we heard someone—presumably the man who had opened the door—inquire if his services would be wanted again that night.

Smith inclined his head and hung over me in a tense attitude, in order to catch Slattin's reply.

"Yes, Burke," it came—"I want you to sit up until I return; I shall be going out shortly."

Evidently the man withdrew at that; for a complete silence followed which prevailed for fully half an hour. I sought cautiously to move my cramped limbs, unlike Smith, who seeming to have sinews of piano-wire, crouched beside me immovable, untiringly. Then loud upon the stillness, broke the strident note of the telephone bell.

I started, nervously, clutching at Smith's arm. It felt hard as iron to my grip.

"Hullo!" I heard Slattin call—"who is speaking?... Yes, yes! This is Mr. A. S.... I am to come at once?... I know where—yes I ... you will meet me there?... Good!—I shall be with you in half an hour.... Good-by!"

Distinctly I heard the creak of the revolving office-chair as Slattin rose; then Smith had me by the arm, and we were flying swiftly away from the door to take up our former post around the angle of the building. This gained:

"He's going to his death!" rapped Smith beside me; "but Carter has a cab from the Yard waiting in the nearest rank. We shall follow to see where he goes—for it is possible that Weymouth may have been thrown off the scent; then, when we are sure of his destination, we can take a hand in the game! We..."

The end of the sentence was lost to me—drowned in such a frightful wave of sound as I despair to describe. It began with a high, thin scream, which was choked off staccato fashion; upon it followed a loud and dreadful cry uttered with all the strength of Slattin's lungs—

"Oh, God!" he cried, and again—"Oh, God!"

This in turn merged into a sort of hysterical sobbing.

I was on my feet now, and automatically making for the door. I had a vague impression of Nayland Smith's face beside me, the eyes glassy with a fearful apprehension. Then the door was flung open, and, in the bright light of the hall-way, I saw Slattin standing—swaying and seemingly fighting with the empty air.

"What is it? For God's sake, what has happened!" reached my ears dimly—and the man Burke showed behind his master. White-faced I saw him to be; for now Smith and I were racing up the steps.

Ere we could reach him, Slattin, uttering another choking cry, pitched forward and lay half across the threshold.

We burst into the hall, where Burke stood with both his hands raised dazedly to his head. I could hear the sound of running feet upon the gravel, and knew that Carter was coming to join us.

Burke, a heavy man with a lowering, bull-dog type of face, collapsed onto his knees beside Slattin, and began softly to laugh in little rising peals.

"Drop that!" snapped Smith, and grasping him by the shoulders, he sent him spinning along the hallway, where he sank upon the bottom step of the stairs, to sit with his outstretched fingers extended before his face, and peering at us grotesquely through the crevices.

There were rustlings and subdued cries from the upper part of the house. Carter came in out of the darkness, carefully stepping over the recumbent figure; and the three of us stood there in the lighted hall looking down at Slattin.

"Help us to move him back," directed Smith, tensely; "far enough to close the door."

Between us we accomplished this, and Carter fastened the door. We were alone with the shadow of Fu-Manchu's vengeance; for as I knelt beside the body on the floor, a look and a touch sufficed to tell me that this was but clay from which the spirit had fled!

Smith met my glance as I raised my head, and his teeth came together with a loud snap; the jaw muscles stood out prominently beneath the dark skin; and his face was grimly set in that odd, half-despairful expression which I knew so well but which boded so ill for whomsoever occasioned it.

"Dead, Petrie!—already?"

"Lightning could have done the work no better. Can I turn him over?"

Smith nodded.

Together we stooped and rolled the heavy body on its back. A flood of whispers came sibilantly from the stairway. Smith spun around rapidly, and glared upon the group of half-dressed servants.

"Return to your rooms!" he rapped, imperiously; "let no one come into the hall without my orders."

The masterful voice had its usual result; there was a hurried retreat to the upper landing. Burke, shaking like a man with an ague, sat on the lower step, pathetically drumming his palms upon his uplifted knees.

"I warned him, I warned him!" he mumbled monotonously, "I warned him, oh, I warned him!"

"Stand up!" shouted Smith—"stand up and come here!"

The man, with his frightened eyes turning to right and left, and seeming to search for something in the shadows about him, advanced obediently.

"Have you a flask?" demanded Smith of Carter.

The detective silently administered to Burke a stiff restorative.

"Now," continued Smith, "you, Petrie, will want to examine him, I suppose?" He pointed to the body. "And in the meantime I have some questions to put to you, my man."

He clapped his hand upon Burke's shoulder.

"My God!" Burke broke out, "I was ten yards from him when it happened!"

"No one is accusing you," said Smith, less harshly; "but since you were the only witness, it is by your aid that we hope to clear the matter up."

Exerting a gigantic effort to regain control of himself, Burke nodded, watching my friend with a childlike eagerness. During the ensuing conversation, I examined Slattin for marks of violence; and of what I found, more anon.

"In the first place," said Smith, "you say that you warned him. When did you warn him and of what?"

"I warned him, sir, that it would come to this—"

"That what would come to this?"

"His dealings with the Chinaman!"

"He had dealings with Chinamen?"

"He accidentally met a Chinaman at an East End gaming-house, a man he had known in Frisco—a man called Singapore Charlie—"

"What! Singapore Charlie!"

"Yes, sir, the same man that had a dope-shop, two years ago, down Ratcliffe way—"

"There was a fire—"

"But Singapore Charlie escaped, sir."

"And he is one of the gang?"

"He is one of what we used to call in New York, the Seven Group."

Smith began to tug at the lobe of his left ear, reflectively, as I saw out of the corner of my eye.

"The Seven Group!" he mused. "That is significant. I always suspected that Dr. Fu-Manchu and the notorious Seven Group were one and the same. Go on, Burke."

"Well, sir," the man continued, more calmly, "the lieutenant—"

"The lieutenant!" began Smith; then: "Oh! of course; Slattin used to be a police lieutenant!"

"Well, sir, he—Mr. Slattin—had a sort of hold on this Singapore Charlie, and two years ago, when he first met him, he thought that with his aid he was going to pull off the biggest thing of his life—"

"Forestall me, in fact?"

"Yes, sir; but you got in first, with the big raid and spoiled it."

Smith nodded grimly, glancing at the Scotland Yard man, who returned his nod with equal grimness.

"A couple of months ago," resumed Burke, "he met Charlie again down East, and the Chinaman introduced him to a girl—some sort of an Egyptian girl."

"Go on!" snapped Smith—"I know her."

"He saw her a good many times—and she came here once or twice. She made out that she and Singapore Charlie were prepared to give away the boss of the Yellow gang—"

"For a price, of course?"

"I suppose so," said Burke; "but I don't know. I only know that I warned him."

"H'm!" muttered Smith. "And now, what took place to-night?"

"He had an appointment here with the girl," began Burke

"I know all that," interrupted Smith. "I merely want to know, what took place after the telephone call?"

"Well, he told me to wait up, and I was dozing in the next room to the study—the dining-room—when the 'phone bell aroused me. I heard the lieutenant—Mr. Slattin, coming out, and I ran out too, but only in time to see him taking his hat from the rack—"

"But he wears no hat!"

"He never got it off the peg! Just as he reached up to take it, he gave a most frightful scream, and turned around like lightning as though some one had attacked him from behind!"

"There was no one else in the hall?"

"No one at all. I was standing down there outside the dining-room just by the stairs, but he didn't turn in my direction, he turned and looked right behind him—where there was no one—nothing. His cries were frightful." Burke's voice broke, and he shuddered feverishly. "Then he made a rush for the front door. It seemed as though he had not seen me. He stood there screaming; but, before I could reach him, he fell...."

Nayland Smith fixed a piercing gaze upon Burke.

"Is that all you know?" he demanded slowly.

"As God is my judge, sir, that's all I know, and all I saw. There was no living thing near him when he met his death."

"We shall see," muttered Smith. He turned to me—"What killed him?" he asked, shortly.

"Apparently, a minute wound on the left wrist," I replied, and, stooping, I raised the already cold hand in mine.

A tiny, inflamed wound showed on the wrist; and a certain puffiness was becoming observable in the injured hand and arm. Smith bent down and drew a quick, sibilant breath.

"You know what this is, Petrie?" he cried.

"Certainly. It was too late to employ a ligature and useless to inject ammonia. Death was practically instantaneous. His heart..."

There came a loud knocking and ringing.

"Carter!" cried Smith, turning to the detective, "open that door to no one—no one. Explain who I am—"

"But if it is the inspector?—"

"I said, open the door to no one!" snapped Smith.

"Burke, stand exactly where you are! Carter, you can speak to whoever knocks, through the letter-box. Petrie, don't move for your life! It may be here, in the hallway!—"

CHAPTER IX.

THE CLIMBER

Our search of the house of Abel Slattin ceased only with the coming of the dawn, and yielded nothing but disappointment. Failure followed upon failure; for, in the gray light of the morning, our own quest concluded, Inspector Weymouth returned to report that the girl, Karamaneh, had thrown him off the scent.

Again he stood before me, the big, burly friend of old and dreadful days, a little grayer above the temples, which I set down for a record of former horrors, but deliberate, stoical, thorough, as ever. His blue eyes melted in the old generous way as he saw me, and he gripped my hand in greeting.

"Once again," he said, "your dark-eyed friend has been too clever for me, Doctor. But the track as far as I could follow, leads to the old spot. In fact,"—he turned to Smith, who, grim-faced and haggard, looked thoroughly ill in that gray light—"I believe Fu-Manchu's lair is somewhere near the former opium-den of Shen-Yan—'Singapore Charlie.'"

Smith nodded.

"We will turn our attention in that direction," he replied, "at a very early date."

Inspector Weymouth looked down at the body of Abel Slattin.

"How was it done?" he asked softly.

"Clumsily for Fu-Manchu," I replied. "A snake was introduced into the house by some means—"

"By Karamaneh!" rapped Smith.

"Very possibly by Karamaneh," I continued firmly. "The thing has escaped us."

"My own idea," said Smith, "is that it was concealed about his clothing. When he fell by the open door it glided out of the house. We must have the garden searched thoroughly by daylight."

"He"—Weymouth glanced at that which lay upon the floor—"must be moved; but otherwise we can leave the place untouched, clear out the servants, and lock the house up."

"I have already given orders to that effect," answered Smith. He spoke wearily and with a note of conscious defeat in his voice. "Nothing has been disturbed;"—he swept his arm around comprehensively—"papers and so forth you can examine at leisure."

Presently we quitted that house upon which the fateful Chinaman had set his seal, as the suburb was awakening to a new day. The clank of milk-cans was my final impression of the avenue to which a dreadful minister of death had come at the bidding of the death lord. We left Inspector Weymouth in charge and returned to my rooms, scarcely exchanging a word upon the way.

Nayland Smith, ignoring my entreaties, composed himself for slumber in the white cane chair in my study. About noon he retired to the bathroom, and returning, made a pretense of breakfast; then resumed his seat in the cane armchair. Carter reported in the afternoon, but his report was merely formal. Returning from my round of professional visits at half past five, I found Nayland Smith in the same position; and so the day waned into evening, and dusk fell uneventfully.

In the corner of the big room by the empty fireplace, Nayland Smith lay, with his long, lean frame extended in the white cane chair. A tumbler, from which two straws protruded, stood by his right elbow, and a perfect continent of tobacco smoke lay between us, wafted toward the door by the draught from an open window. He had littered the hearth with matches and tobacco ash, being the most untidy smoker I have ever met; and save for his frequent rapping-out of his pipe bowl and perpetual striking of matches, he had shown no sign of activity for the past hour. Collarless and wearing an old tweed jacket, he had spent the evening, as he had spent the day, in the cane chair, only quitting it for some ten minutes, or less, to toy with dinner.

My several attempts at conversation had elicited nothing but growls; therefore, as dusk descended, having dismissed my few patients, I busied myself collating my notes upon the renewed activity of the Yellow Doctor, and was thus engaged when the 'phone bell disturbed me. It was Smith who was wanted, however; and he went out eagerly, leaving me to my task.

At the end of a lengthy conversation, he returned from the 'phone and began, restlessly, to pace the room. I made a pretense of continuing my labors, but covertly I was watching him. He was twitching at the lobe of his left ear, and his face was a study in perplexity. Abruptly he burst out:

"I shall throw the thing up, Petrie! Either I am growing too old to cope with such an adversary as Fu-Manchu, or else my intellect has become dull. I cannot seem to think clearly or consistently. For the Doctor, this crime, this removal of Slattin, is clumsy—unfinished. There are two explanations. Either he, too, is losing his old cunning or he has been interrupted!"

"Interrupted!"

"Take the facts, Petrie,"—Smith clapped his hands upon my table and bent down, peering into my eyes—"is it characteristic of Fu-Manchu to kill a man by the direct agency of a snake and to implicate one of his own damnable servants in this way?"

"But we have found no snake!"

"Karamaneh introduced one in some way. Do you doubt it?"

"Certainly Karamaneh visited him on the evening of his death, but you must be perfectly well aware that even if she had been arrested, no jury could convict her."

Smith resumed his restless pacings up and down.

"You are very useful to me, Petrie," he replied; "as a counsel for the defense you constantly rectify my errors of prejudice. Yet I am convinced that our presence at Slattin's house last night prevented Fu-Manchu from finishing off this little matter as he had designed to do."

"What has given you this idea?"

"Weymouth is responsible. He has rung me up from the Yard. The constable on duty at the house where the murder was committed, reports that some one, less than an hour ago, attempted to break in."

"Break in!"

"Ah! you are interested? I thought the circumstance illuminating, also!"

"Did the officer see this person?"

"No; he only heard him. It was some one who endeavored to enter by the bathroom window, which, I am told, may be reached fairly easily by an agile climber."

"The attempt did not succeed?"

"No; the constable interrupted, but failed to make a capture or even to secure a glimpse of the man."

We were both silent for some moments; then:

"What do you propose to do?" I asked.

"We must not let Fu-Manchu's servants know," replied Smith, "but to-night I shall conceal myself in Slattin's house and remain there for a week or a day—it matters not how long—until that attempt is repeated. Quite obviously, Petrie, we have overlooked something which implicates the murderer with the murder! In short, either by accident, by reason of our superior vigilance, or by the clumsiness of his plans, Fu-Manchu for once in an otherwise blameless career, has left a clue!"

◆

CHAPTER X.

THE CLIMBER RETURNS

In utter darkness we groped our way through into the hallway of Slattin's house, having entered, stealthily, from the rear; for Smith had selected the study as a suitable base of operations. We reached it without mishap, and presently I found myself seated in the very chair which Karamaneh had occupied; my companion took up a post just within the widely opened door.

So we commenced our ghostly business in the house of the murdered man—a house from which, but a few hours since, his body had been removed. This was such a vigil as I had endured once before, when, with Nayland Smith and another, I had waited for the coming of one of Fu-Manchu's death agents.

Of all the sounds which, one by one, now began to detach themselves from the silence, there was a particular sound, homely enough at another time, which spoke to me more dreadfully than the rest. It was the ticking of the clock upon the mantelpiece; and I thought how this sound must have been familiar to Abel Slattin, how it must have formed part and parcel of his life, as it were, and how it went on now—tick-tick-tick-tick—whilst he, for whom it had ticked, lay unheeding—would never heed it more.

As I grew more accustomed to the gloom, I found myself staring at his office chair; once I found myself expecting Abel Slattin to enter the room and occupy it. There was a little China Buddha upon the bureau in one corner, with a gilded cap upon its head, and as some reflection of the moonlight sought out this little cap, my thoughts grotesquely turned upon the murdered man's gold tooth.

Vague creakings from within the house, sounds as though of stealthy footsteps upon the stair, set my nerves tingling; but Nayland Smith gave no sign, and I knew that my imagination was magnifying these ordinary night sounds out of all proportion to their actual significance. Leaves rustled faintly outside the window at my back: I construed their sibilant whispers into the dreaded name—Fu-Manchu-Fu-Manchu—Fu-Manchu!

So wore on the night; and, when the ticking clock hollowly boomed the hour of one, I almost leaped out of my chair, so highly strung were my nerves, and so appallingly did the sudden clangor beat upon them. Smith, like a man of stone, showed no sign. He was capable of so subduing his constitutionally high-strung temperament, at times, that temporarily he became immune from human dreads. On such occasions he would be icily cool amid universal panic; but, his object accomplished, I have seen him in such a state of collapse, that utter nervous exhaustion is the only term by which I can describe it.

Tick-tick-tick-tick went the clock, and, with my heart still thumping noisily in my breast, I began to count the tickings; one, two, three, four, five, and so on to a hundred, and from one hundred to many hundreds.

Then, out from the confusion of minor noises, a new, arresting sound detached itself. I ceased my counting; no longer I noted the tick-tick of the clock, nor the vague creakings, rustlings and whispers. I saw Smith, shadowly, raise his hand in warning—in needless warning, for I was almost holding my breath in an effort of acute listening.

From high up in the house this new sound came from above the topmost room, it seemed, up under the roof; a regular squeaking, oddly familiar, yet elusive. Upon it followed a very soft and muffled thud; then a metallic sound as of a rusty hinge in motion; then a new silence, pregnant with a thousand possibilities more eerie than any clamor.

My mind was rapidly at work. Lighting the topmost landing of the house was a sort of glazed trap, evidently set in the floor of a loft-like place extending over the entire building. Somewhere in the red-tiled roof above, there presumably existed a corresponding skylight or lantern.

So I argued; and, ere I had come to any proper decision, another sound, more intimate, came to interrupt me.

This time I could be in no doubt; some one was lifting the trap above the stairhead—slowly, cautiously, and all but silently. Yet to my ears, attuned to trifling disturbances, the trap creaked and groaned noisily.

Nayland Smith waved to me to take a stand on the other side of the opened door—behind it, in fact, where I should be concealed from the view of any one descending the stair.

I stood up and crossed the floor to my new post.

A dull thud told of the trap fully raised and resting upon some supporting joist. A faint rustling (of discarded garments, I told myself) spoke to my newly awakened, acute perceptions, of the visitor preparing to lower himself to the landing. Followed a groan of woodwork submitted to sudden strain—and the unmistakable pad of bare feet upon the linoleum of the top corridor.

I knew now that one of Dr. Fu-Manchu's uncanny servants had gained the roof of the house by some means, had broken through the skylight and had descended by means of the trap beneath on to the landing.

In such a tensed-up state as I cannot describe, nor, at this hour mentally reconstruct, I waited for the creaking of the stairs which should tell of the creature's descent.

I was disappointed. Removed scarce a yard from me as he was, I could hear Nayland Smith's soft, staccato breathing; but my eyes were all for the darkened hallway, for the smudgy outline of the stair-rail with the faint patterning in the background which, alone, indicated the wall.

It was amid an utter silence, unheralded by even so slight a sound as those which I had acquired the power of detecting—that I saw the continuity of the smudgy line of stair-rail to be interrupted.

A dark patch showed upon it, just within my line of sight, invisible to Smith on the other side of the doorway, and some ten or twelve stairs up.

No sound reached me, but the dark patch vanished and reappeared three feet lower down.

Still I knew that this phantom approach must be unknown to my companion—and I knew that it was impossible for me to advise him of it unseen by the dreaded visitor.

A third time the dark patch—the hand of one who, ghostly, silent, was creeping down into the hallway—vanished and reappeared on a level with my eyes. Then a vague shape became visible; no more than a blur upon the dim design of the wall-paper... and Nayland Smith got his first sight of the stranger.

The clock on the mantelpiece boomed out the half-hour.

At that, such was my state (I blush to relate it) I uttered a faint cry!

It ended all secrecy—that hysterical weakness of mine. It might have frustrated our hopes; that it did not do so was in no measure due to me. But in a sort of passionate whirl, the ensuing events moved swiftly.

Smith hesitated not one instant. With a panther-like leap he hurled himself into the hall.

"The lights, Petrie!" he cried—"the lights! The switch is near the street-door!"

I clenched my fists in a swift effort to regain control of my treacherous nerves, and, bounding past Smith, and past the foot of the stair, I reached out my hand to the switch, the situation of which, fortunately, I knew.

Around I came, in response to a shrill cry from behind me—an inhuman cry, less a cry than the shriek of some enraged animal....

With his left foot upon the first stair, Nayland Smith stood, his lean body bent perilously backward, his arms rigidly thrust out, and his sinewy fingers gripping the throat of an almost naked man—a man whose brown body glistened unctuously, whose shaven head was apish low, whose bloodshot eyes were the eyes of a mad dog! His teeth, upper and lower, were bared; they glistened, they gnashed, and a froth was on his lips. With both his hands, he clutched a heavy stick, and once—twice, he brought it down upon Nayland Smith's head!

I leaped forward to my friend's aid; but as though the blows had been those of a feather, he stood like some figure of archaic statuary, nor for an instant relaxed the death grip which he had upon his adversary's throat.

Thrusting my way up the stairs, I wrenched the stick from the hand of the dacoit—for in this glistening brown man, I recognized one of that deadly brotherhood who hailed Dr. Fu-Manchu their Lord and Master.

I cannot dwell upon the end of that encounter; I cannot hope to make acceptable to my readers an account of how Nayland Smith, glassy-eyed, and with consciousness ebbing from him instant by instant, stood there, a realization of Leighton's "Athlete," his arms rigid as iron bars even after Fu-Manchu's servant hung limply in that frightful grip.

In his last moments of consciousness, with the blood from his wounded head trickling down into his eyes, he pointed to the stick which I had torn from the grip of the dacoit, and which I still held in my hand.

"Not Aaron's rod, Petrie!" he gasped hoarsely—"the rod of Moses!—Slattin's stick!"

Even in upon my anxiety for my friend, amazement intruded.

"But," I began—and turned to the rack in which Slattin's favorite cane at that moment reposed—had reposed at the time of his death.

Yes!—there stood Slattin's cane; we had not moved it; we had disturbed nothing in that stricken house; there it stood, in company with an umbrella and a malacca.

I glanced at the cane in my hand. Surely there could not be two such in the world?

Smith collapsed on the floor at my feet.

"Examine the one in the rack, Petrie," he whispered, almost inaudibly, "but do not touch it. It may not be yet...."

I propped him up against the foot of the stairs, and as the constable began knocking violently at the street door, crossed to the rack and lifted out the replica of the cane which I held in my hand.

A faint cry from Smith—and as if it had been a leprous thing, I dropped the cane instantly.

"Merciful God!" I groaned.

Although, in every other particular, it corresponded with that which I held—which I had taken from the dacoit—which he had come to substitute for the cane now lying upon the floor—in one dreadful particular it differed.

Up to the snake's head it was an accurate copy; but the head lived!

Either from pain, fear or starvation, the thing confined in the hollow tube of this awful duplicate was become torpid. Otherwise, no power on earth could have saved me from the fate of Abel Slattin; for the creature was an Australian death-adder.

◆◆◆◆◆◆◆

CHAPTER XI.

THE WHITE PEACOCK

Nayland Smith wasted no time in pursuing the plan of campaign which he had mentioned to Inspector Weymouth. Less than forty-eight hours after quitting the house of the murdered Slattin, I found myself bound along Whitechapel Road upon strange enough business.

A very fine rain was falling, which rendered it difficult to see clearly from the windows; but the weather apparently had little effect upon the commercial activities of the district. The cab was threading a hazardous way through the cosmopolitan throng crowding the street. On either side of me extended a row of stalls, seemingly established in opposition to the more legitimate shops upon the inner side of the pavement.

Jewish hawkers, many of them in their shirt-sleeves, acclaimed the rarity of the bargains which they had to offer; and, allowing for the difference of costume, these tireless Israelites, heedless of climatic conditions, sweating at their mongery, might well have stood, not in a squalid London thoroughfare, but in an equally squalid market-street of the Orient.

They offered linen and fine raiment; from footgear to hair-oil their wares ranged. They enlivened their auctioneering with conjuring tricks and witty stories, selling watches by the aid of legerdemain, and fancy vests by grace of a seasonable anecdote.

Poles, Russians, Serbs, Roumanians, Jews of Hungary, and Italians of Whitechapel mingled in the throng. Near East and Far East rubbed shoulders. Pidgin English contested with Yiddish for the ownership of some tawdry article offered by an auctioneer whose nationality defied conjecture, save that always some branch of his ancestry had drawn nourishment from the soil of Eternal Judea.

Some wearing mens' caps, some with shawls thrown over their oily locks, and some, more true to primitive instincts, defying, bare-headed, the unkindly elements, bedraggled women—more often than not burdened with muffled infants—crowded the pavements and the roadway, thronged about the stalls like white ants about some choicer carrion.

And the fine drizzling rain fell upon all alike, pattering upon the hood of the taxi-cab, trickling down the front windows; glistening upon the unctuous hair of those in the street who were hatless; dewing the bare arms of the auctioneers, and dripping, melancholy, from the tarpaulin coverings of the stalls. Heedless of the rain above and of the mud beneath, North, South, East, and West mingled their cries, their bids, their blandishments, their raillery, mingled their persons in that joyless throng.

Sometimes a yellow face showed close to one of the streaming windows; sometimes a black-eyed, pallid face, but never a face wholly sane and healthy. This was an underworld where squalor and vice went hand in hand through the beautiless streets, a melting-pot of the world's outcasts; this was the shadowland, which last night had swallowed up Nayland Smith.

Ceaselessly I peered to right and left, searching amid that rain-soaked company for any face known to me. Whom I expected to find there, I know not, but I should have counted it no matter for surprise had I detected amid that ungracious ugliness the beautiful face of Karamaneh the Eastern slave-girl, the leering yellow face of a Burmese dacoit, the gaunt, bronzed features of Nayland Smith; a hundred times I almost believed that I had seen the ruddy countenance of Inspector Weymouth, and once (at which instant my heart seemed to stand still) I suffered from the singular delusion that the oblique green eyes of Dr. Fu-Manchu peered out from the shadows between two stalls.

It was mere phantasy, of course, the sick imaginings of a mind overwrought. I had not slept and had scarcely tasted food for more than thirty hours; for, following up a faint clue supplied by Burke, Slattin's man, and, like his master, an ex-officer of New York Police, my friend, Nayland Smith, on the previous evening had set out in quest of some obscene den where the man called Shen-Yan—former keeper of an opium-shop—was now said to be in hiding.

Shen-Yan we knew to be a creature of the Chinese doctor, and only a most urgent call had prevented me from joining Smith upon this promising, though hazardous expedition.

At any rate, Fate willing it so, he had gone without me; and now—although Inspector Weymouth, assisted by a number of C. I. D. men, was sweeping the district about me—to the time of my departure nothing whatever had been heard of Smith. The ordeal of waiting finally had proved too great to be borne. With no definite idea of what I proposed to do, I had thrown myself into the search, filled with such dreadful apprehensions as I hope never again to experience.

I did not know the exact situation of the place to which Smith was gone, for owing to the urgent case which I have mentioned, I had been absent at the time of his departure; nor could Scotland Yard enlighten me upon this point. Weymouth was in charge of the case—under Smith's direction—and since the inspector had left the Yard, early that morning, he had disappeared as completely as Smith, no report having been received from him.

As my driver turned into the black mouth of a narrow, ill-lighted street, and the glare and clamor of the greater thoroughfare died behind me, I sank into the corner of the cab burdened with such a sense of desolation as mercifully comes but rarely.

We were heading now for that strange settlement off the West India Dock Road, which, bounded by Limehouse Causeway and Pennyfields, and narrowly confined within four streets, composes an unique Chinatown, a miniature of that at Liverpool, and of the greater one in San Francisco. Inspired with an idea which promised hopefully, I raised the speaking tube.

"Take me first to the River Police Station," I directed; "along Ratcliffe Highway."

The man turned and nodded comprehendingly, as I could see through the wet pane.

Presently we swerved to the right and into an even narrower street. This inclined in an easterly direction, and proved to communicate with a wide thoroughfare along which passed brilliantly lighted electric trams. I had lost all sense of direction, and when, swinging to the left and to the right again, I looked through the window and perceived that we were before the door of the Police Station, I was dully surprised.

In quite mechanical fashion I entered the depot. Inspector Ryman, our associate in one of the darkest episodes of the campaign with the Yellow Doctor two years before, received me in his office.

By a negative shake of the head, he answered my unspoken question.

"The ten o'clock boat is lying off the Stone Stairs, Doctor," he said, "and co-operating with some of the Scotland Yard men who are dragging that district—"

I shuddered at the word "dragging"; Ryman had not used it literally, but nevertheless it had conjured up a dread possibility—a possibility in accordance with the methods of Dr. Fu-Manchu. All within space of an instant I saw the tide of Limehouse Reach, the Thames lapping about the green-coated timbers of a dock pier; and rising—falling—sometimes disclosing to the pallid light a rigid hand, sometimes a horribly bloated face—I saw the body of Nayland Smith at the mercy of those oily waters. Ryman continued:

"There is a launch out, too, patrolling the riverside from here to Tilbury. Another lies at the breakwater"—he jerked his thumb over his shoulder. "Should you care to take a run down and see for yourself?"

"No, thanks," I replied, shaking my head. "You are doing all that can be done. Can you give me the address of the place to which Mr. Smith went last night?"

"Certainly," said Ryman; "I thought you knew it. You remember Shen-Yan's place—by Limehouse Basin? Well, further east—east of the Causeway, between Gill Street and Three Colt Street—is a block of wooden buildings. You recall them?"

"Yes," I replied. "Is the man established there again, then?"

"It appears so, but, although you have evidently not been informed of the fact, Weymouth raided the establishment in the early hours of this morning!"

"Well?" I cried.

"Unfortunately with no result," continued the inspector. "The notorious Shen-Yan was missing, and although there is no real doubt that the place is used as a gaming-house, not a particle of evidence to that effect could be obtained. Also—there was no sign of Mr. Nayland Smith, and no sign of the American, Burke, who had led him to the place."

"Is it certain that they went there?"

"Two C. I. D. men who were shadowing, actually saw the pair of them enter. A signal had been arranged, but it was never given; and at about half past four, the place was raided."

"Surely some arrests were made?"

"But there was no evidence!" cried Ryman. "Every inch of the rat-burrow was searched. The Chinese gentleman who posed as the proprietor of what he claimed to be a respectable lodging-house offered every facility to the police. What could we do?"

"I take it that the place is being watched?"

"Certainly," said Ryman. "Both from the river and from the shore. Oh! they are not there! God knows where they are, but they are not there!"

I stood for a moment in silence, endeavoring to determine my course; then, telling Ryman that I hoped to see him later, I walked out slowly into the rain and mist, and nodding to the taxi-driver to proceed to our original destination, I re-entered the cab.

As we moved off, the lights of the River Police depot were swallowed up in the humid murk, and again I found myself being carried through the darkness of those narrow streets, which, like a maze, hold secret within their labyrinth mysteries as great, and at least as foul, as that of Pasiphae.

The marketing centers I had left far behind me; to my right stretched the broken range of riverside buildings, and beyond them flowed the Thames, a stream more heavily burdened with secrets than ever was Tiber or Tigris. On my left, occasional flickering lights broke through the mist, for the most part the lights of taverns; and saving these rents in the veil, the darkness was punctuated with nothing but the faint and yellow luminance of the street lamps.

Ahead was a black mouth, which promised to swallow me up as it had swallowed up my friend.

In short, what with my lowered condition and consequent frame of mind, and what with the traditions, for me inseparable from that gloomy quarter of London, I was in the grip of a shadowy menace which at any moment might become tangible—I perceived, in the most commonplace objects, the yellow hand of Dr. Fu-Manchu.

When the cab stopped in a place of utter darkness, I aroused myself with an effort, opened the door, and stepped out into the mud of a narrow lane. A high brick wall frowned upon me from one side, and, dimly perceptible, there towered a smoke stack, beyond. On my right uprose the side of a wharf building, shadowly, and some distance ahead, almost obscured by the drizzling rain, a solitary lamp flickered. I turned up the collar of my raincoat, shivering, as much at the prospect as from physical chill.

"You will wait here," I said to the man; and, feeling in my breast-pocket, I added: "If you hear the note of a whistle, drive on and rejoin me."

He listened attentively and with a certain eagerness. I had selected him that night for the reason that he had driven Smith and myself on previous occasions and had proved himself a man of intelligence. Transferring a Browning pistol from my hip-pocket to that of my raincoat, I trudged on into the mist.

The headlights of the taxi were swallowed up behind me, and just abreast of the street lamp I stood listening.

Save for the dismal sound of rain, and the trickling of water along the gutters, all about me was silent. Sometimes this silence would be broken by the distant, muffled note of a steam siren; and always, forming a sort of background to the near stillness, was the remote din of riverside activity.

I walked on to the corner just beyond the lamp. This was the street in which the wooden buildings were situated. I had expected to detect some evidences of surveillances, but if any were indeed being observed, the fact was effectively masked. Not a living creature was visible, peer as I could.

Plans, I had none, and perceiving that the street was empty, and that no lights showed in any of the windows, I passed on, only to find that I had entered a cul-de-sac.

A rickety gate gave access to a descending flight of stone steps, the bottom invisible in the denser shadows of an archway, beyond which, I doubted not, lay the river.

Still uninspired by any definite design, I tried the gate and found that it was unlocked. Like some wandering soul, as it has since seemed to me, I descended. There was a lamp over the archway, but the glass was broken, and the rain apparently had extinguished the light; as I passed under it, I could hear the gas whistling from the burner.

Continuing my way, I found myself upon a narrow wharf with the Thames flowing gloomily beneath me. A sort of fog hung over the river, shutting me in. Then came an incident.

Suddenly, quite near, there arose a weird and mournful cry—a cry indescribable, and inexpressibly uncanny!

I started back so violently that how I escaped falling into the river I do not know to this day. That cry, so eerie and so wholly unexpected, had unnerved me; and realizing the nature of my surroundings, and the folly of my presence alone in such a place, I began to edge back toward the foot of the steps, away from the thing that cried; when—a great white shape uprose like a phantom before me!...

There are few men, I suppose, whose lives have been crowded with so many eerie happenings as mine, but this phantom thing which grew out of the darkness, which seemed about to envelope me, takes rank in my memory amongst the most fearsome apparitions which I have witnessed.

I knew that I was frozen with a sort of supernatural terror. I stood there with hands clenched, staring—staring at that white shape, which seemed to float.

As I stared, every nerve in my body thrilling, I distinguished the outline of the phantom. With a subdued cry, I stepped forward. A new sensation claimed me. In that one stride I passed from the horrible to the bizarre.

I found myself confronted with something tangible, certainly, but something whose presence in that place was utterly extravagant—could only be reconcilable in the dreams of an opium slave.

Was I awake, was I sane? Awake and sane beyond doubt, but surely moving, not in the purlieus of Limehouse, but in the fantastic realms of fairyland.

Swooping, with open arms, I rounded up in an angle against the building and gathered in this screaming thing which had inspired in me so keen a terror.

The great, ghostly fan was closed as I did so, and I stumbled back toward the stair with my struggling captive tucked under my arm; I mounted into one of London's darkest slums, carrying a beautiful white peacock!

◆

CHAPTER XII.

DARK EYES LOOKED INTO MINE

My adventure had done nothing to relieve the feeling of unreality which held me enthralled. Grasping the struggling bird firmly by the body, and having the long white tail fluttering a yard or so behind me, I returned to where the taxi waited.

"Open the door!" I said to the man—who greeted me with such a stare of amazement that I laughed outright, though my mirth was but hollow.

He jumped into the road and did as I directed. Making sure that both windows were closed, I thrust the peacock into the cab and shut the door upon it.

"For God's sake, sir!" began the driver—

"It has probably escaped from some collector's place on the riverside," I explained, "but one never knows. See that it does not escape again, and if at the end of an hour, as arranged, you do not hear from me, take it back with you to the River Police Station."

"Right you are, sir," said the man, remounting his seat. "It's the first time I ever saw a peacock in Limehouse!"

It was the first time I had seen one, and the incident struck me as being more than odd; it gave me an idea, and a new, faint hope. I returned to the head of the steps, at the foot of which I had met with this singular experience, and gazed up at the dark building beneath which they led. Three windows were visible, but they were broken and neglected. One, immediately above the arch, had been pasted up with brown paper, and this was now peeling off in the rain, a little stream of which trickled down from the detached corner to drop, drearily, upon the stone stairs beneath.

Where were the detectives? I could only assume that they had directed their attention elsewhere, for had the place not been utterly deserted, surely I had been challenged.

In pursuit of my new idea, I again descended the steps. The persuasion (shortly to be verified) that I was close upon the secret hold of the Chinaman, grew stronger, unaccountably. I had descended some eight steps, and was at the darkest part of the archway or tunnel, when confirmation of my theories came to me.

A noose settled accurately upon my shoulders, was snatched tightly about my throat, and with a feeling of insupportable agony at the base of my skull, and a sudden supreme knowledge that I was being strangled—hanged—I lost consciousness!

How long I remained unconscious, I was unable to determine at the time, but I learned later, that it was for no more than half an hour; at any rate, recovery was slow.

The first sensation to return to me was a sort of repetition of the asphyxia. The blood seemed to be forcing itself into my eyes—I choked—I felt that my end was come. And, raising my hands to my throat, I found it to be swollen and inflamed. Then the floor upon which I lay seemed to be rocking like the deck of a ship, and I glided back again into a place of darkness and forgetfulness.

My second awakening was heralded by a returning sense of smell; for I became conscious of a faint, exquisite perfume.

It brought me to my senses as nothing else could have done, and I sat upright with a hoarse cry. I could have distinguished that perfume amid a thousand others, could have marked it apart from the rest in a scent bazaar. For me it had one meaning, and one meaning only—Karamaneh.

She was near to me, or had been near to me!

And in the first moments of my awakening, I groped about in the darkness blindly seeking her.

Then my swollen throat and throbbing head, together with my utter inability to move my neck even slightly, reminded me of the facts as they were. I knew in that bitter moment that Karamaneh was no longer my friend; but, for all her beauty and charm, was the most heartless, the most fiendish creature in the service of Dr. Fu-Manchu. I groaned aloud in my despair and misery.

Something stirred, near to me in the room, and set my nerves creeping with a new apprehension. I became fully alive to the possibilities of the darkness.

To my certain knowledge, Dr. Fu-Manchu at this time had been in England for fully three months, which meant that by now he must be equipped with all the instruments of destruction, animate and inanimate, which dread experience had taught me to associate with him.

Now, as I crouched there in that dark apartment listening for a repetition of the sound, I scarcely dared to conjecture what might have occasioned it, but my imagination peopled the place with reptiles which writhed upon the floor, with tarantulas and other deadly insects which crept upon the walls, which might drop upon me from the ceiling at any moment.

Then, since nothing stirred about me, I ventured to move, turning my shoulders, for I was unable to move my aching head; and I looked in the direction from which a faint, very faint, light proceeded.

A regular tapping sound now began to attract my attention, and, having turned about, I perceived that behind me was a broken window, in places patched with brown paper; the corner of one sheet of paper was detached, and the rain trickled down upon it with a rhythmical sound.

In a flash I realized that I lay in the room immediately above the archway; and listening intently, I perceived above the other faint sounds of the night, or thought that I perceived, the hissing of the gas from the extinguished lamp-burner.

Unsteadily I rose to my feet, but found myself swaying like a drunken man. I reached out for support, stumbling in the direction of the wall. My foot came in contact with something that lay there, and I pitched forward and fell....

I anticipated a crash which would put an end to my hopes of escape, but my fall was comparatively noiseless—for I fell upon the body of a man who lay bound up with rope close against the wall!

A moment I stayed as I fell, the chest of my fellow captive rising and falling beneath me as he breathed. Knowing that my life depended upon retaining a firm hold upon myself, I succeeded in overcoming the dizziness and nausea which threatened to drown my senses, and, moving back so that I knelt upon the floor, I fumbled in my pocket for the electric lamp which I had placed there. My raincoat had been removed whilst I was unconscious, and with it my pistol, but the lamp was untouched.

I took it out, pressed the button, and directed the ray upon the face of the man beside me.

It was Nayland Smith!

Trussed up and fastened to a ring in the wall he lay, having a cork gag strapped so tightly between his teeth that I wondered how he had escaped suffocation.

But, although a grayish pallor showed through the tan of his skin, his eyes were feverishly bright, and there, as I knelt beside him, I thanked heaven, silently but fervently.

Then, in furious haste, I set to work to remove the gag. It was most ingeniously secured by means of leather straps buckled at the back of his head, but I unfastened these without much difficulty, and he spat out the gag, uttering an exclamation of disgust.

"Thank God, old man!" he said, huskily. "Thank God that you are alive! I saw them drag you in, and I thought…"

"I have been thinking the same about you for more than twenty-four hours," I said, reproachfully. "Why did you start without—"

"I did not want you to come, Petrie," he replied. "I had a sort of premonition. You see it was realized; and instead of being as helpless as I, Fate has made you the instrument of my release. Quick! You have a knife? Good!" The old, feverish energy was by no means extinguished in him. "Cut the ropes about my wrists and ankles, but don't otherwise disturb them—"

I set to work eagerly.

"Now," Smith continued, "put that filthy gag in place again—but you need not strap it so tightly! Directly they find that you are alive, they will treat you the same—you understand? She has been here three times—"

"Karamaneh?"...

"Ssh!"

I heard a sound like the opening of a distant door.

"Quick! the straps of the gag!" whispered Smith, "and pretend to recover consciousness just as they enter—"

Clumsily I followed his directions, for my fingers were none too steady, replaced the lamp in my pocket, and threw myself upon the floor.

Through half-shut eyes, I saw the door open and obtained a glimpse of a desolate, empty passage beyond. On the threshold stood Karamaneh. She held in her hand a common tin oil lamp which smoked and flickered with every movement, filling the already none too cleanly air with an odor of burning paraffin. She personified the outre; nothing so incongruous as her presence in that place could well be imagined. She was dressed as I remembered once to have seen her two years before, in the gauzy silks of the harem. There were pearls glittering like great tears amid the cloud of her wonderful hair. She wore broad gold bangles upon her bare arms, and her fingers were laden with jewelry. A heavy girdle swung from her hips, defining the lines of her slim shape, and about one white ankle was a gold band.

As she appeared in the doorway I almost entirely closed my eyes, but my gaze rested fascinatedly upon the little red slippers which she wore.

Again I detected the exquisite, elusive perfume, which, like a breath of musk, spoke of the Orient; and, as always, it played havoc with my reason, seeming to intoxicate me as though it were the very essence of her loveliness.

But I had a part to play, and throwing out one clenched hand so that my fist struck upon the floor, I uttered a loud groan, and made as if to rise upon my knees.

One quick glimpse I had of her wonderful eyes, widely opened and turned upon me with such an enigmatical expression as set my heart leaping wildly—then, stepping back, Karamaneh placed the lamp upon the boards of the passage and clapped her hands.

As I sank upon the floor in assumed exhaustion, a Chinaman with a perfectly impassive face, and a Burman, whose pock-marked, evil countenance was set in an apparently habitual leer, came running into the room past the girl.

With a hand which trembled violently, she held the lamp whilst the two yellow ruffians tied me. I groaned and struggled feebly, fixing my gaze upon the lamp-bearer in a silent reproach which was by no means without its effect.

She lowered her eyes, and I could see her biting her lip, whilst the color gradually faded from her cheeks. Then, glancing up again quickly, and still meeting that reproachful stare, she turned her head aside altogether, and rested one hand upon the wall, swaying slightly as she did so.

It was a singular ordeal for more than one of that incongruous group; but in order that I may not be charged with hypocrisy or with seeking to hide my own folly, I confess, here, that when again I found myself in darkness, my heart was leaping not because of the success of my strategy, but because of the success of that reproachful glance which I had directed toward the lovely, dark-eyed Karamaneh, toward the faithless, evil Karamaneh! So much for myself.

The door had not been closed ten seconds, ere Smith again was spitting out the gag, swearing under his breath, and stretching his cramped limbs free from their binding. Within a minute from the time of my trussing, I was a free man again; save that look where I would—to right, to left, or inward, to my own conscience—two dark eyes met mine, enigmatically.

"What now?" I whispered.

"Let me think," replied Smith. "A false move would destroy us."

"How long have you been here?"

"Since last night."

"Is Fu-Manchu—"

"Fu-Manchu is here!" replied Smith, grimly—"and not only Fu-Manchu, but—another."

"Another!"

"A higher than Fu-Manchu, apparently. I have an idea of the identity of this person, but no more than an idea. Something unusual is going on, Petrie; otherwise I should have been a dead man twenty-four hours ago. Something even more important than my death engages Fu-Manchu's attention—and this can only be the presence of the mysterious visitor. Your seductive friend, Karamaneh, is arrayed in her very becoming national costume in his honor, I presume." He stopped abruptly; then added: "I would give five hundred pounds for a glimpse of that visitor's face!"

"Is Burke—"

"God knows what has become of Burke, Petrie! We were both caught napping in the establishment of the amiable Shen-Yan, where, amid a very mixed company of poker players, we were losing our money like gentlemen."

"But Weymouth—"

"Burke and I had both been neatly sand-bagged, my dear Petrie, and removed elsewhere, some hours before Weymouth raided the gaming-house. Oh! I don't know how they smuggled us away with the police watching the place; but my presence here is sufficient evidence of the fact. Are you armed?"

"No; my pistol was in my raincoat, which is missing."

In the dim light from the broken window, I could see Smith tugging reflectively at the lobe of his left ear.

"I am without arms, too," he mused. "We might escape from the window—"

"It's a long drop!"

"Ah! I imagined so. If only I had a pistol, or a revolver—"

"What should you do?"

"I should present myself before the important meeting, which, I am assured, is being held somewhere in this building; and to-night would see the end of my struggle with the Fu-Manchu group—the end of the whole Yellow menace! For not only is Fu-Manchu here, Petrie, with all his gang of assassins, but he whom I believe to be the real head of the group—a certain mandarin—is here also!"

◆

CHAPTER XIII.

THE SACRED ORDER

Smith stepped quietly across the room and tried the door. It proved to be unlocked, and an instant later, we were both outside in the passage. Coincident with our arrival there, arose a sudden outcry from some place at the westward end. A high-pitched, grating voice, in which guttural notes alternated with a serpent-like hissing, was raised in anger.

"Dr. Fu-Manchu!" whispered Smith, grasping my arm.

Indeed, it was the unmistakable voice of the Chinaman, raised hysterically in one of those outbursts which in the past I had diagnosed as symptomatic of dangerous mania.

The voice rose to a scream, the scream of some angry animal rather than anything human. Then, chokingly, it ceased. Another short sharp cry followed—but not in the voice of Fu-Manchu—a dull groan, and the sound of a fall.

With Smith still grasping my wrist, I shrank back into the doorway, as something that looked in the darkness like a great ball of fluff came rapidly along the passage toward me. Just at my feet the thing stopped and I made it out for a small animal. The tiny, gleaming eyes looked up at me, and, chattering wickedly, the creature bounded past and was lost from view.

It was Dr. Fu-Manchu's marmoset.

Smith dragged me back into the room which we had just left. As he partly reclosed the door, I heard the clapping of hands. In a condition of most dreadful suspense, we waited; until a new, ominous sound proclaimed itself. Some heavy body was being dragged into the passage. I heard the opening of a trap. Exclamations in guttural voices told of a heavy task in progress; there was a great straining and creaking—whereupon the trap was softly reclosed.

Smith bent to my ear.

"Fu-Manchu has chastised one of his servants," he whispered. "There will be food for the grappling-irons to-night!"

I shuddered violently, for, without Smith's words, I knew that a bloody deed had been done in that house within a few yards of where we stood.

In the new silence, I could hear the drip, drip, drip of the rain outside the window; then a steam siren hooted dismally upon the river, and I thought how the screw of that very vessel, even as we listened, might be tearing the body of Fu-Manchu's servant!

"Have you some one waiting?" whispered Smith, eagerly.

"How long was I insensible?"

"About half an hour."

"Then the cabman will be waiting."

"Have you a whistle with you?"

I felt in my coat pocket.

"Yes," I reported.

"Good! Then we will take a chance."

Again we slipped out into the passage and began a stealthy progress to the west. Ten paces amid absolute darkness, and we found ourselves abreast of a branch corridor. At the further end, through a kind of little window, a dim light shone.

"See if you can find the trap," whispered Smith; "light your lamp."

I directed the ray of the pocket-lamp upon the floor, and there at my feet was a square wooden trap. As I stooped to examine it, I glanced back, painfully, over my shoulder—and saw Nayland Smith tiptoeing away from me along the passage toward the light!

Inwardly I cursed his folly, but the temptation to peep in at that little window proved too strong for me, as it had proved too strong for him.

Fearful that some board would creak beneath my tread, I followed; and side by side we two crouched, looking into a small rectangular room. It was a bare and cheerless apartment with unpapered walls and carpetless floor. A table and a chair constituted the sole furniture.

Seated in the chair, with his back toward us, was a portly Chinaman who wore a yellow, silken robe. His face, it was impossible to see; but he was beating his fist upon the table, and pouring out a torrent of words in a thin, piping voice. So much I perceived at a glance; then, into view at the distant end of the room, paced a tall, high-shouldered figure—a figure unforgettable, at once imposing and dreadful, stately and sinister.

With the long, bony hands behind him, fingers twining and intertwining serpentinely about the handle of a little fan, and with the pointed chin resting on the breast of the yellow robe, so that the light from the lamp swinging in the center of the ceiling gleamed upon the great, dome-like brow, this tall man paced somberly from left to right.

He cast a sidelong, venomous glance at the voluble speaker out of half-shut eyes; in the act they seemed to light up as with an internal luminance; momentarily they sparkled like emeralds; then their brilliance was filmed over as in the eyes of a bird when the membrane is lowered.

My blood seemed to chill, and my heart to double its pulsations; beside me Smith was breathing more rapidly than usual. I knew now the explanation of the feeling which had claimed me when first I had descended the stone stairs. I knew what it was that hung like a miasma over that house. It was the aura, the glamour, which radiated from this wonderful and evil man as light radiates from radium. It was the vril, the force, of Dr. Fu-Manchu.

I began to move away from the window. But Smith held my wrist as in a vise. He was listening raptly to the torrential speech of the Chinaman who sat in the chair; and I perceived in his eyes the light of a sudden comprehension.

As the tall figure of the Chinese doctor came pacing into view again, Smith, his head below the level of the window, pushed me gently along the passage.

Regaining the site of the trap, he whispered to me: "We owe our lives, Petrie, to the national childishness of the Chinese! A race of ancestor worshipers is capable of anything, and Dr. Fu-Manchu, the dreadful being who has rained terror upon Europe stands in imminent peril of disgrace for having lost a decoration."

"What do you mean, Smith?"

"I mean that this is no time for delay, Petrie! Here, unless I am greatly mistaken, lies the rope by means of which you made your entrance. It shall be the means of your exit. Open the trap!"

Handling the lamp to Smith, I stooped and carefully raised the trap-door. At which moment, a singular and dramatic thing happened.

A softly musical voice—the voice of my dreams!—spoke.

"Not that way! O God, not that way!"

In my surprise and confusion I all but let the trap fall, but I retained sufficient presence of mind to replace it gently. Standing upright, I turned... and there, with her little jeweled hand resting upon Smith's arm, stood Karamaneh!

In all my experience of him, I had never seen Nayland Smith so utterly perplexed. Between anger, distrust and dismay, he wavered; and each passing emotion was written legibly upon the lean bronzed features. Rigid with surprise, he stared at the beautiful face of the girl. She, although her hand still rested upon Smith's arm, had her dark eyes turned upon me with that same enigmatical expression. Her lips were slightly parted, and her breast heaved tumultuously.

This ten seconds of silence in which we three stood looking at one another encompassed the whole gamut of human emotion. The silence was broken by Karamaneh.

"They will be coming back that way!" she whispered, bending eagerly toward me. (How, in the most desperate moments, I loved to listen to that odd, musical accent!) "Please, if you would save your life, and spare mine, trust me!"—She suddenly clasped her hands together and looked up into my face, passionately—"Trust me—just for once— and I will show you the way!"

Nayland Smith never removed his gaze from her for a moment, nor did he stir.

"Oh!" she whispered, tremulously, and stamped one little red slipper upon the floor. "Won't you heed me? Come, or it will be too late!"

I glanced anxiously at my friend; the voice of Dr. Fu-Manchu, now raised in anger, was audible above the piping tones of the other Chinaman. And as I caught Smith's eye, in silent query—the trap at my feet began slowly to lift!

Karamaneh stifled a little sobbing cry; but the warning came too late. A hideous yellow face with oblique squinting eyes, appeared in the aperture.

I found myself inert, useless; I could neither think nor act. Nayland Smith, however, as if instinctively, delivered a pitiless kick at the head protruding above the trap.

A sickening crushing sound, with a sort of muffled snap, spoke of a broken jaw-bone; and with no word or cry, the Chinaman fell. As the trap descended with a bang, I heard the thud of his body on the stone stairs beneath.

But we were lost. Karamaneh fled along one of the passages lightly as a bird, and disappeared as Dr. Fu-Manchu, his top lip drawn up above his teeth in the manner of an angry jackal, appeared from the other.

"This way!" cried Smith, in a voice that rose almost to a shriek—"this way!"—and he led toward the room overhanging the steps.

Off we dashed with panic swiftness, only to find that this retreat also was cut off. Dimly visible in the darkness was a group of yellow men, and despite the gloom, the curved blades of the knives which they carried glittered menacingly. The passage was full of dacoits!

Smith and I turned, together. The trap was raised again, and the Burman, who had helped to tie me, was just scrambling up beside Dr. Fu-Manchu, who stood there watching us, a shadowy, sinister figure.

"The game's up, Petrie!" muttered Smith. "It has been a long fight, but Fu-Manchu wins!"

"Not entirely!" I cried. I whipped the police whistle from my pocket, and raised it to my lips; but brief as the interval had been, the dacoits were upon me.

A sinewy brown arm shot over my shoulder and the whistle was dashed from my grasp. Then came a whirl of maelstrom fighting with Smith and myself ever sinking lower amid a whirlpool, as it seemed, of blood-lustful eyes, yellow fangs, and gleaming blades.

I had some vague idea that the rasping voice of Fu-Manchu broke once through the turmoil, and when, with my wrists tied behind me, I emerged from the strife to find myself lying beside Smith in the passage, I could only assume that the Chinaman had ordered his bloody servants to take us alive; for saving numerous bruises and a few superficial cuts, I was unwounded.

The place was utterly deserted again, and we two panting captives found ourselves alone with Dr. Fu-Manchu. The scene was unforgettable; that dimly lighted passage, its extremities masked in shadow, and the tall, yellow-robed figure of the Satanic Chinaman towering over us where we lay.

He had recovered his habitual calm, and as I peered at him through the gloom I was impressed anew with the tremendous intellectual force of the man. He had the brow of a genius, the features of a born ruler; and even in that moment I could find time to search my memory, and to discover that the face, saving the indescribable evil of its expression, was identical with that of Seti, the mighty Pharaoh who lies in the Cairo Museum.

Down the passage came leaping and gamboling the doctor's marmoset. Uttering its shrill, whistling cry, it leaped onto his shoulder, clutched with its tiny fingers at the scanty, neutral-colored hair upon his crown, and bent forward, peering grotesquely into that still, dreadful face.

Dr. Fu-Manchu stroked the little creature; and crooned to it, as a mother to her infant. Only this crooning, and the labored breathing of Smith and myself, broke that impressive stillness.

Suddenly the guttural voice began:

"You come at an opportune time, Mr. Commissioner Nayland Smith, and Dr. Petrie; at a time when the greatest man in China flatters me with a visit. In my absence from home, a tremendous honor has been conferred upon me, and, in the hour of this supreme honor, dishonor and calamity have befallen! For my services to China—the

New China, the China of the future—I have been admitted by the Sublime Prince to the Sacred Order of the White Peacock."

Warming to his discourse, he threw wide his arms, hurling the chattering marmoset fully five yards along the corridor.

"O god of Cathay!" he cried, sibilantly, "in what have I sinned that this catastrophe has been visited upon my head! Learn, my two dear friends, that the sacred white peacock brought to these misty shores for my undying glory, has been lost to me! Death is the penalty of such a sacrilege; death shall be my lot, since death I deserve."

Covertly Smith nudged me with his elbow. I knew what the nudge was designed to convey; he would remind me of his words—anent the childish trifles which sway the life of intellectual China.

Personally, I was amazed. That Fu-Manchu's anger, grief, sorrow and resignation were real, no one watching him, and hearing his voice, could doubt.

He continued:

"By one deed, and one deed alone, may I win a lighter punishment. By one deed, and the resignation of all my titles, all my lands, and all my honors, may I merit to be spared to my work—which has only begun."

I knew now that we were lost, indeed; these were confidences which our graves should hold inviolate! He suddenly opened fully those blazing green eyes and directed their baneful glare upon Nayland Smith.

"The Director of the Universe," he continued, softly, "has relented toward me. To-night, you die! To-night, the arch-enemy of our caste shall be no more. This is my offering—the price of redemption..."

My mind was working again, and actively. I managed to grasp the stupendous truth—and the stupendous possibility.

Dr. Fu-Manchu was in the act of clapping his hands, when I spoke.

"Stop!" I cried.

He paused, and the weird film, which sometimes became visible in his eyes, now obscured their greenness, and lent him the appearance of a blind man.

"Dr. Petrie," he said, softly, "I shall always listen to you with respect."

"I have an offer to make," I continued, seeking to steady my voice. "Give us our freedom, and I will restore your shattered honor—I will restore the sacred peacock!"

Dr. Fu-Manchu bent forward until his face was so close to mine that I could see the innumerable lines which, an intricate network, covered his yellow skin.

"Speak!" he hissed. "You lift up my heart from a dark pit!"

"I can restore your white peacock," I said; "I and I alone, know where it is!"—and I strove not to shrink from the face so close to mine.

Upright shot the tall figure; high above his head Fu-Manchu threw his arms—and a light of exaltation gleamed in the now widely opened, catlike eyes.

"O god!" he screamed, frenziedly—"O god of the Golden Age! like a phoenix I arise from the ashes of myself!" He turned to me. "Quick! Quick! make your bargain! End my suspense!"

Smith stared at me like a man dazed; but, ignoring him, I went on:

"You will release me, now, immediately. In another ten minutes it will be too late; my friend will remain. One of your—servants—can accompany me, and give the signal when I return with the peacock. Mr. Nayland Smith and yourself, or another, will join me at the corner of the street where the raid took place last night. We shall then give you ten minutes grace, after which we shall take whatever steps we choose."

"Agreed!" cried Fu-Manchu. "I ask but one thing from an Englishman; your word of honor?"

"I give it."

"I, also," said Smith, hoarsely.

Ten minutes later, Nayland Smith and I, standing beside the cab, whose lights gleamed yellowly through the mist, exchanged a struggling, frightened bird for our lives—capitulated with the enemy of the white race.

With characteristic audacity—and characteristic trust in the British sense of honor—Dr. Fu-Manchu came in person with Nayland Smith, in response to the wailing signal of the dacoit who had accompanied me. No word was spoken, save that the cabman suppressed a curse of amazement; and the Chinaman, his sinister servant at his elbow, bowed low—and left us, surely to the mocking laughter of the gods!

◆

CHAPTER XIV.

THE COUGHING HORROR

I leaped up in bed with a great start.

My sleep was troubled often enough in these days, which immediately followed our almost miraculous escape, from the den of Fu-Manchu; and now as I crouched there, nerves aquiver—listening—listening—I could not be sure if this dank panic which possessed me had its origin in nightmare or in something else.

Surely a scream, a choking cry for help, had reached my ears; but now, almost holding my breath in that sort of nervous tensity peculiar to one aroused thus, I listened, and the silence seemed complete. Perhaps I had been dreaming...

"Help! Petrie! Help!..."

It was Nayland Smith in the room above me!

My doubts were dissolved; this was no trick of an imagination disordered. Some dreadful menace threatened my friend. Not delaying even to snatch my dressing-gown, I rushed out on to the landing, up the stairs, bare-footed as I was, threw open the door of Smith's room and literally hurled myself in.

Those cries had been the cries of one assailed, had been uttered, I judged, in the brief interval of a life and death struggle; had been choked off...

A certain amount of moonlight found access to the room, without spreading so far as the bed in which my friend lay. But at the moment of my headlong entrance, and before I had switched on the light, my gaze automatically was directed to the pale moonbeam streaming through the window and down on to one corner of the sheep-skin rug beside the bed.

There came a sound of faint and muffled coughing.

What with my recent awakening and the panic at my heart, I could not claim that my vision was true; but across this moonbeam passed a sort of gray streak, for all the world as though some long thin shape had been withdrawn, snakelike, from the room, through the open window... From somewhere outside the house, and below, I heard the cough again, followed by a sharp cracking sound like the lashing of a whip.

I depressed the switch, flooding the room with light, and as I leaped forward to the bed a word picture of what I had seen formed in my mind; and I found that I was thinking of a gray feather boa.

"Smith!" I cried (my voice seemed to pitch itself, unwilled, in a very high key), "Smith, old man!"

He made no reply, and a sudden, sorrowful fear clutched at my heart-strings. He was lying half out of bed flat upon his back, his head at a dreadful angle with his body. As I bent over him and seized him by the shoulders, I could see the whites of his eyes. His arms hung limply, and his fingers touched the carpet.

"My God!" I whispered—"what has happened?"

I heaved him back onto the pillow, and looked anxiously into his face. Habitually gaunt, the flesh so refined away by the consuming nervous energy of the man as to reveal the cheekbones in sharp prominence, he now looked truly ghastly. His skin was so sunbaked as to have changed constitutionally; nothing could ever eradicate that tan. But to-night a fearful grayness was mingled with the brown, his lips were purple... and there were marks of strangulation upon the lean throat—ever darkening weals made by clutching fingers.

He began to breathe stentoriously and convulsively, inhalation being accompanied by a significant gurgling in the throat. But now my calm was restored in face of a situation which called for professional attention.

I aided my friend's labored respirations by the usual means, setting to work vigorously; so that presently he began to clutch at his inflamed throat which that murderous pressure had threatened to close.

I could hear sounds of movement about the house, showing that not I alone had been awakened by those hoarse screams.

"It's all right, old man," I said, bending over him; "brace up!"

He opened his eyes—they looked bleared and bloodshot—and gave me a quick glance of recognition.

"It's all right, Smith!" I said—"no! don't sit up; lie there for a moment."

I ran across to the dressing-table, whereon I perceived his flask to lie, and mixed him a weak stimulant with which I returned to the bed.

As I bent over him again, my housekeeper appeared in the doorway, pale and wide-eyed.

"There is no occasion for alarm," I said over my shoulder; "Mr. Smith's nerves are overwrought and he was awakened by some disturbing dream. You can return to bed, Mrs. Newsome."

Nayland Smith seemed to experience much difficulty in swallowing the contents of the tumbler which I held to his lips; and, from the way in which he fingered the swollen glands, I could see that his throat, which I had vigorously massaged, was occasioning him great pain. But the danger was past, and already that glassy look was disappearing from his eyes, nor did they protrude so unnaturally.

"God, Petrie!" he whispered, "that was a near shave! I haven't the strength of a kitten!"

"The weakness will pass off," I replied; "there will be no collapse, now. A little more fresh air..."

I stood up, glancing at the windows, then back at Smith, who forced a wry smile in answer to my look.

"Couldn't be done, Petrie," he said, huskily.

His words referred to the state of the windows. Although the night was oppressively hot, these were only opened some four inches at top and bottom. Further opening was impossible because of iron brackets screwed firmly into the casements which prevented the windows being raised or lowered further.

It was a precaution adopted after long experience of the servants of Dr. Fu-Manchu.

Now, as I stood looking from the half-strangled man upon the bed to those screwed-up windows, the fact came home to my mind that this precaution had proved futile. I thought of the thing which I had likened to a feather boa; and I looked at the swollen weals made by clutching fingers upon the throat of Nayland Smith.

The bed stood fully four feet from the nearest window.

I suppose the question was written in my face; for, as I turned again to Smith, who, having struggled upright, was still fingering his injured throat ruefully:

"God only knows, Petrie!" he said; "no human arm could have reached me..."

For us, the night was ended so far as sleep was concerned. Arrayed in his dressing-gown, Smith sat in the white cane chair in my study with a glass of brandy-and-water beside him, and (despite my official prohibition) with the cracked briar which had sent up its incense in many strange and dark places of the East and which yet survived to perfume these prosy rooms in suburban London, steaming between his teeth. I stood with my elbow resting upon the mantelpiece looking down at him where he sat.

"By God! Petrie," he said, yet again, with his fingers straying gently over the surface of his throat, "that was a narrow shave—a damned narrow shave!"

"Narrower than perhaps you appreciate, old man," I replied. "You were a most unusual shade of blue when I found you..."

"I managed," said Smith evenly, "to tear those clutching fingers away for a moment and to give a cry for help. It was only for a moment, though. Petrie! they were fingers of steel—of steel!"

"The bed," I began...

"I know that," rapped Smith. "I shouldn't have been sleeping in it, had it been within reach of the window; but, knowing that the doctor avoids noisy methods, I had thought myself fairly safe so long as I made it impossible for any one actually to enter the room..."

"I have always insisted, Smith," I cried, "that there was danger! What of poisoned darts? What of the damnable reptiles and insects which form part of the armory of Fu-Manchu?"

"Familiarity breeds contempt, I suppose," he replied. "But as it happened none of those agents was employed. The very menace that I sought to avoid reached me somehow. It would almost seem that Dr. Fu-Manchu deliberately accepted the challenge of those screwed-up windows! Hang it all, Petrie! one cannot sleep in a room hermetically sealed, in weather like this! It's positively Burmese; and although I can stand tropical heat, curiously enough the heat of London gets me down almost immediately."

"The humidity; that's easily understood. But you'll have to put up with it in the future. After nightfall our windows must be closed entirely, Smith."

Nayland Smith knocked out his pipe upon the side of the fireplace. The bowl sizzled furiously, but without delay he stuffed broad-cut mixture into the hot pipe, dropping a liberal quantity upon the carpet during the process. He raised his eyes to me, and his face was very grim.

"Petrie," he said, striking a match on the heel of his slipper, "the resources of Dr. Fu-Manchu are by no means exhausted. Before we quit this room it is up to us to come to a decision upon a certain point." He got his pipe well alight. "What kind of thing, what unnatural, distorted creature, laid hands upon my throat to-night? I owe my life, primarily, to you, old man, but, secondarily, to the fact that I was awakened, just before the attack—by the creature's coughing—by its vile, high-pitched coughing..."

I glanced around at the books upon my shelves. Often enough, following some outrage by the brilliant Chinese doctor whose genius was directed to the discovery of new and unique death agents, we had obtained a clue in those works of a scientific nature which bulk largely in the library of a medical man. There are creatures, there are drugs, which, ordinarily innocuous, may be so employed as to become inimical to human life; and in the distorting of nature, in the disturbing of balances and the diverting of beneficent forces into strange and dangerous channels, Dr. Fu-Manchu excelled. I had known him to enlarge, by artificial culture, a minute species of fungus so as to render it a powerful agent capable of attacking man; his knowledge of venomous insects has probably never been paralleled in the history of the world; whilst, in the sphere of pure toxicology, he had, and has, no rival; the Borgias were children by comparison. But, look where I would, think how I might, no adequate explanation of this latest outrage seemed possible along normal lines.

"There's the clue," said Nayland Smith, pointing to a little ash-tray upon the table near by. "Follow it if you can."

But I could not.

"As I have explained," continued my friend, "I was awakened by a sound of coughing; then came a death grip on my throat, and instinctively my hands shot out in search of my attacker. I could not reach him; my hands came in contact with nothing palpable. Therefore I clutched at the fingers which were dug into my windpipe, and found them to be small—as the marks show—and hairy. I managed to give that first cry for help, then with all my strength I tried to unfasten the grip that was throttling the life out of me. At last I contrived to move one of the hands, and I called out again, though not so loudly. Then both the hands were back again; I was weakening; but I clawed like a madman at the thin, hairy arms of the strangling thing, and with a blood-red mist dancing before my eyes, I seemed to be whirling madly round and round until all became a blank. Evidently I used my nails pretty freely—and there's the trophy."

For the twentieth time, I should think, I carried the ash-tray in my hand and laid it immediately under the table-lamp in order to examine its contents. In the little brass bowl lay a blood-stained fragment of grayish hair attached to a tatter of skin. This fragment of epidermis had an odd bluish tinge, and the attached hair was much darker at the roots than elsewhere. Saving its singular color, it might have been torn from the forearm of a very hirsute human; but although my thoughts wandered unfettered, north, south, east and west; although, knowing the resources of Fu-Manchu, I considered all the recognized Mongolian types, and, in quest of hirsute mankind, even roamed far north among the blubbering Esquimo; although I glanced at Australasia, at Central Africa, and passed in mental review the dark places of the Congo, nowhere in the known world, nowhere in the history of the human species, could I come upon a type of man answering to the description suggested by our strange clue.

Nayland Smith was watching me curiously as I bent over the little brass ash-tray.

"You are puzzled," he rapped in his short way.

"So am I—utterly puzzled. Fu-Manchu's gallery of monstrosities clearly has become reinforced; for even if we identified the type, we should not be in sight of our explanation."

"You mean," I began...

"Fully four feet from the window, Petrie, and that window but a few inches open! Look"—he bent forward, resting his chest against the table, and stretched out his hand toward me. "You have a rule there; just measure."

Setting down the ash-tray, I opened out the rule and measured the distance from the further edge of the table to the tips of Smith's fingers.

"Twenty-eight inches—and I have a long reach!" snapped Smith, withdrawing his arm and striking a match to relight his pipe. "There's one thing, Petrie, often proposed before, which now we must do without delay. The ivy must be stripped from the walls at the back. It's a pity, but we can not afford to sacrifice our lives to our sense of the aesthetic. What do you make of the sound like the cracking of a whip?"

"I make nothing of it, Smith," I replied, wearily. "It might have been a thick branch of ivy breaking beneath the weight of a climber."

"Did it sound like it?"

"I must confess that the explanation does not convince me, but I have no better one."

Smith, permitting his pipe to go out, sat staring straight before him, and tugging at the lobe of his left ear.

"The old bewilderment is seizing me," I continued. "At first, when I realized that Dr. Fu-Manchu was back in England, when I realized that an elaborate murder-machine was set up somewhere in London, it seemed unreal, fantastical. Then I met—Karamaneh! She, whom we thought to be his victim, showed herself again to be his slave. Now, with Weymouth and Scotland Yard at work, the old secret evil is established again in our midst, unaccountably—our lives are menaced—sleep is a danger—every shadow threatens death... oh! it is awful."

Smith remained silent; he did not seem to have heard my words. I knew these moods and had learnt that it was useless to seek to interrupt them. With his brows drawn down, and his deep-set eyes staring into space, he sat there gripping his cold pipe so tightly that my own jaw muscles ached sympathetically. No man was better equipped than this gaunt British Commissioner to stand between society and the menace of the Yellow Doctor; I respected his meditations, for, unlike my own, they were informed by an intimate knowledge of the dark and secret things of the East, of that mysterious East out of which Fu-Manchu came, of that jungle of noxious things whose miasma had been wafted Westward with the implacable Chinaman.

I walked quietly from the room, occupied with my own bitter reflections.

◆

CHAPTER XV.

BEWITCHMENT

"You say you have two items of news for me?" said Nayland Smith, looking across the breakfast table to where Inspector Weymouth sat sipping coffee.

"There are two points—yes," replied the Scotland Yard man, whilst Smith paused, egg-spoon in hand, and fixed his keen eyes upon the speaker. "The first is this: the headquarters of the Yellow group is no longer in the East End."

"How can you be sure of that?"

"For two reasons. In the first place, that district must now be too hot to hold Dr. Fu-Manchu; in the second place, we have just completed a house-to-house inquiry which has scarcely overlooked a rathole or a rat. That place where you say Fu-Manchu was visited by some Chinese mandarin; where you, Mr. Smith," and—glancing in my direction—"you, Doctor, were confined for a time—"

"Yes?" snapped Smith, attacking his egg.

"Well," continued the inspector, "it is all deserted, now. There is not the slightest doubt that the Chinaman has fled to some other abode. I am certain of it. My second piece of news will interest you very much, I am sure. You were taken to the establishment of the Chinaman, Shen-Yan, by a certain ex-officer of New York Police—Burke..."

"Good God!" cried Smith, looking up with a start; "I thought they had him!"

"So did I," replied Weymouth grimly; "but they haven't! He got away in the confusion following the raid, and has been hiding ever since with a cousin, a nurseryman out Upminster way..."

"Hiding?" snapped Smith.

"Exactly—hiding. He has been afraid to stir ever since, and has scarcely shown his nose outside the door. He says he is watched night and day."

"Then how..."

"He realized that something must be done," continued the inspector, "and made a break this morning. He is so convinced of this constant surveillance that he came away secretly, hidden under the boxes of a market-wagon. He landed at Covent Garden in the early hours of this morning and came straight away to the Yard."

"What is he afraid of exactly?"

Inspector Weymouth put down his coffee cup and bent forward slightly.

"He knows something," he said in a low voice, "and they are aware that he knows it!"

"And what is this he knows?"

Nayland Smith stared eagerly at the detective.

"Every man has his price," replied Weymouth with a smile, "and Burke seems to think that you are a more likely market than the police authorities."

"I see," snapped Smith. "He wants to see me?"

"He wants you to go and see him," was the reply. "I think he anticipates that you may make a capture of the person or persons spying upon him."

"Did he give you any particulars?"

"Several. He spoke of a sort of gipsy girl with whom he had a short conversation one day, over the fence which divides his cousin's flower plantations from the lane adjoining."

"Gipsy girl!" I whispered, glancing rapidly at Smith.

"I think you are right, Doctor," said Weymouth with his slow smile; "it was Karamaneh. She asked him the way to somewhere or other and got him to write it upon a loose page of his notebook, so that she should not forget it."

"You hear that, Petrie?" rapped Smith.

"I hear it," I replied, "but I don't see any special significance in the fact."

"I do!" rapped Smith; "I didn't sit up the greater part of last night thrashing my weary brains for nothing! But I am going to the British Museum to-day, to confirm a certain suspicion." He turned to Weymouth. "Did Burke go back?" he demanded abruptly.

"He returned hidden under the empty boxes," was the reply. "Oh! you never saw a man in such a funk in all your life!"

"He may have good reasons," I said.

"He has good reasons!" replied Nayland Smith grimly; "if that man really possesses information inimical to the safety of Fu-Manchu, he can only escape doom by means of a miracle similar to that which has hitherto protected you and me."

"Burke insists," said Weymouth at this point, "that something comes almost every night after dusk, slinking about the house—it's an old farmhouse, I understand; and on two or three occasions he has been awakened (fortunately for him he is a light sleeper) by sounds of coughing immediately outside his window. He is a man who sleeps with a pistol under his pillow, and more than once, on running to the window, he has had a vague glimpse of some creature leaping down from the tiles of the roof, which slopes up to his room, into the flower beds below..."

"Creature!" said Smith, his gray eyes ablaze now—"you said creature!"

"I used the word deliberately," replied Weymouth, "because Burke seems to have the idea that it goes on all fours."

There was a short and rather strained silence. Then:

"In descending a sloping roof," I suggested, "a human being would probably employ his hands as well as his feet."

"Quite so," agreed the inspector. "I am merely reporting the impression of Burke."

"Has he heard no other sound?" rapped Smith; "one like the cracking of dry branches, for instance?"

"He made no mention of it," replied Weymouth, staring.

"And what is the plan?"

"One of his cousin's vans," said Weymouth, with his slight smile, "has remained behind at Covent Garden and will return late this afternoon. I propose that you and I, Mr. Smith, imitate Burke and ride down to Upminster under the empty boxes!"

Nayland Smith stood up, leaving his breakfast half finished, and began to wander up and down the room, reflectively tugging at his ear. Then he began to fumble in the pockets of his dressing-gown and finally produced the inevitable pipe, dilapidated pouch, and box of safety matches. He began to load the much-charred agent of reflection.

"Do I understand that Burke is actually too afraid to go out openly even in daylight?" he asked suddenly.

"He has not hitherto left his cousin's plantations at all," replied Weymouth. "He seems to think that openly to communicate with the authorities, or with you, would be to seal his death warrant."

"He's right," snapped Smith.

"Therefore he came and returned secretly," continued the inspector; "and if we are to do any good, obviously we must adopt similar precautions. The market wagon, loaded in such a way as to leave ample space in the interior for us, will be drawn up outside the office of Messrs. Pike and Pike, in Covent Garden, until about five o'clock this afternoon. At, say, half past four, I propose that we meet there and embark upon the journey."

The speaker glanced in my direction interrogatively.

"Include me in the program," I said. "Will there be room in the wagon?"

"Certainly," was the reply; "it is most commodious, but I cannot guarantee its comfort."

Nayland Smith promenaded the room, unceasingly, and presently he walked out altogether, only to return ere the inspector and I had had time to exchange more than a glance of surprise, carrying a brass ash-tray. He placed this on a corner of the breakfast table before Weymouth.

"Ever seen anything like that?" he inquired.

The inspector examined the gruesome relic with obvious curiosity, turning it over with the tip of his little finger and manifesting considerable repugnance—in touching it at all. Smith and I watched him in silence, and, finally, placing the tray again upon the table, he looked up in a puzzled way.

"It's something like the skin of a water rat," he said.

Nayland Smith stared at him fixedly.

"A water rat? Now that you come to mention it, I perceive a certain resemblance—yes. But"—he had been wearing a silk scarf about his throat and now he unwrapped it—"did you ever see a water rat that could make marks like these?"

Weymouth started to his feet with some muttered exclamation.

"What is this?" he cried. "When did it happen, and how?"

In his own terse fashion, Nayland Smith related the happenings of the night. At the conclusion of the story:

"By heaven!" whispered Weymouth, "the thing on the roof—the coughing thing that goes on all fours, seen by Burke..."

"My own idea exactly!" cried Smith...

"Fu-Manchu," I said excitedly, "has brought some new, some dreadful creature, from Burma..."

"No, Petrie," snapped Smith, turning upon me suddenly. "Not from Burma—from Abyssinia."

That day was destined to be an eventful one; a day never to be forgotten by any of us concerned in those happenings which I have to record. Early in the morning Nayland Smith set off for the British Museum to pursue his mysterious investigations, and having performed my brief professional round (for, as Nayland Smith had remarked on one occasion, this was a beastly healthy district), I found, having made the necessary arrangements, that, with over three hours to spare, I had nothing to occupy my time until the appointment in Covent Garden Market. My lonely lunch completed, a restless fit seized me, and I felt unable to remain longer in the house. Inspired by this restlessness, I attired myself for the adventure of the evening, not neglecting to place a pistol in my pocket, and, walking to the neighboring Tube station, I booked to Charing Cross, and presently found myself rambling aimlessly along the crowded streets. Led on by what link of memory I know not, I presently drifted into New Oxford Street, and looked up with a start—to learn that I stood before the shop of a second-hand book-seller where once two years before I had met Karamaneh.

The thoughts conjured up at that moment were almost too bitter to be borne, and without so much as glancing at the books displayed for sale, I crossed the roadway, entered Museum Street, and, rather in order to distract my mind than because I contemplated any purchase, began to examine the Oriental Pottery, Egyptian statuettes, Indian armor, and other curios, displayed in the window of an antique dealer.

But, strive as I would to concentrate my mind upon the objects in the window, my memories persistently haunted me, and haunted me to the exclusion even of the actualities. The crowds thronging the Pavement, the traffic in New Oxford Street, swept past unheeded; my eyes saw nothing of pot nor statuette, but only met, in a misty imaginative world, the glance of two other eyes—the dark and beautiful eyes of Karamaneh. In the exquisite tinting of a Chinese vase dimly perceptible in the background of the shop, I perceived only the blushing cheeks of Karamaneh; her face rose up, a taunting phantom, from out of the darkness between a hideous, gilded idol and an Indian sandalwood screen.

I strove to dispel this obsessing thought, resolutely fixing my attention upon a tall Etruscan vase in the corner of the window, near to the shop door. Was I losing my senses indeed? A doubt of my own sanity momentarily possessed me. For, struggle as I would to dispel the illusion—there, looking out at me over that ancient piece of pottery, was the bewitching face of the slave-girl!

Probably I was glaring madly, and possibly I attracted the notice of the passers-by; but of this I cannot be certain, for all my attention was centered upon that phantasmal face, with the cloudy hair, slightly parted red lips, and the brilliant dark eyes which looked into mine out of the shadows of the shop.

It was bewildering—it was uncanny; for, delusion or verity, the glamour prevailed. I exerted a great mental effort, stepped to the door, turned the handle, and entered the shop with as great a show of composure as I could muster.

A curtain draped in a little door at the back of one counter swayed slightly, with no greater violence than may have been occasioned by the draught. But I fixed my eyes upon this swaying curtain almost fiercely... as an impassive half-caste of some kind who appeared to be a strange cross between a Graeco-Hebrew and a Japanese, entered and quite unemotionally faced me, with a slight bow.

So wholly unexpected was this apparition that I started back.

"Can I show you anything, sir?" inquired the new arrival, with a second slight inclination of the head.

I looked at him for a moment in silence. Then:

"I thought I saw a lady of my acquaintance here a moment ago," I said. "Was I mistaken?"

"Quite mistaken, sir," replied the shopman, raising his black eyebrows ever so slightly; "a mistake possibly due to a reflection in the window. Will you take a look around now that you are here?"

"Thank you," I replied, staring him hard in the face; "at some other time."

I turned and quitted the shop abruptly. Either I was mad, or Karamaneh was concealed somewhere therein.

However, realizing my helplessness in the matter, I contented myself with making a mental note of the name which appeared above the establishment—J. Salaman—and walked on, my mind in a chaotic condition and my heart beating with unusual rapidity.

◆

CHAPTER XVI.

THE QUESTING HANDS

Within my view, from the corner of the room where I sat in deepest shadow, through the partly opened window (it was screwed, like our own) were rows of glass-houses gleaming in the moonlight, and, beyond them, orderly ranks of flower-beds extending into a blue haze of distance. By reason of the moon's position, no light entered the room, but my eyes, from long watching, were grown familiar with the darkness, and I could see Burke quite clearly as he lay in the bed between my post and the window. I seemed to be back again in those days of the troubled past when first Nayland Smith and I had come to grips with the servants of Dr. Fu-Manchu. A more peaceful scene than this flower-planted corner of Essex it would be difficult to imagine; but, either because of my knowledge that its peace was chimerical, or because of that outflung consciousness of danger which, actually, or in my imagination, preceded the coming of the Chinaman's agents, to my seeming the silence throbbed electrically and the night was laden with stilly omens.

Already cramped by my journey in the market-cart, I found it difficult to remain very long in any one position. What information had Burke to sell? He had refused, for some reason, to discuss the matter that evening, and now, enacting the part allotted him by Nayland Smith, he feigned sleep consistently, although at intervals he would whisper to me his doubts and fears.

All the chances were in our favor to-night; for whilst I could not doubt that Dr. Fu-Manchu was set upon the removal of the ex-officer of New York police, neither could I doubt that our presence in the farm was unknown to the agents of the Chinaman. According to Burke, constant attempts had been made to achieve Fu-Manchu's purpose, and had only been frustrated by his (Burke's) wakefulness.

There was every probability that another attempt would be made to-night.

Any one who has been forced by circumstance to undertake such a vigil as this will be familiar with the marked changes (corresponding with phases of the earth's movement) which take place in the atmosphere, at midnight, at two o'clock, and again at four o'clock. During those fours hours falls a period wherein all life is at its lowest ebb, and every Physician is aware that there is a greater likelihood of a patient's passing between midnight and four A. M., than at any other period during the cycle of the hours.

To-night I became specially aware of this lowering of vitality, and now, with the night at that darkest phase which precedes the dawn, an indescribable dread, such as I had known before in my dealings with the Chinaman, assailed me, when I was least prepared to combat it. The stillness was intense. Then:

"Here it is!" whispered Burke from the bed.

The chill at the very center of my being, which but corresponded with the chill of all surrounding nature at that hour, became intensified, keener, at the whispered words.

I rose stealthily out of my chair, and from my nest of shadows watched—watched intently, the bright oblong of the window...

Without the slightest heralding sound—a black silhouette crept up against the pane... the silhouette of a small, malformed head, a dog-like head, deep-set in square shoulders. Malignant eyes peered intently in. Higher it arose—that wicked head—against the window, then crouched down on the sill and became less sharply defined as the creature stooped to the opening below. There was a faint sound of sniffing.

Judging from the stark horror which I experienced, myself, I doubted, now, if Burke could sustain the role allotted him. In beneath the slightly raised window came a hand, perceptible to me despite the darkness of the room. It seemed to project from the black silhouette outside the pane, to be thrust forward—and forward—and forward... that small hand with the outstretched fingers.

The unknown possesses unique terrors; and since I was unable to conceive what manner of thing this could be, which, extending its incredibly long arms, now sought the throat of the man upon the bed, I tasted of that sort of terror which ordinarily one knows only in dreams.

"Quick, sir—quick!" screamed Burke, starting up from the pillow.

The questing hands had reached his throat!

Choking down an urgent dread that I had of touching the thing which reached through the window to kill the sleeper, I sprang across the room and grasped the rigid, hairy forearms.

Heavens! Never have I felt such muscles, such tendons, as those beneath the hirsute skin! They seemed to be of steel wire, and with a sudden frightful sense of impotence, I realized that I was as powerless as a child to relax that strangle-hold. Burke was making the most frightful sounds and quite obviously was being asphyxiated before my eyes!

"Smith!" I cried, "Smith! Help! help! for God's sake!"

Despite the confusion of my mind I became aware of sounds outside and below me. Twice the thing at the window coughed; there was an incessant, lash-like cracking, then some shouted words which I was unable to make out; and finally the staccato report of a pistol.

Snarling like that of a wild beast came from the creature with the hairy arms, together with renewed coughing. But the steel grip relaxed not one iota.

I realized two things: the first, that in my terror at the suddenness of the attack I had omitted to act as pre-arranged: the second, that I had discredited the strength of the visitant, whilst Smith had foreseen it.

Desisting in my vain endeavor to pit my strength against that of the nameless thing, I sprang back across the room and took up the weapon which had been left in my charge earlier in the night, but which I had been unable to believe it would be necessary to employ. This was a sharp and heavy axe, which Nayland Smith, when I had met him in Covent Garden, had brought with him, to the great amazement of Weymouth and myself.

As I leaped back to the window and uplifted this primitive weapon, a second shot sounded from below, and more fierce snarling, coughing, and guttural mutterings assailed my ears from beyond the pane.

Lifting the heavy blade, I brought it down with all my strength upon the nearer of those hairy arms where it crossed the window-ledge, severing muscle, tendon and bone as easily as a knife might cut cheese....

A shriek—a shriek neither human nor animal, but gruesomely compounded of both—followed... and merged into a choking cough. Like a flash the other shaggy arm was withdrawn, and some vaguely-seen body went rolling down the sloping red tiles and crashed on to the ground beneath.

With a second piercing shriek, louder than that recently uttered by Burke, wailing through the night from somewhere below, I turned desperately to the man on the bed, who now was become significantly silent. A candle, with matches, stood upon a table hard by, and, my fingers far from steady, I set about obtaining a light. This accomplished, I stood the candle upon the little chest-of-drawers and returned to Burke's side.

"Merciful God!" I cried.

Of all the pictures which remain in my memory, some of them dark enough, I can find none more horrible than that which now confronted me in the dim candle-light. Burke lay crosswise on the bed, his head thrown back and sagging; one rigid hand he held in the air, and with the other grasped the hairy forearm which I had severed with the ax; for, in a death-grip, the dead fingers were still fastened, vise-like, at his throat.

His face was nearly black, and his eyes projected from their sockets horribly. Mastering my repugnance, I seized the hideous piece of bleeding anatomy and strove to release it. It defied all my efforts; in death it was as implacable as in life. I took a knife from my pocket, and, tendon by tendon, cut away that uncanny grip from Burke's throat...

But my labor was in vain. Burke was dead!

I think I failed to realize this for some time. My clothes were sticking clammily to my body; I was bathed in perspiration, and, shaking furiously, I clutched at the edge of the window, avoiding the bloody patch upon the ledge, and looked out over the roofs to where, in the more distant plantations, I could hear excited voices. What had been the meaning of that scream which I had heard but to which in my frantic state of mind I had paid comparatively little attention?

There was a great stirring all about me.

"Smith!" I cried from the window; "Smith, for mercy's sake where are you?"

Footsteps came racing up the stairs. Behind me the door burst open and Nayland Smith stumbled into the room.

"God!" he said, and started back in the doorway.

"Have you got it, Smith?" I demanded hoarsely. "In sanity's name what is it—what is it?"

"Come downstairs," replied Smith quietly, "and see for yourself." He turned his head aside from the bed.

Very unsteadily I followed him down the stairs and through the rambling old house out into the stone-paved courtyard. There were figures moving at the end of a long alleyway between the glass houses, and one, carrying a lantern, stooped over something which lay upon the ground.

"That's Burke's cousin with the lantern," whispered Smith in my ear; "don't tell him yet."

I nodded, and we hurried up to join the group. I found myself looking down at one of those thick-set Burmans whom I always associated with Fu-Manchu's activities. He lay quite flat, face downward; but the back of his head was a shapeless blood-dotted mass, and a heavy stock-whip, the butt end ghastly because of the blood and hair which clung to it, lay beside him. I started back appalled as Smith caught my arm.

"It turned on its keeper!" he hissed in my ear. "I wounded it twice from below, and you severed one arm; in its insensate fury, its unreasoning malignity, it returned—and there lies its second victim..."

"Then..."

"It's gone, Petrie! It has the strength of four men even now. Look!"

He stooped, and from the clenched left hand of the dead Burman, extracted a piece of paper and opened it.

"Hold the lantern a moment," he said.

In the yellow light he glanced at the scrap of paper.

"As I expected—a leaf of Burke's notebook; it worked by scent." He turned to me with an odd expression in his gray eyes. "I wonder what piece of my personal property Fu-Manchu has pilfered," he said, "in order to enable it to sleuth me?"

He met the gaze of the man holding the lantern.

"Perhaps you had better return to the house," he said, looking him squarely in the eyes.

The other's face blanched.

"You don't mean, sir—you don't mean..."

"Brace up!" said Smith, laying his hand upon his shoulder. "Remember—he chose to play with fire!"

One wild look the man cast from Smith to me, then went off, staggering, toward the farm.

"Smith," I began...

He turned to me with an impatient gesture.

"Weymouth has driven into Upminster," he snapped; "and the whole district will be scoured before morning. They probably motored here, but the sounds of the shots will have enabled whoever was with the car to make good his escape. And exhausted from loss of blood, its capture is only a matter of time, Petrie."

CHAPTER XVII.

ONE DAY IN RANGOON

Nayland Smith returned from the telephone. Nearly twenty-four hours had elapsed since the awful death of Burke.

"No news, Petrie," he said, shortly. "It must have crept into some inaccessible hole to die."

I glanced up from my notes. Smith settled into the white cane armchair, and began to surround himself with clouds of aromatic smoke. I took up a half-sheet of foolscap covered with penciled writing in my friend's cramped characters, and transcribed the following, in order to complete my account of the latest Fu-Manchu outrage:

"The Amharun, a Semitic tribe allied to the Falashas, who have been settled for many generations in the southern province of Shoa (Abyssinia) have been regarded as unclean and outcast, apparently since the days of Menelek—son of Suleyman and the Queen of Sheba—from whom they claim descent. Apart from their custom of eating meat cut from living beasts, they are accursed because of their alleged association with the Cynocephalus hamadryas (Sacred Baboon). I, myself, was taken to a hut on the banks of the Hawash and shown a creature... whose predominant trait was an unreasoning malignity toward... and a ferocious tenderness for the society of its furry brethren. Its powers of scent were fully equal to those of a bloodhound, whilst its abnormally long forearms possessed incredible strength... a Cynocephalyte such as this, contracts phthisis even in the more northern provinces of Abyssinia..."

"You have not explained to me, Smith," I said, having completed this note, "how you got in touch with Fu-Manchu; how you learnt that he was not dead, as we had supposed, but living—active."

Nayland Smith stood up and fixed his steely eyes upon me with an indefinable expression in them. Then:

"No," he replied; "I haven't. Do you wish to know?"

"Certainly," I said with surprise; "is there any reason why I should not?"

"There is no real reason," said Smith; "or"—staring at me very hard—"I hope there is no real reason."

"What do you mean?"

"Well"—he grabbed up his pipe from the table and began furiously to load it—"I blundered upon the truth one day in Rangoon. I was walking out of a house which I occupied there for a time, and as I swung around the corner into the main street, I ran into—literally ran into..."

Again he hesitated oddly; then closed up his pouch and tossed it into the cane chair. He struck a match.

"I ran into Karamaneh," he continued abruptly, and began to puff away at his pipe, filling the air with clouds of tobacco smoke.

I caught my breath. This was the reason why he had kept me so long in ignorance of the story. He knew of my hopeless, uncrushable sentiments toward the gloriously beautiful but utterly hypocritical and evil Eastern girl who was perhaps the most dangerous of all Dr. Fu-Manchu's servants; for the power of her loveliness was magical, as I knew to my cost.

"What did you do?" I asked quietly, my fingers drumming upon the table.

"Naturally enough," continued Smith, "with a cry of recognition I held out both my hands to her, gladly. I welcomed her as a dear friend regained; I thought of the joy with which you would learn that I had found the missing one; I thought how you would be in Rangoon just as quickly as the fastest steamer could get you there..."

"Well?"

"Karamaneh started back and treated me to a glance of absolute animosity. No recognition was there, and no friendliness—only a sort of scornful anger."

He shrugged his shoulders and began to walk up and down the room.

"I do not know what you would have done in the circumstances, Petrie, but I—"

"Yes?"

"I dealt with the situation rather promptly, I think. I simply picked her up without another word, right there in the public street, and raced back into the house, with her kicking and fighting like a little demon! She did not shriek or do anything of that kind, but fought silently like a vicious wild animal. Oh! I had some scars, I assure you; but I carried her up into my office, which fortunately was empty at the time, plumped her down in a chair, and stood looking at her."

"Go on," I said rather hollowly; "what next?"

"She glared at me with those wonderful eyes, an expression of implacable hatred in them! Remembering all that we had done for her; remembering our former friendship; above all, remembering you—this look of hers almost made me shiver. She was dressed very smartly in European fashion, and the whole thing had been so sudden that as I stood looking at her I half expected to wake up presently and find it all a day-dream. But it was real—as real as her enmity. I felt the need for reflection, and having vainly endeavored to draw her into conversation, and elicited no other answer than this glare of hatred—I left her there, going out and locking the door behind me."

"Very high-handed?"

"A commissioner has certain privileges, Petrie, and any action I might choose to take was not likely to be questioned. There was only one window to the office, and it was fully twenty feet above the level; it overlooked a narrow street off the main thoroughfare (I think I have explained that the house stood on a corner) so I did not fear her escaping. I had an important engagement which I had been on my way to fulfil when the encounter took place, and now, with a word to my native servant—who chanced to be downstairs—I hurried off."

Smith's pipe had gone out as usual, and he proceeded to relight it, whilst, with my eyes lowered, I continued to drum upon the table.

"This boy took her some tea later in the afternoon," he continued, "and apparently found her in a more placid frame of mind. I returned immediately after dusk, and he reported that when last he had looked in, about half an hour earlier, she had been seated in an armchair reading a newspaper (I may mention that everything of value in the office was securely locked up!) I was determined upon a certain course by this time, and I went slowly upstairs, unlocked the door, and walked into the darkened office. I turned up the light... the place was empty!"

"Empty!"

"The window was open, and the bird flown! Oh! it was not so simple a flight—as you would realize if you knew the place. The street, which the window overlooked, was bounded by a blank wall, on the opposite side, for thirty or forty yards along; and as we had been having heavy rains, it was full of glutinous mud. Furthermore, the boy whom I had left in charge had been sitting in the doorway immediately below the office window watching for my return ever since his last visit to the room above..."

"She must have bribed him," I said bitterly—"or corrupted him with her infernal blandishments."

"I'll swear she did not," rapped Smith decisively. "I know my man, and I'll swear she did not. There were no marks in the mud of the road to show that a ladder had been placed there; moreover, nothing of the kind could have been attempted whilst the boy was sitting in the doorway; that was evident. In short, she did not descend into the roadway and did not come out by the door..."

"Was there a gallery outside the window?"

"No; it was impossible to climb to right or left of the window or up on to the roof. I convinced myself of that."

"But, my dear man!" I cried, "you are eliminating every natural mode of egress! Nothing remains but flight."

"I am aware, Petrie, that nothing remains but flight; in other words I have never to this day understood how she quitted the room. I only know that she did."

"And then?"

"I saw in this incredible escape the cunning hand of Dr. Fu-Manchu—saw it at once. Peace was ended; and I set to work along certain channels without delay. In this manner I got on the track at last, and learned, beyond the possibility of doubt, that the Chinese doctor lived—nay! was actually on his way to Europe again!"

There followed a short silence. Then:

"I suppose it's a mystery that will be cleared up some day," concluded Smith; "but to date the riddle remains intact." He glanced at the clock. "I have an appointment with Weymouth; therefore, leaving you to the task of solving this problem which thus far has defied my own efforts, I will get along."

He read a query in my glance.

"Oh! I shall not be late," he added; "I think I may venture out alone on this occasion without personal danger."

Nayland Smith went upstairs to dress, leaving me seated at my writing table, deep in thought. My notes upon the renewed activity of Dr. Fu-Manchu were stacked at my left hand, and, opening a new writing block, I commenced to add to them particulars of this surprising event in Rangoon which properly marked the opening of the Chinaman's second campaign. Smith looked in at the door on his way out, but seeing me thus engaged, did not disturb me.

I think I have made it sufficiently evident in these records that my practice was not an extensive one, and my hour for receiving patients arrived and passed with only two professional interruptions.

My task concluded, I glanced at the clock, and determined to devote the remainder of the evening to a little private investigation of my own. From Nayland Smith I had preserved the matter a secret, largely because I feared his ridicule; but I had by no means forgotten that I had seen, or had strongly imagined that I had seen, Karamaneh—that beautiful anomaly, who (in modern London) asserted herself to be a slave—in the shop of an antique dealer not a hundred yards from the British Museum!

A theory was forming in my brain, which I was burningly anxious to put to the test. I remembered how, two years before, I had met Karamaneh near to this same spot; and I had heard Inspector Weymouth assert positively that Fu-Manchu's headquarters were no longer in the East End, as of yore. There seemed to me to be a distinct probability that a suitable center had been established for his reception in this place, so much less likely to be suspected by the authorities. Perhaps I attached too great a value to what may have been a delusion; perhaps my theory rested upon no more solid foundation than the belief that I had seen Karamaneh in the shop of the curio dealer. If her appearance there should prove to have been phantasmal, the structure of my theory would be shattered at its base. To-night I should test my premises, and upon the result of my investigations determine my future action.

CHAPTER XVIII.

THE SILVER BUDDHA

Museum Street certainly did not seem a likely spot for Dr. Fu-Manchu to establish himself, yet, unless my imagination had strangely deceived me, from the window of the antique dealer who traded under the name of J. Salaman, those wonderful eyes of Karamaneh like the velvet midnight of the Orient, had looked out at me.

As I paced slowly along the pavement toward that lighted window, my heart was beating far from normally, and I cursed the folly which, in spite of all, refused to die, but lingered on, poisoning my life. Comparative quiet reigned in Museum Street, at no time a busy thoroughfare, and, excepting another shop at the Museum end, commercial activities had ceased there. The door of a block of residential chambers almost immediately opposite to the shop which was my objective, threw out a beam of light across the pavement, but not more than two or three people were visible upon either side of the street.

I turned the knob of the door and entered the shop.

The same dark and immobile individual whom I had seen before, and whose nationality defied conjecture, came out from the curtained doorway at the back to greet me.

"Good evening, sir," he said monotonously, with a slight inclination of the head; "is there anything which you desire to inspect?"

"I merely wish to take a look around," I replied. "I have no particular item in view."

The shop man inclined his head again, swept a yellow hand comprehensively about, as if to include the entire stock, and seated himself on a chair behind the counter.

I lighted a cigarette with such an air of nonchalance as I could summon to the operation, and began casually to inspect the varied objects of interest loading the shelves and tables about me. I am bound to confess that I retain no one definite impression of this tour. Vases I handled, statuettes, Egyptian scarabs, bead necklaces, illuminated missals, portfolios of old prints, jade ornaments, bronzes, fragments of rare lace, early printed books, Assyrian tablets, daggers, Roman rings, and a hundred other curiosities, leisurely, and I trust with apparent interest, yet without forming the slightest impression respecting any one of them.

Probably I employed myself in this way for half an hour or more, and whilst my hands busied themselves among the stock of J. Salaman, my mind was occupied entirely elsewhere. Furtively I was studying the shopman himself, a human presentment of a Chinese idol; I was listening and watching; especially I was watching the curtained doorway at the back of the shop.

"We close at about this time, sir," the man interrupted me, speaking in the emotionless, monotonous voice which I had noted before.

I replaced upon the glass counter a little Sekhet boat, carved in wood and highly colored, and glanced up with a start. Truly my methods were amateurish; I had learnt nothing; I was unlikely to learn anything. I wondered how Nayland Smith would have conducted such an inquiry, and I racked my brains for some means of penetrating into the recesses of the establishment. Indeed, I had been seeking such a plan for the past half an hour, but my mind had proved incapable of suggesting one.

Why I did not admit failure I cannot imagine, but, instead, I began to tax my brains anew for some means of gaining further time; and, as I looked about the place, the shopman very patiently awaiting my departure, I observed an open case at the back of the counter. The three lower shelves were empty, but upon the fourth shelf squatted a silver Buddha.

"I should like to examine the silver image yonder," I said; "what price are you asking for it?"

"It is not for sale, sir," replied the man, with a greater show of animation than he had yet exhibited.

"Not for sale!" I said, my eyes ever seeking the curtained doorway; "how's that?"

"It is sold."

"Well, even so, there can be no objection to my examining it?"

"It is not for sale, sir."

Such a rebuff from a tradesman would have been more than sufficient to call for a sharp retort at any other time, but now it excited the strangest suspicions. The street outside looked comparatively deserted, and prompted, primarily, by an emotion which I did not pause to analyze, I adopted a singular measure; without doubt I relied upon the unusual powers vested in Nayland Smith to absolve me in the event of error. I made as if to go out into the street, then turned, leaped past the shopman, ran behind the counter, and grasped at the silver Buddha!

That I was likely to be arrested for attempted larceny I cared not; the idea that Karamaneh was concealed somewhere in the building ruled absolutely, and a theory respecting this silver image had taken possession of my mind. Exactly what I expected to happen at that moment I cannot say, but what actually happened was far more startling than anything I could have imagined.

At the instant that I grasped the figure I realized that it was attached to the woodwork; in the next I knew that it was a handle ... as I tried to pull it toward me I became aware that this handle was the handle of a door. For that door swung open before me, and I found myself at the foot of a flight of heavily carpeted stairs.

Anxious as I had been to proceed a moment before, I was now trebly anxious to retire, and for this reason: on the bottom step of the stair, facing me, stood Dr. Fu-Manchu!

CHAPTER XIX.

DR. FU-MANCHU'S LABORATORY

I cannot conceive that any ordinary mortal ever attained to anything like an intimacy with Dr. Fu-Manchu; I cannot believe that any man could ever grow used to his presence, could ever cease to fear him. I suppose I had set eyes upon Fu-Manchu some five or six times prior to this occasion, and now he was dressed in the manner which I always associated with him, probably because it was thus I first saw him. He wore a plain yellow robe, and, with his pointed chin resting upon his bosom, he looked down at me, revealing a great expanse of the marvelous brow with its sparse, neutral-colored hair.

Never in my experience have I known such force to dwell in the glance of any human eye as dwelt in that of this uncanny being. His singular affliction (if affliction it were), the film or slight membrane which sometimes obscured the oblique eyes, was particularly evident at the moment that I crossed the threshold, but now, as I looked up at Dr. Fu-Manchu, it lifted—revealing the eyes in all their emerald greenness.

The idea of physical attack upon this incredible being seemed childish—inadequate. But, following that first instant of stupefaction, I forced myself to advance upon him.

A dull, crushing blow descended on the top of my skull, and I became oblivious of all things.

My return to consciousness was accompanied by tremendous pains in my head, whereby, from previous experience, I knew that a sandbag had been used against me by some one in the shop, presumably by the immobile shopman. This awakening was accompanied by none of those hazy doubts respecting previous events and present surroundings which are the usual symptoms of revival from sudden unconsciousness; even before I opened my eyes, before I had more than a partial command of my senses, I knew that, with my wrists handcuffed behind me, I lay in a room which was also occupied by Dr. Fu-Manchu. This absolute certainty of the Chinaman's presence was evidenced, not by my senses, but only by an inner consciousness, and the same that always awoke into life at the approach not only of Fu-Manchu in person but of certain of his uncanny servants.

A faint perfume hung in the air about me; I do not mean that of any essence or of any incense, but rather the smell which is suffused by Oriental furniture, by Oriental draperies; the indefinable but unmistakable perfume of the East.

Thus, London has a distinct smell of its own, and so has Paris, whilst the difference between Marseilles and Suez, for instance, is even more marked.

Now, the atmosphere surrounding me was Eastern, but not of the East that I knew; rather it was Far Eastern. Perhaps I do not make myself very clear, but to me there was a mysterious significance in that perfumed atmosphere. I opened my eyes.

I lay upon a long low settee, in a fairly large room which was furnished as I had anticipated in an absolutely Oriental fashion. The two windows were so screened as to have lost, from the interior point of view, all resemblance to European windows, and the whole structure of the room had been altered in conformity, bearing out my idea that the place had been prepared for Fu-Manchu's reception some time before his actual return. I doubt if, East or West, a duplicate of that singular apartment could be found.

The end in which I lay, was, as I have said, typical of an Eastern house, and a large, ornate lantern hung from the ceiling almost directly above me. The further end of the room was occupied by tall cases, some of them containing books, but the majority filled with scientific paraphernalia; rows of flasks and jars, frames of test-tubes, retorts, scales, and other objects of the laboratory. At a large and very finely carved table sat Dr. Fu-Manchu, a yellow and faded volume open before him, and some dark red fluid, almost like blood, bubbling in a test-tube which he held over the flame of a Bunsen-burner.

The enormously long nail of his right index finger rested upon the opened page of the book to which he seemed constantly to refer, dividing his attention between the volume, the contents of the test-tube, and the progress of a second experiment, or possibly a part of the same, which was taking place upon another corner of the littered table.

A huge glass retort (the bulb was fully two feet in diameter), fitted with a Liebig's Condenser, rested in a metal frame, and within the bulb, floating in an oily substance, was a fungus some six inches high, shaped like a toadstool, but of a brilliant and venomous orange color. Three flat tubes of light were so arranged as to cast violet rays upward into the retort, and the receiver, wherein condensed the product of this strange experiment, contained some drops of a red fluid which may have been identical with that boiling in the test-tube.

These things I perceived at a glance: then the filmy eyes of Dr. Fu-Manchu were raised from the book, turned in my direction, and all else was forgotten.

"I regret," came the sibilant voice, "that unpleasant measures were necessary, but hesitation would have been fatal. I trust, Dr. Petrie, that you suffer no inconvenience?"

To this speech no reply was possible, and I attempted none.

"You have long been aware of my esteem for your acquirements," continued the Chinaman, his voice occasionally touching deep guttural notes, "and you will appreciate the pleasure which this visit affords me. I kneel at the feet of my silver Buddha. I look to you, when you shall have overcome your prejudices—due to ignorance of my true motives—to assist me in establishing that intellectual control which is destined to be the new World Force. I bear you no malice for your ancient enmity, and even now"—he waved one yellow hand toward the retort—"I am conducting an experiment designed to convert you from your misunderstanding, and to adjust your perspective."

Quite unemotionally he spoke, then turned again to his book, his test-tube and retort, in the most matter-of-fact way imaginable. I do not think the most frenzied outburst on his part, the most fiendish threats, could have produced such effect upon me as those cold and carefully calculated words, spoken in that unique voice which rang about the room sibilantly. In its tones, in the glance of the green eyes, in the very pose of the gaunt, high-shouldered body, there was power—force.

I counted myself lost, and in view of the doctor's words, studied the progress of the experiment with frightful interest. But a few moments sufficed in which to realize that, for all my training, I knew as little of chemistry—of chemistry as understood by this man's genius—as a junior student in surgery knows of trephining. The process in operation was a complete mystery to me; the means and the end alike incomprehensible.

Thus, in the heavy silence of that room, a silence only broken by the regular bubbling from the test tube, I found my attention straying from the table to the other objects surrounding it; and at one of them my gaze stopped and remained chained with horror.

It was a glass jar, some five feet in height and filled with viscous fluid of a light amber color. Out from this peered a hideous, dog-like face, low browed, with pointed ears and a nose almost hoggishly flat. By the death-grin of the face the gleaming fangs were revealed; and the body, the long yellow-gray body, rested, or seemed to rest, upon short, malformed legs, whilst one long limp arm, the right, hung down straightly in the preservative. The left arm had been severed above the elbow.

Fu-Manchu, finding his experiment to be proceeding favorably, lifted his eyes to me again.

"You are interested in my poor Cynocephalyte?" he said; and his eyes were filmed like the eyes of one afflicted with cataract. "He was a devoted servant, Dr. Petrie, but the lower influences in his genealogy, sometimes conquered. Then he got out of hand; and at last he was so ungrateful toward those who had educated him, that, in one of those paroxysms of his, he attacked and killed a most faithful Burman, one of my oldest followers."

Fu-Manchu returned to his experiment.

Not the slightest emotion had he exhibited thus far, but had chatted with me as any other scientist might chat with a friend who casually visits his laboratory. The horror of the thing was playing havoc with my own composure, however. There I lay, fettered, in the same room with this man whose existence was a menace to the entire white race, whilst placidly he pursued an experiment designed, if his own words were believable, to cut me off from my kind—to wreak some change, psychological or physiological I knew not; to place me, it might be, upon a level with such brute-things as that which now hung, half floating, in the glass jar!

Something I knew of the history of that ghastly specimen, that thing neither man nor ape; for within my own knowledge had it not attempted the life of Nayland Smith, and was it not I who, with an ax, had maimed it in the instant of one of its last slayings?

Of these things Dr. Fu-Manchu was well aware, so that his placid speech was doubly, trebly horrible to my ears. I sought, furtively, to move my arms, only to realize that, as I had anticipated, the handcuffs were chained to a ring in the wall behind me. The establishments of Dr. Fu-Manchu were always well provided with such contrivances as these.

I uttered a short, harsh laugh. Fu-Manchu stood up slowly from the table, and, placing the test-tube in a rack, stood the latter carefully upon a shelf at his side.

"I am happy to find you in such good humor," he said softly. "Other affairs call me; and, in my absence, that profound knowledge of chemistry, of which I have had evidence in the past, will enable you to follow with intelligent interest the action of these violet rays upon this exceptionally fine specimen of Siberian amanita muscaria. At some future time, possibly when you are my guest in China—which country I am now making arrangements for you to visit—I shall discuss with you some lesser-known properties of this species; and I may say that one of your first tasks when you commence your duties as assistant in my laboratory in Kiang-su, will be to conduct a series of twelve experiments, which I have outlined, into other potentialities of this unique fungus."

He walked quietly to a curtained doorway, with his cat-like yet awkward gait, lifted the drapery, and, with a slight nod in my direction, went out of the room.

✦

CHAPTER XX.

THE CROSS BAR

How long I lay there alone I had no means of computing. My mind was busy with many matters, but principally concerned with my fate in the immediate future. That Dr. Fu-Manchu entertained for me a singular kind of regard, I had had evidence before. He had formed the erroneous opinion that I was an advanced scientist who could be of use to him in his experiments and I was aware that he cherished a project of transporting me to some place in China where his principal laboratory was situated. Respecting the means which he proposed to employ, I was unlikely to forget that this man, who had penetrated further along certain byways of science than seemed humanly possible, undoubtedly was master of a process for producing artificial catalepsy. It was my lot, then, to be packed in a chest (to all intents and purposes a dead man for the time being) and despatched to the interior of China!

What a fool I had been. To think that I had learned nothing from my long and dreadful experience of the methods of Dr. Fu-Manchu; to think that I had come alone in quest of him; that, leaving no trace behind me, I had deliberately penetrated to his secret abode!

I have said that my wrists were manacled behind me, the manacles being attached to a chain fastened in the wall. I now contrived, with extreme difficulty, to reverse the position of my hands; that is to say, I climbed backward through the loop formed by my fettered arms, so that instead of their being locked behind me, they now were locked in front.

Then I began to examine the fetters, learning, as I had anticipated, that they fastened with a lock. I sat gazing at the steel bracelets in the light of the lamp which swung over my head, and it became apparent to me that I had gained little by my contortion.

A slight noise disturbed these unpleasant reveries. It was nothing less than the rattling of keys!

For a moment I wondered if I had heard aright, or if the sound portended the coming of some servant of the doctor, who was locking up the establishment for the night. The jangling sound was repeated, and in such a way that I could not suppose it to be accidental. Some one was deliberately rattling a small bunch of keys in an adjoining room.

And now my heart leaped wildly—then seemed to stand still.

With a low whistling cry a little gray shape shot through the doorway by which Fu-Manchu had retired, and rolled, like a ball of fluff blown by the wind, completely under the table which bore the weird scientific appliances of the Chinaman; the advent of the gray object was accompanied by a further rattling of keys.

My fear left me, and a mighty anxiety took its place. This creature which now crouched chattering at me from beneath the big table was Fu-Manchu's marmoset, and in the intervals of its chattering and grimacing, it nibbled, speculatively, at the keys upon the ring which it clutched in its tiny hands. Key after key it sampled in this manner, evincing a growing dissatisfaction with the uncrackable nature of its find.

One of those keys might be that of the handcuffs!

I could not believe that the tortures of Tantulus were greater than were mine at this moment. In all my hopes of rescue or release, I had included nothing so strange, so improbable as this. A sort of awe possessed me; for if by this means the key which should release me should come into my possession, how, ever again, could I doubt a beneficent Providence?

But they were not yet in my possession; moreover, the key of the handcuffs might not be amongst the bunch.

Were there no means whereby I could induce the marmoset to approach me?

Whilst I racked my brains for some scheme, the little animal took the matter out of my hands. Tossing the ring with its jangling contents a yard or so across the carpet in my direction, it leaped in pursuit, picked up the ring, whirled it over its head, and then threw a complete somersault around it. Now it snatched up the keys again, and holding them close to its ear, rattled them furiously. Finally, with an incredible spring, it leaped onto the chain supporting the lamp above my head, and with the garish shade swinging and spinning wildly, clung there looking down at me like an acrobat on a trapeze. The tiny, bluish face, completely framed in grotesque whiskers, enhanced the illusion of an acrobatic comedian. Never for a moment did it release its hold upon the key-ring.

My suspense now was intolerable. I feared to move, lest, alarming the marmoset, it should run off again, taking the keys with it. So as I lay there, looking up at the little creature swinging above me, the second wonder of the night came to pass.

A voice that I could never forget, strive how I would, a voice that haunted my dreams by night, and for which by day I was ever listening, cried out from some adjoining room.

"Ta'ala hina!" it called. "Ta'ala hina, Peko!"

It was Karamaneh!

The effect upon the marmoset was instantaneous. Down came the bunch of keys upon one side of the shade, almost falling on my head, and down leaped the ape upon the other. In two leaps it had traversed the room and had vanished through the curtained doorway.

If ever I had need of coolness it was now; the slightest mistake would be fatal. The keys had slipped from the mattress of the divan, and now lay just beyond reach of my fingers. Rapidly I changed my position, and sought, without undue noise, to move the keys with my foot.

I had actually succeeded in sliding them back on to the mattress, when, unheralded by any audible footstep, Karamaneh came through the doorway, holding the marmoset in her arms. She wore a dress of fragile muslin material, and out from its folds protruded one silk-stockinged foot, resting in a high-heeled red shoe....

For a moment she stood watching me, with a sort of enforced composure; then her glance strayed to the keys lying upon the floor. Slowly, and with her eyes fixed again upon my face, she crossed the room, stooped, and took up the key-ring.

It was one of the poignant moments of my life; for by that simple act all my hopes had been shattered!

Any poor lingering doubt that I may have had, left me now. Had the slightest spark of friendship animated the bosom of Karamaneh most certainly she would have overlooked the presence of the keys—of the keys which represented my one hope of escape from the clutches of the fiendish Chinaman.

There is a silence more eloquent than words. For half a minute or more, Karamaneh stood watching me—forcing herself to watch me—and I looked up at her with a concentrated gaze in which rage and reproach must have been strangely mingled. What eyes she had!—of that blackly lustrous sort nearly always associated with unusually dark complexions; but Karamaneh's complexion was peachlike, or rather of an exquisite and delicate fairness which reminded me of the petal of a rose. By some I had been accused of raving about this girl's beauty, but only by those who had not met her; for indeed she was astonishingly lovely.

At last her eyes fell, the long lashes drooped upon her cheeks. She turned and walked slowly to the chair in which Fu-Manchu had sat. Placing the keys upon the table amid the scientific litter, she rested one dimpled elbow upon the yellow page of the book, and with her chin in her palm, again directed upon me that enigmatical gaze.

I dared not think of the past, of the past in which this beautiful, treacherous girl had played a part; yet, watching her, I could not believe, even now, that she was false! My state was truly a pitiable one; I could have cried out in sheer anguish. With her long lashes partly lowered, she watched me awhile, then spoke; and her voice was music which seemed to mock me; every inflection of that elusive accent reopened, lancet-like, the ancient wound.

"Why do you look at me so?" she said, almost in a whisper. "By what right do you reproach me?—Have you ever offered me friendship, that I should repay you with friendship? When first you came to the house where I was, by the river—came to save some one from" (there was the familiar hesitation which always preceded the name of Fu-Manchu) "from—him, you treated me as your enemy, although—I would have been your friend..."

There was appeal in the soft voice, but I laughed mockingly, and threw myself back upon the divan.

Karamaneh stretched out her hands toward me, and I shall never forget the expression which flashed into those glorious eyes; but, seeing me intolerant of her appeal, she drew back and quickly turned her head aside. Even in this hour of extremity, of impotent wrath, I could find no contempt in my heart for her feeble hypocrisy; with all the old wonder I watched that exquisite profile, and Karamaneh's very deceitfulness was a salve—for had she not cared she would not have attempted it!

Suddenly she stood up, taking the keys in her hands, and approached me.

"Not by word, nor by look," she said, quietly, "have you asked for my friendship, but because I cannot bear you to think of me as you do, I will prove that I am not the hypocrite and the liar you think me. You will not trust me, but I will trust you."

I looked up into her eyes, and knew a pagan joy when they faltered before my searching gaze. She threw herself upon her knees beside me, and the faint exquisite perfume inseparable from my memories of her, became perceptible, and seemed as of old to intoxicate me. The lock clicked... and I was free.

Karamaneh rose swiftly to her feet as I stood upright and outstretched my cramped arms. For one delirious moment her bewitching face was close to mine, and the dictates of madness almost ruled; but I clenched my teeth and turned sharply aside. I could not trust myself to speak.

With Fu-Manchu's marmoset again gamboling before us, she walked through the curtained doorway into the room beyond. It was in darkness, but I could see the slave-girl in front of me, a slim silhouette, as she walked to a screened window, and, opening the screen in the manner of a folding door, also threw up the window.

"Look!" she whispered.

I crept forward and stood beside her. I found myself looking down into Museum Street from a first-floor window! Belated traffic still passed along New Oxford Street on the left, but not a solitary figure was visible to the right, as far as I could see, and that was nearly to the railings of the Museum. Immediately opposite, in one of the flats which I had noticed earlier in the evening, another window was opened. I turned, and in the reflected light saw that Karamaneh held a cord in her hand. Our eyes met in the semi-darkness.

She began to haul the cord into the window, and, looking upward, I perceived that it was looped in some way over the telegraph cables which crossed the street at that point. It was a slender cord, and it appeared to be passed across a joint in the cables almost immediately above the center of the roadway. As it was hauled in, a second and stronger line attached to it was pulled, in turn, over the cables, and thence in by the window. Karamaneh twisted a length of it around a metal bracket fastened in the wall, and placed a light wooden crossbar in my hand.

"Make sure that there is no one in the street," she said, craning out and looking to right and left, "then swing across. The length of the rope is just sufficient to enable you to swing through the open window opposite, and there is a mattress inside to drop upon. But release the bar immediately, or you may be dragged back. The door of the room in which you will find yourself is unlocked, and you have only to walk down the stairs and out into the street."

I peered at the crossbar in my hand, then looked hard at the girl beside me. I missed something of the old fire of her nature; she was very subdued, tonight.

"Thank you, Karamaneh," I said, softly.

She suppressed a little cry as I spoke her name, and drew back into the shadows.

"I believe you are my friend," I said, "but I cannot understand. Won't you help me to understand?"

I took her unresisting hand, and drew her toward me. My very soul seemed to thrill at the contact of her lithe body...

She was trembling wildly and seemed to be trying to speak, but although her lips framed the words no sound followed. Suddenly comprehension came to me. I looked down into the street, hitherto deserted... and into the upturned face of Fu-Manchu.

Wearing a heavy fur-collared coat, and with his yellow, malignant countenance grotesquely horrible beneath the shade of a large tweed motor cap, he stood motionless, looking up at me. That he had seen me, I could not doubt; but had he seen my companion?

In a choking whisper Karamaneh answered my unspoken question.

"He has not seen me! I have done much for you; do in return a small thing for me. Save my life!"

She dragged me back from the window and fled across the room to the weird laboratory where I had lain captive. Throwing herself upon the divan, she held out her white wrists and glanced significantly at the manacles.

"Lock them upon me!" she said, rapidly. "Quick! quick!"

Great as was my mental disturbance, I managed to grasp the purpose of this device. The very extremity of my danger found me cool. I fastened the manacles, which so recently had confined my own wrists, upon the slim wrists of Karamaneh. A faint and muffled disturbance, doubly ominous because there was nothing to proclaim its nature, reached me from some place below, on the ground floor.

"Tie something around my mouth!" directed Karamaneh with nervous rapidity. As I began to look about me:—"Tear a strip from my dress," she said; "do not hesitate—be quick! be quick!"

I seized the flimsy muslin and tore off half a yard or so from the hem of the skirt. The voice of Dr Fu-Manchu became audible. He was speaking rapidly, sibilantly, and evidently was approaching—would be upon me in a matter of moments. I fastened the strip of fabric over the girl's mouth and tied it behind, experiencing a pang half pleasurable and half fearful as I found my hands in contact with the foamy luxuriance of her hair.

Dr. Fu-Manchu was entering the room immediately beyond.

Snatching up the bunch of keys, I turned and ran, for in another instant my retreat would be cut off. As I burst once more into the darkened room I became aware that a door on the further side of it was open; and framed in the opening was the tall, high-shouldered figure of the Chinaman, still enveloped in his fur coat and wearing the grotesque cap. As I saw him, so he perceived me; and as I sprang to the window, he advanced.

I turned desperately and hurled the bunch of keys with all my force into the dimly-seen face...

Either because they possessed a chatoyant quality of their own (as I had often suspected), or by reason of the light reflected through the open window, the green eyes gleamed upon me vividly like those of a giant cat. One short guttural exclamation paid tribute to the accuracy of my aim; then I had the crossbar in my hand. I threw one leg across the sill, and dire as was my extremity, hesitated for an instant ere trusting myself to the flight...

A vise-like grip fastened upon my left ankle.

Hazily I became aware that the dark room was flooded with figures. The whole yellow gang were upon me—the entire murder-group composed of units recruited from the darkest place of the East!

I have never counted myself a man of resource, and have always envied Nayland Smith his possession of that quality, in him extraordinarily developed; but on this occasion the gods were kind to me, and I resorted to the only device, perhaps, which could have saved me. Without releasing my hold upon the crossbar, I clutched at the ledge with the fingers of both hands and swung back into the room my right leg, which was already across the sill. With all my strength I kicked out. My heel came in contact, in sickening contact, with a human head; beyond doubt that I had split the skull of the man who held me.

The grip upon my ankle was released automatically; and now consigning all my weight to the rope I slipped forward, as a diver, across the broad ledge and found myself sweeping through the night like a winged thing...

The line, as Karamaneh had assured me, was of well-judged length. Down I swept to within six or seven feet of the street level, then up, at ever decreasing speed, toward the vague oblong of the open window beyond.

I hope I have been successful, in some measure, in portraying the varied emotions which it was my lot to experience that night, and it may well seem that nothing more exquisite could remain for me. Yet it was written otherwise; for as I swept up to my goal, describing the inevitable arc which I had no power to check, I saw that one awaited me.

Crouching forward half out of the open window was a Burmese dacoit, a cross-eyed, leering being whom I well remembered to have encountered two years before in my dealings with Dr. Fu-Manchu. One bare, sinewy arm held rigidly at right angles before his breast, he clutched a long curved knife and waited—waited—for the critical moment when my throat should be at his mercy!

I have said that a strange coolness had come to my aid; even now it did not fail me, and so incalculably rapid are the workings of the human mind that I remember complimenting myself upon an achievement which Smith himself could not have bettered, and this in the immeasurable interval which intervened between the commencement of my upward swing and my arrival on a level with the window.

I threw my body back and thrust my feet forward. As my legs went through the opening, an acute pain in one calf told me that I was not to escape scatheless from the night's melee. But the dacoit went rolling over in the darkness of the room, as helpless in face of that ramrod stroke as the veriest infant...

Back I swept upon my trapeze, a sight to have induced any passing citizen to question his sanity. With might and main I sought to check the swing of the pendulum, for if I should come within reach of the window behind I doubted not that other knives awaited me. It was no difficult feat, and I succeeded in checking my flight. Swinging there above Museum Street I could even appreciate, so lucid was my mind, the ludicrous element of the situation.

I dropped. My wounded leg almost failed me; and greatly shaken, but with no other serious damage, I picked myself up from the dust of the roadway. It was a mockery of Fate that the problem which Nayland Smith had set me to solve, should have been solved thus; for I could not doubt that by means of the branch of a tall tree or some other suitable object situated opposite to Smith's house in Rangoon, Karamaneh had made her escape as tonight I had made mine.

Apart from the acute pain in my calf I knew that the dacoit's knife had bitten deeply, by reason of the fact that a warm liquid was trickling down into my boot. Like any drunkard I stood there in the middle of the road looking up at the vacant window where the dacoit had been, and up at the window above the shop of J. Salaman where I knew Fu-Manchu to be. But for some reason the latter window had been closed or almost closed, and as I stood there this reason became apparent to me.

The sound of running footsteps came from the direction of New Oxford Street. I turned—to see two policemen bearing down upon me!

This was a time for quick decisions and prompt action. I weighed all the circumstances in the balance, and made the last vital choice of the night; I turned and ran toward the British Museum as though the worst of Fu-Manchu's creatures, and not my allies the police, were at my heels!

No one else was in sight, but, as I whirled into the Square, the red lamp of a slowly retreating taxi became visible some hundred yards to the left. My leg was paining me greatly, but the nature of the wound did not interfere with my progress; therefore I continued my headlong career, and ere the police had reached the end of Museum Street I had my hand upon the door handle of the cab—for, the Fates being persistently kind to me, the vehicle was for hire.

"Dr. Cleeve's, Harley Street!" I shouted at the man. "Drive like hell! It's an urgent case."

I leaped into the cab.

Within five seconds from the time that I slammed the door and dropped back panting upon the cushions, we were speeding westward toward the house of the famous pathologist, thereby throwing the police hopelessly off the track.

Faintly to my ears came the purr of a police whistle. The taxi-man evidently did not hear the significant sound. Merciful Providence had rung down the curtain; for to-night my role in the yellow drama was finished.

CHAPTER XXI.

CRAGMIRE TOWER

Less than two hours later, Inspector Weymouth and a party of men from Scotland Yard raided the house in Museum Street. They found the stock of J. Salaman practically intact, and, in the strangely appointed rooms above, every evidence of a hasty outgoing. But of the instruments, drugs and other laboratory paraphernalia not one item remained. I would gladly have given my income for a year, to have gained possession of the books, alone; for, beyond all shadow of doubt, I knew them to contain formula calculated to revolutionize the science of medicine.

Exhausted, physically and mentally, and with my mind a whispering-gallery of conjectures (it were needless for me to mention whom respecting) I turned in, gratefully, having patched up the slight wound in my calf.

I seemed scarcely to have closed my eyes, when Nayland Smith was shaking me into wakefulness.

"You are probably tired out," he said; "but your crazy expedition of last night entitles you to no sympathy. Read this; there is a train in an hour. We will reserve a compartment and you can resume your interrupted slumbers in a corner seat."

As I struggled upright in bed, rubbing my eyes sleepily, Smith handed me the Daily Telegraph, pointing to the following paragraph upon the literary page:

Messrs. M—— announce that they will publish shortly the long delayed work of Kegan Van Roon, the celebrated American traveler, Orientalist and psychic investigator, dealing with his recent inquiries in China. It will be remembered that Mr. Van Roon undertook to motor from Canton to Siberia last winter, but met with unforeseen difficulties in the province of Ho-Nan. He fell into the hands of a body of fanatics and was fortunate to escape with his life. His book will deal in particular with his experiences in Ho-Nan, and some sensational revelations regarding the awakening of that most mysterious race, the Chinese, are promised. For reasons of his own he has decided to remain in England until the completion of his book (which will be published simultaneously in New York and London) and has leased Cragmire Tower, Somersetshire, in which romantic and historical residence he will collate his notes and prepare for the world a work ear-marked as a classic even before it is published.

I glanced up from the paper, to find Smith's eyes fixed upon me, inquiringly.

"From what I have been able to learn," he said, evenly, "we should reach Saul, with decent luck, just before dusk."

As he turned, and quitted the room without another word, I realized, in a flash, the purport of our mission; I understood my friend's ominous calm, betokening suppressed excitement.

The Fates were with us (or so it seemed); and whereas we had not hoped to gain Saul before sunset, as a matter of fact, the autumn afternoon was in its most glorious phase as we left the little village with its oldtime hostelry behind us and set out in an easterly direction, with the Bristol Channel far away on our left and a gently sloping upland on our right.

The crooked high-street practically constituted the entire hamlet of Saul, and the inn, "The Wagoners," was the last house in the street. Now, as we followed the ribbon of moor-path to the top of the rise, we could stand and look back upon the way we had come; and although we had covered fully a mile of ground, it was possible to detect the sunlight gleaming now and then upon the gilt lettering of the inn sign as it swayed in the breeze. The day had been unpleasantly warm, but was relieved by this same sea breeze, which, although but slight, had in it the tang of the broad Atlantic. Behind us, then, the foot-path sloped down to Saul, unpeopled by any living thing; east and northeast swelled the monotony of the moor right out to the hazy distance where the sky began and the sea remotely lay hidden; west fell the gentle gradient from the top of the slope which we had mounted, and here, as far as the eye could reach, the country had an appearance suggestive of a huge and dried-up lake. This idea was borne out by an odd blotchiness, for sometimes there would be half a mile or more of seeming moorland, then a sharply defined change (or it seemed sharply defined from that bird's-eye point of view). A vivid greenness marked these changes, which merged into a dun-colored smudge and again into the brilliant green; then the moor would begin once more.

"That will be the Tor of Glastonbury, I suppose," said Smith, suddenly peering through his field-glasses in an easterly direction; "and yonder, unless I am greatly mistaken, is Cragmire Tower."

Shading my eyes with my hand, I also looked ahead, and saw the place for which we were bound; one of those round towers, more common in Ireland, which some authorities have declared to be of Phoenician origin. Ramshackle buildings clustered untidily about its base, and to it a sort of tongue of that oddly venomous green which patched the lowlands, shot out and seemed almost to reach the towerbase. The land for miles around was as flat as the palm of my hand, saving certain hummocks, lesser tors, and irregular piles of boulders which dotted its expanse. Hills and uplands there were in the hazy distance, forming a sort of mighty inland bay which I doubted not in some past age had been covered by the sea. Even in the brilliant sunlight the place had something of a mournful aspect, looking like a great dried-up pool into which the children of giants had carelessly cast stones.

We met no living soul upon the moor. With Cragmire Tower but a quarter of a mile off, Smith paused again, and raising his powerful glasses swept the visible landscape.

"Not a sign, Petrie," he said, softly; "yet…"

Dropping the glasses back into their case, my companion began to tug at his left ear.

"Have we been over-confident?" he said, narrowing his eyes in speculative fashion. "No less than three times I have had the idea that something, or some one, has just dropped out of sight, behind me, as I focused..."

"What do you mean, Smith?"

"Are we"—he glanced about him as though the vastness were peopled with listening Chinamen—"followed?"

Silently we looked into one another's eyes, each seeking for the dread which neither had named. Then:

"Come on Petrie!" said Smith, grasping my arm; and at quick march we were off again.

Cragmire Tower stood upon a very slight eminence, and what had looked like a green tongue, from the moorland slopes above, was in fact a creek, flanked by lush land, which here found its way to the sea. The house which we were come to visit consisted in a low, two-story building, joining the ancient tower on the east with two smaller outbuildings. There was a miniature kitchen-garden, and a few stunted fruit trees in the northwest corner; the whole being surrounded by a gray stone wall.

The shadow of the tower fell sharply across the path, which ran up almost alongside of it. We were both extremely warm by reason of our long and rapid walk on that hot day, and this shade should have been grateful to us. In short, I find it difficult to account for the unwelcome chill which I experienced at the moment that I found myself at the foot of the time-worn monument. I know that we both pulled up sharply and looked at one another as though acted upon by some mutual disturbance.

But not a sound broke the stillness save a remote murmuring, until a solitary sea gull rose in the air and circled directly over the tower, uttering its mournful and unmusical cry. Automatically to my mind sprang the lines of the poem:

Far from all brother-men, in the weird of the fen,
With God's creatures I bide, 'mid the birds that I ken;
Where the winds ever dree, where the hymn of the sea
Brings a message of peace from the ocean to me.

Not a soul was visible about the premises; there was no sound of human activity and no dog barked. Nayland Smith drew a long breath, glanced back along the way we had come, then went on, following the wall, I beside him, until we came to the gate. It was unfastened, and we walked up the stone path through a wilderness of weeds. Four windows of the house were visible, two on the ground floor and two above. Those on the ground floor were heavily boarded up, those above, though glazed, boasted neither blinds nor curtains. Cragmire Tower showed not the slightest evidence of tenancy.

We mounted three steps and stood before a tremendously massive oaken door. An iron bell-pull, ancient and rusty, hung on the right of the door, and Smith, giving me an odd glance, seized the ring and tugged it.

From somewhere within the building answered a mournful clangor, a cracked and toneless jangle, which, seeming to echo through empty apartments, sought and found an exit apparently by way of one of the openings in the round tower; for it was from above our heads that the noise came to us.

It died away, that eerie ringing—that clanging so dismal that it could chill my heart even then with the bright sunlight streaming down out of the blue; it awoke no other response than the mournful cry of the sea gull circling over our heads. Silence fell. We looked at one another, and we were both about to express a mutual doubt when, unheralded by any unfastening of bolts or bars, the oaken door was opened, and a huge mulatto, dressed in white, stood there regarding us.

I started nervously, for the apparition was so unexpected, but Nayland Smith, without evidence of surprise, thrust a card into the man's hand.

"Take my card to Mr. Van Roon, and say that I wish to see him on important business," he directed, authoritatively.

The mulatto bowed and retired. His white figure seemed to be swallowed up by the darkness within, for beyond the patch of uncarpeted floor revealed by the peeping sunlight, was a barn-like place of densest shadow. I was about to speak, but Smith laid his hand upon my arm warningly, as, out from the shadows the mulatto returned. He stood on the right of the door and bowed again.

"Be pleased to enter," he said, in his harsh, negro voice. "Mr. Van Roon will see you."

The gladness of the sun could no longer stir me; a chill and sense of foreboding bore me company, as beside Nayland Smith I entered Cragmire Tower.

CHAPTER XXII.

THE MULATTO

The room in which Van Roon received us was roughly of the shape of an old-fashioned keyhole; one end of it occupied the base of the tower, upon which the remainder had evidently been built. In many respects it was a singular room, but the feature which caused me the greatest amazement was this:—it had no windows!

In the deep alcove formed by the tower sat Van Roon at a littered table, upon which stood an oil reading-lamp, green shaded, of the "Victoria" pattern, to furnish the entire illumination of the apartment. That bookshelves lined the rectangular portion of this strange study I divined, although that end of the place was dark as a catacomb. The walls were wood-paneled, and the ceiling was oaken beamed. A small bookshelf and tumble-down cabinet stood upon either side of the table, and the celebrated American author and traveler lay propped up in a long split-cane chair. He wore smoked glasses, and had a clean-shaven, olive face, with a profusion of jet black hair. He was garbed in a dirty red dressing-gown, and a perfect fog of cigar smoke hung in the room. He did not rise to greet us, but merely extended his right hand, between two fingers whereof he held Smith's card.

"You will excuse the seeming discourtesy of an invalid, gentlemen?" he said; "but I am suffering from undue temerity in the interior of China!"

He waved his hand vaguely, and I saw that two rough deal chairs stood near the table. Smith and I seated ourselves, and my friend, leaning his elbow upon the table, looked fixedly at the face of the man whom we had come from London to visit. Although comparatively unfamiliar to the British public, the name of Van Roon was well-known in American literary circles; for he enjoyed in the United States a reputation somewhat similar to that which had rendered the name of our mutual friend, Sir Lionel Barton, a household word in England. It was Van Roon who, following in the footsteps of Madame Blavatsky, had sought out the haunts of the fabled mahatmas in the Himalayas, and Van Roon who had essayed to explore the fever swamps of Yucatan in quest of the secret of lost Atlantis; lastly, it was Van Roon, who, with an overland car specially built for him by a celebrated American firm, had undertaken the journey across China.

I studied the olive face with curiosity. Its natural impassivity was so greatly increased by the presence of the colored spectacles that my study was as profitless as if I had scrutinized the face of a carven Buddha. The mulatto had withdrawn, and in an atmosphere of gloom and tobacco smoke, Smith and I sat staring, perhaps rather rudely, at the object of our visit to the West Country.

"Mr. Van Roon," began my friend abruptly, "you will no doubt have seen this paragraph. It appeared in this morning's Daily Telegraph."

He stood up, and taking out the cutting from his notebook, placed it on the table.

"I have seen this—yes," said Van Roon, revealing a row of even, white teeth in a rapid smile. "Is it to this paragraph that I owe the pleasure of seeing you here?"

"The paragraph appeared in this morning's issue," replied Smith. "An hour from the time of seeing it, my friend, Dr. Petrie, and I were entrained for Bridgewater."

"Your visit delights me, gentlemen, and I should be ungrateful to question its cause; but frankly I am at a loss to understand why you should have honored me thus. I am a poor host, God knows; for what with my tortured limb, a legacy from the Chinese devils whose secrets I surprised, and my semi-blindness, due to the same cause, I am but sorry company."

Nayland Smith held up his right hand deprecatingly. Van Roon tendered a box of cigars and clapped his hands, whereupon the mulatto entered.

"I see that you have a story to tell me, Mr. Smith," he said; "therefore I suggest whisky-and-soda—or you might prefer tea, as it is nearly tea time?"

Smith and I chose the former refreshment, and the soft-footed half-breed having departed upon his errand, my companion, leaning forward earnestly across the littered table, outlined for Van Roon the story of Dr. Fu-Manchu, the great and malign being whose mission in England at that moment was none other than the stoppage of just such information as our host was preparing to give to the world.

"There is a giant conspiracy, Mr. Van Roon," he said, "which had its birth in this very province of Ho-Nan, from which you were so fortunate to escape alive; whatever its scope or limitations, a great secret society is established among the yellow races. It means that China, which has slumbered for so many generations, now stirs in that age-long sleep. I need not tell you how much more it means, this seething in the pot..."

"In a word," interrupted Van Roon, pushing Smith's glass across the table "you would say?—"

"That your life is not worth that!" replied Smith, snapping his fingers before the other's face.

A very impressive silence fell. I watched Van Roon curiously as he sat propped up among his cushions, his smooth face ghastly in the green light from the lamp-shade. He held the stump of a cigar between his teeth, but, apparently unnoticed by him, it had long since gone out. Smith, out of the shadows, was watching him, too. Then:

"Your information is very disturbing," said the American. "I am the more disposed to credit your statement because I am all too painfully aware of the existence of such a group as you mention, in China, but that they had an agent here in England is something I had never conjectured. In seeking out this solitary residence I have unwittingly done much to assist their designs... But—my dear Mr. Smith, I am very remiss! Of course you will remain tonight, and I trust for some days to come?"

Smith glanced rapidly across at me, then turned again to our host.

"It seems like forcing our company upon you," he said, "but in your own interests I think it will be best to do as you are good enough to suggest. I hope and believe that our arrival here has not been noticed by the enemy; therefore it will be well if we remain concealed as much as possible for the present, until we have settled upon some plan."

"Hagar shall go to the station for your baggage," said the American rapidly, and clapped his hands, his usual signal to the mulatto.

Whilst the latter was receiving his orders I noticed Nayland Smith watching him closely; and when he had departed:

"How long has that man been in your service?" snapped my friend.

Van Roon peered blindly through his smoked glasses.

"For some years," he replied; "he was with me in India—and in China."

"Where did you engage him?"

"Actually, in St. Kitts."

"H'm," muttered Smith, and automatically he took out and began to fill his pipe.

"I can offer you no company but my own, gentlemen," continued Van Roon, "but unless it interferes with your plans, you may find the surrounding district of interest and worthy of inspection, between now and dinner time. By the way, I think I can promise you quite a satisfactory meal, for Hagar is a model chef."

"A walk would be enjoyable," said Smith, "but dangerous."

"Ah! perhaps you are right. Evidently you apprehend some attempt upon me?"

"At any moment!"

"To one in my crippled condition, an alarming outlook! However, I place myself unreservedly in your hands. But really, you must not leave this interesting district before you have made the acquaintance of some of its historical spots. To me, steeped as I am in what I may term the lore of the odd, it is a veritable wonderland, almost as interesting, in its way, as the caves and jungles of Hindustan depicted by Madame Blavatsky."

His high-pitched voice, with a certain labored intonation, not quite so characteristically American as was his accent, rose even higher; he spoke with the fire of the enthusiast.

"When I learned that Cragmire Tower was vacant," he continued, "I leaped at the chance (excuse the metaphor, from a lame man!). This is a ghost hunter's paradise. The tower itself is of unknown origin, though probably Phoenician, and the house traditionally sheltered Dr. Macleod, the necromancer, after his flight from the persecution of James of Scotland. Then, to add to its interest, it borders on Sedgemoor, the scene of the bloody battle during the Monmouth rising, whereat a thousand were slain on the field. It is a local legend that the unhappy Duke and his staff may be seen, on stormy nights, crossing the path which skirts the mire, after which this building is named, with flaming torches held aloft."

"Merely marsh-lights, I take it?" interjected Smith, gripping his pipe hard between his teeth.

"Your practical mind naturally seeks a practical explanation," smiled Van Roon, "but I myself have other theories. Then in addition to the charms of Sedgemoor—haunted Sedgemoor—on a fine day it is quite possible to see the ruins of Glastonbury Abbey from here; and Glastonbury Abbey, as you may know, is closely bound up with the history of alchemy. It was in the ruins of Glastonbury Abbey that the adept Kelly, companion of Dr. Dee, discovered, in the reign of Elizabeth, the famous caskets of St. Dunstan, containing the two tinctures..."

So he ran on, enumerating the odd charms of his residence, charms which for my part I did not find appealing. Finally:

"We cannot presume further upon your kindness," said Nayland Smith, standing up. "No doubt we can amuse ourselves in the neighborhood of the house until the return of your servant."

"Look upon Cragmire Tower as your own, gentlemen!" cried Van Roon. "Most of the rooms are unfurnished, and the garden is a wilderness, but the structure of the brickwork in the tower may interest you archaeologically, and the view across the moor is at least as fine as any in the neighborhood."

So, with his brilliant smile and a gesture of one thin yellow hand, the crippled traveler made us free of his odd dwelling. As I passed out from the room close at Smith's heels, I glanced back, I cannot say why. Van Roon already was bending over his papers, in his green shadowed sanctuary, and the light shining down upon his smoked glasses created the odd illusion that he was looking over the tops of the lenses and not down at the table as his attitude suggested. However, it was probably ascribable to the weird chiaroscuro of the scene, although it gave the seated figure an oddly malignant appearance, and I passed out through the utter darkness of the outer room to the front door. Smith opening it, I was conscious of surprise to find dusk come—to meet darkness where I had looked for sunlight.

The silver wisps which had raced along the horizon, as we came to Cragmire Tower, had been harbingers of other and heavier banks. A stormy sunset smeared crimson streaks across the skyline, where a great range of clouds, like the oily smoke of a city burning, was banked, mountain topping mountain, and lighted from below by this angry red. As we came down the steps and out by the gate, I turned and looked across the moor behind us. A sort of reflection from this distant blaze encrimsoned the whole landscape. The inland bay glowed sullenly, as if internal fires and not reflected light were at work; a scene both wild and majestic.

Nayland Smith was staring up at the cone-like top of the ancient tower in a curious, speculative fashion. Under the influence of our host's conversation I had forgotten the reasonless dread which had touched me at the moment of our arrival, but now, with the red light blazing over Sedgemoor, as if in memory of the blood which had been shed there, and with the tower of unknown origin looming above me, I became very uncomfortable again, nor did I envy Van Roon his eerie residence. The proximity of a tower of any kind, at night, makes in some inexplicable way for awe, and to-night there were other agents, too.

"What's that?" snapped Smith suddenly, grasping my arm.

He was peering southward, toward the distant hamlet, and, starting violently at his words and the sudden grasp of his hand, I, too, stared in that direction.

"We were followed, Petrie," he almost whispered. "I never got a sight of our follower, but I'll swear we were followed. Look! there's something moving over yonder!"

Together we stood staring into the dusk; then Smith burst abruptly into one of his rare laughs, and clapped me upon the shoulder.

"It's Hagar, the mulatto!" he cried—"and our grips. That extraordinary American with his tales of witch-lights and haunted abbeys has been playing the devil with our nerves."

Together we waited by the gate until the half-caste appeared on the bend of the path with a grip in either hand. He was a great, muscular fellow with a stoic face, and, for the purpose of visiting Saul, presumably, he had doffed his white raiment and now wore a sort of livery, with a peaked cap.

Smith watched him enter the house. Then:

"I wonder where Van Roon obtains his provisions and so forth," he muttered. "It's odd they knew nothing about the new tenant of Cragmire Tower at 'The Wagoners.'"

There came a sort of sudden expectancy into his manner for which I found myself at a loss to account. He turned his gaze inland and stood there tugging at his left ear and clicking his teeth together. He stared at me, and his eyes looked very bright in the dusk, for a sort of red glow from the sunset touched them; but he spoke no word, merely taking my arm and leading me off on a rambling walk around and about the house. Neither of us spoke a word until we stood at the gate of Cragmire Tower again; then:

"I'll swear, now, that we were followed here today!" muttered Smith.

The lofty place immediately within the doorway proved, in the light of a lamp now fixed in an iron bracket, to be a square entrance hall meagerly furnished. The closed study door faced the entrance, and on the left of it ascended an open staircase up which the mulatto led the way. We found ourselves on the floor above, in a corridor traversing the house from back to front. An apartment on the immediate left was indicated by the mulatto as that allotted to Smith. It was a room of fair size, furnished quite simply but boasting a wardrobe cupboard, and Smith's grip stood beside the white enameled bed. I glanced around, and then prepared to follow the man, who had awaited me in the doorway.

He still wore his dark livery, and as I followed the lithe, broad-shouldered figure along the corridor, I found myself considering critically his breadth of shoulder and the extraordinary thickness of his neck.

I have repeatedly spoken of a sort of foreboding, an elusive stirring in the depths of my being of which I became conscious at certain times in my dealings with Dr. Fu-Manchu and his murderous servants. This sensation, or something akin to it, claimed me now, unaccountably, as I stood looking into the neat bedroom, on the same side of the corridor but at the extreme end, wherein I was to sleep.

A voiceless warning urged me to return; a kind of childish panic came fluttering about my heart, a dread of entering the room, of allowing the mulatto to come behind me.

Doubtless this was no more than a sub-conscious product of my observations respecting his abnormal breadth of shoulder. But whatever the origin of the impulse, I found myself unable to disobey it. Therefore, I merely nodded, turned on my heel and went back to Smith's room.

I closed the door, then turned to face Smith, who stood regarding me.

"Smith," I said, "that man sends cold water trickling down my spine!"

Still regarding me fixedly, my friend nodded his head.

"You are curiously sensitive to this sort of thing," he replied slowly; "I have noticed it before as a useful capacity. I don't like the look of the man myself. The fact that he has been in Van Roon's employ for some years goes for nothing. We are neither of us likely to forget Kwee, the Chinese servant of Sir Lionel Barton, and it is quite possible that Fu-Manchu has corrupted this man as he corrupted the other. It is quite possible..."

His voice trailed off into silence, and he stood looking across the room with unseeing eyes, meditating deeply. It was quite dark now outside, as I could see through the uncurtained window, which opened upon the dreary expanse stretching out to haunted Sedgemoor. Two candles were burning upon the dressing table; they were but recently lighted, and so intense was the stillness that I could distinctly hear the spluttering of one of the wicks, which was damp. Without giving the slightest warning of his intention, Smith suddenly made two strides forward, stretched out his long arms, and snuffed the pair of candles in a twinkling.

The room became plunged in impenetrable darkness.

"Not a word, Petrie!" whispered my companion.

I moved cautiously to join him, but as I did so, perceived that he was moving too. Vaguely, against the window I perceived him silhouetted. He was looking out across the moor, and:

"See! see!" he hissed.

With my heart thumping furiously in my breast, I bent over him; and for the second time since our coming to Cragmire Tower, my thoughts flew to "The Fenman."

There are shades in the fen; ghosts of women and men
Who have sinned and have died, but are living again.
O'er the waters they tread, with their lanterns of dread,
And they peer in the pools – in the pools of the dead...

A light was dancing out upon the moor, a witchlight that came and went unaccountably, up and down, in and out, now clearly visible, now masked in the darkness!

"Lock the door!" snapped my companion—"if there's a key."

I crept across the room and fumbled for a moment; then:

"There is no key," I reported.

"Then wedge the chair under the knob and let no one enter until I return!" he said, amazingly.

With that he opened the window to its fullest extent, threw his leg over the sill, and went creeping along a wide concrete ledge, in which ran a leaded gutter, in the direction of the tower on the right!

Not pausing to follow his instructions respecting the chair, I craned out of the window, watching his progress, and wondering with what sudden madness he was bitten. Indeed, I could not credit my senses, could not believe that I heard and saw aright. Yet there out in the darkness on the moor moved the will-o'-the-wisp, and ten yards along the gutter crept my friend, like a great gaunt cat. Unknown to me he must have prospected the route by daylight, for now I saw his design. The ledge terminated only where it met the ancient wall of the tower, and it was possible for an agile climber to step from it to the edge of the unglazed window some four feet below, and to scramble from that point to the stone fence and thence on to the path by which we had come from Saul.

This difficult operation Nayland Smith successfully performed, and, to my unbounded amazement, went racing into the darkness toward the dancing light, headlong, like a madman! The night swallowed him up, and between my wonder and my fear my hands trembled so violently that I could scarce support myself where I rested, with my full weight upon the sill.

I seemed now to be moving through the fevered phases of a nightmare. Around and below me Cragmire Tower was profoundly silent, but a faint odor of cookery was now perceptible. Outside, from the night, came a faint whispering as of the distant sea, but no moon and no stars relieved the impenetrable blackness. Only out over the moor the mysterious light still danced and moved.

One—two—three—four—five minutes passed. The light vanished and did not appear again. Five more age-long minutes elapsed in absolute silence, whilst I peered into the darkness of the night and listened, every nerve in my body tense, for the return of Nayland Smith. Yet two more minutes, which embraced an agony of suspense, passed in the same fashion; then a shadowy form grew, phantomesque, out of the gloom; a moment more, and I distinctly heard the heavy breathing of a man nearly spent, and saw my friend scrambling up toward the black embrasure in the tower. His voice came huskily, pantingly:

"Creep along and lend me a hand, Petrie! I am nearly winded."

I crept through the window, steadied my quivering nerves by an effort of the will, and reached the end of the ledge in time to take Smith's extended hand and to draw him up beside me against the wall of the tower. He was shaking with his exertions, and must have fallen, I think, without my assistance. Inside the room again:

"Quick! light the candles!" he breathed hoarsely.

"Did any one come?"

"No one—nothing."

Having expended several matches in vain, for my fingers twitched nervously, I ultimately succeeded in relighting the candles.

"Get along to your room!" directed Smith. "Your apprehensions are unfounded at the moment, but you may as well leave both doors wide open!"

I looked into his face—it was very drawn and grim, and his brow was wet with perspiration, but his eyes had the fighting glint, and I knew that we were upon the eve of strange happenings.

◆

CHAPTER XXIII.

A CRY ON THE MOOR

Of the events intervening between this moment and that when death called to us out of the night, I have the haziest recollections. An excellent dinner was served in the bleak and gloomy dining-room by the mulatto, and the crippled author was carried to the head of the table by this same Herculean attendant, as lightly as though he had but the weight of a child.

Van Roon talked continuously, revealing a deep knowledge of all sorts of obscure matters; and in the brief intervals, Nayland Smith talked also, with almost feverish rapidity. Plans for the future were discussed. I can recall no one of them.

I could not stifle my queer sentiments in regard to the mulatto, and every time I found him behind my chair I was hard put to repress a shudder. In this fashion the strange evening passed; and to the accompaniment of distant, muttering thunder, we two guests retired to our chambers in Cragmire Tower. Smith had contrived to give me my instructions in a whisper, and five minutes after entering my own room, I had snuffed the candles, slipped a wedge, which he had given me, under the door, crept out through the window onto the guttered ledge, and joined Smith in his room. He, too, had extinguished his candles, and the place was in darkness. As I climbed in, he grasped my wrist to silence me, and turned me forcibly toward the window.

"Listen!" he said.

I turned and looked out upon a prospect which had been a fit setting for the witch scene in Macbeth. Thunder clouds hung low over the moor, but through them ran a sort of chasm, or rift, allowing a bar of lurid light to stretch across the drear, from east to west—a sort of lane walled by darkness. There came a remote murmuring, as of a troubled sea—a hushed and distant chorus; and sometimes in upon it broke the drums of heaven. In the west lightning flickered, though but faintly, intermittently.

Then came the call.

Out of the blackness of the moor it came, wild and distant—"Help! help!"

"Smith!" I whispered—"what is it? What..."

"Mr. Smith!" came the agonized cry... "Nayland Smith, help! for God's sake...."

"Quick, Smith!" I cried, "quick, man! It's Van Roon—he's been dragged out... they are murdering him..."

Nayland Smith held me in a vise-like grip, silent, unmoved!

Louder and more agonized came the cry for aid, and I became more than ever certain that it was poor Van Roon who uttered it.

"Mr. Smith! Dr. Petrie! for God's sake come... or... it will be ... too... late..."

"Smith!" I said, turning furiously upon my friend, "if you are going to remain here whilst murder is done, I am not!"

My blood boiled now with hot resentment. It was incredible, inhuman, that we should remain there inert whilst a fellow man, and our host to boot, was being done to death out there in the darkness. I exerted all my strength to break away; but although my efforts told upon him, as his loud breathing revealed, Nayland Smith clung to me tenaciously. Had my hands been free, in my fury, I could have struck him, for the pitiable cries, growing fainter, now, told their own tale. Then Smith spoke shortly and angrily—breathing hard between the words.

"Be quiet, you fool!" he snapped; "it's little less than an insult, Petrie, to think me capable of refusing help where help is needed!"

Like a cold douche his words acted; in that instant I knew myself a fool.

"You remember the Call of Siva?" he said, thrusting me away irritably, "—two years ago, and what it meant to those who obeyed it?"

"You might have told me..."

"Told you! You would have been through the window before I had uttered two words!"

I realized the truth of his assertion, and the justness of his anger.

"Forgive me, old man," I said, very crestfallen, "but my impulse was a natural one, you'll admit. You must remember that I have been trained never to refuse aid when aid is asked."

"Shut up, Petrie!" he growled; "forget it."

The cries had ceased now, entirely, and a peal of thunder, louder than any yet, echoed over distant Sedgemoor. The chasm of light splitting the heavens closed in, leaving the night wholly black.

"Don't talk!" rapped Smith; "act! You wedged your door?"

"Yes."

"Good. Get into that cupboard, have your Browning ready, and keep the door very slightly ajar."

He was in that mood of repressed fever which I knew and which always communicated itself to me. I spoke no further word, but stepped into the wardrobe indicated and drew the door nearly shut. The recess just accommodated me, and through the aperture I could see the bed, vaguely, the open window, and part of the opposite wall. I saw Smith cross the floor, as a mighty clap of thunder boomed over the house.

A gleam of lightning flickered through the gloom.

I saw the bed for a moment, distinctly, and it appeared to me that Smith lay therein, with the sheets pulled up over his head. The light was gone, and I could hear big drops of rain pattering upon the leaden gutter below the open window.

My mood was strange, detached, and characterized by vagueness. That Van Roon lay dead upon the moor I was convinced; and—although I recognized that it must be a sufficient one—I could not even dimly divine the reason why we had refrained from lending him aid. To have failed to save him, knowing his peril, would have been bad enough; to have refused, I thought was shameful. Better to have shared his fate—yet...

The downpour was increasing, and beating now a regular tattoo upon the gutterway. Then, splitting the oblong of greater blackness which marked the casement, quivered dazzlingly another flash of lightning in which I saw the bed again, with that impression of Smith curled up in it. The blinding light died out; came the crash of thunder, harsh and fearsome, more imminently above the tower than ever. The building seemed to shake.

Coming as they did, horror and the wrath of heaven together, suddenly, crashingly, black and angry after the fairness of the day, these happenings and their setting must have terrorized the stoutest heart; but somehow I seemed detached, as I have said, and set apart from the whirl of events; a spectator. Even when a vague yellow light crept across the room from the direction of the door, and flickered unsteadily on the bed, I remained unmoved to a certain degree, although passively alive to the significance of the incident. I realized that the ultimate issue was at hand, but either because I was emotionally exhausted, or from some other cause, the pending climax failed to disturb me.

Going on tiptoe, in stockinged feet, across my field of vision, passed Kegan Van Roon! He was in his shirt-sleeves and held a lighted candle in one hand whilst with the other he shaded it against the draught from the window. He was a cripple no longer, and the smoked glasses were discarded; most of the light, at the moment when first I saw him, shone upon his thin, olive face, and at sight of his eyes much of the mystery of Cragmire Tower was resolved. For they were oblique, very slightly, but nevertheless unmistakably oblique. Though highly educated, and possibly an American citizen, Van Roon was a Chinaman!

Upon the picture of his face as I saw it then, I do not care to dwell. It lacked the unique horror of Dr. Fu-Manchu's unforgettable countenance, but possessed a sort of animal malignancy which the latter lacked... He approached within three or four feet of the bed, peering—peering. Then, with a timidity which spoke well for Nayland Smith's reputation, paused and beckoned to some one who evidently stood in the doorway behind him. As he did so I noted that the legs of his trousers were caked with greenish brown mud nearly up to the knees.

The huge mulatto, silent-footed, crossed to the bed in three strides. He was stripped to the waist, and, excepting some few professional athletes, I had never seen a torso to compare with that which, brown and glistening, now bent over Nayland Smith. The muscular development was simply enormous; the man had a neck like a column, and the thews around his back and shoulders were like ivy tentacles wreathing some gnarled oak.

Whilst Van Roon, his evil gaze upon the bed, held the candle aloft, the mulatto, with a curious preparatory writhing movement of the mighty shoulders, lowered his outstretched fingers to the disordered bed linen...

I pushed open the cupboard door and thrust out the Browning. As I did so a dramatic thing happened. A tall, gaunt figure shot suddenly upright from beyond the bed. It was Nayland Smith!

Upraised in his hand he held a heavy walking cane. I knew the handle to be leaded, and I could judge of the force with which he wielded it by the fact that it cut the air with a keen swishing sound. It descended upon the back of the mulatto's skull with a sickening thud, and the great brown body dropped inert upon the padded bed—in which not Smith, but his grip, reposed. There was no word, no cry. Then:

"Shoot, Petrie! Shoot the fiend! Shoot..."

Van Roon, dropping the candle, in the falling gleam of which I saw the whites of the oblique eyes turned and leaped from the room with the agility of a wild cat. The ensuing darkness was split by a streak of lightning... and there was Nayland Smith scrambling around the foot of the bed and making for the door in hot pursuit.

We gained it almost together. Smith had dropped the cane, and now held his pistol in his hand. Together we fired into the chasm of the corridor, and in the flash, saw Van Roon hurling himself down the stairs. He went silently in his stockinged feet, and our own clatter was drowned by the awful booming of the thunder which now burst over us again.

Crack!—crack!—crack! Three times our pistols spat venomously after the flying figure... then we had crossed the hall below and were in the wilderness of the night with the rain descending upon us in sheets. Vaguely I saw the white shirt-sleeves of the fugitive near the corner of the stone fence. A moment he hesitated, then darted away inland, not toward Saul, but toward the moor and the cup of the inland bay.

"Steady, Petrie! steady!" cried Nayland Smith. He ran, panting, beside me. "It is the path to the mire." He breathed sibilantly between every few words. "It was out there... that he hoped to lure us... with the cry for help."

A great blaze of lightning illuminated the landscape as far as the eye could see. Ahead of us a flying shape, hair lank and glistening in the downpour, followed a faint path skirting that green tongue of morass which we had noted from the upland. It was Kegan Van Roon. He glanced over his shoulder, showing a yellow, terror-stricken face. We were gaining upon him. Darkness fell, and the thunder cracked and boomed as though the very moor were splitting about us.

"Another fifty yards, Petrie," breathed Nayland Smith, "and after that it's unchartered ground."

On we went through the rain and the darkness; then:

"Slow up! slow up!" cried Smith. "It feels soft!"

Indeed, already I had made one false step—and the hungry mire had fastened upon my foot, almost tripping me.

"Lost the path!"

We stopped dead. The falling rain walled us in. I dared not move, for I knew that the mire, the devouring mire, stretched, eager, close about my feet. We were both waiting for the next flash of lightning, I think, but, before it came, out of the darkness ahead of us rose a cry that sometimes rings in my ears to this hour. Yet it was no more than a repetition of that which had called to us, deathfully, awhile before.

"Help! help! for God's sake help! Quick! I am sinking..."

Nayland Smith grasped my arm furiously.

"We dare not move, Petrie—we dare not move!" he breathed. "It's God's justice—visible for once."

Then came the lightning; and—ignoring a splitting crash behind us—we both looked ahead, over the mire.

Just on the edge of the venomous green path, not thirty yards away, I saw the head and shoulders and upstretched, appealing arms of Van Roon. Even as the lightning flickered and we saw him, he was gone; with one last, long, drawn-out cry, horribly like the mournful wail of a sea gull, he was gone!

That eerie light died, and in the instant before the sound of the thunder came shatteringly, we turned about... in time to see Cragmire Tower, a blacker silhouette against the night, topple and fall! A red glow began to be perceptible above the building. The thunder came booming through the caverns of space. Nayland Smith lowered his wet face close to mine and shouted in my ear:

"Kegan Van Roon never returned from China. It was a trap. Those were two creatures of Dr. Fu-Manchu..."

The thunder died away, hollowly, echoing over the distant sea...

"That light on the moor to-night?"

"You have not learned the Morse Code, Petrie. It was a signal, and it read:—S M I T H... SOS."

"Well?"

"I took the chance, as you know. And it was Karamaneh! She knew of the plot to bury us in the mire. She had followed from London, but could do nothing until dusk. God forgive me if I've misjudged her—for we owe her our lives to-night."

Flames were bursting up from the building beside the ruin of the ancient tower which had faced the storms of countless ages only to succumb at last. The lightning literally had cloven it in twain.

"The mulatto?..."

Again the lightning flashed, and we saw the path and began to retrace our steps. Nayland Smith turned to me; his face was very grim in that unearthly light, and his eyes shone like steel.

"I killed him, Petrie... as I meant to do."

From out over Sedgemoor it came, cracking and rolling and booming toward us, swelling in volume to a stupendous climax, that awful laughter of Jove the destroyer of Cragmire Tower.

◆◆◆◆◆

CHAPTER XXIV.

STORY OF THE GABLES

In looking over my notes dealing with the second phase of Dr. Fu-Manchu's activities in England, I find that one of the worst hours of my life was associated with the singular and seemingly inconsequent adventure of the fiery hand. I shall deal with it in this place, begging you to bear with me if I seem to digress.

Inspector Weymouth called one morning, shortly after the Van Roon episode, and entered upon a surprising account of a visit to a house at Hampstead which enjoyed the sinister reputation of being uninhabitable.

"But in what way does the case enter into your province?" inquired Nayland Smith, idly tapping out his pipe on a bar of the grate.

We had not long finished breakfast, but from an early hour Smith had been at his eternal smoking, which only the advent of the meal had interrupted.

"Well," replied the inspector, who occupied a big armchair near the window, "I was sent to look into it, I suppose, because I had nothing better to do at the moment."

"Ah!" jerked Smith, glancing over his shoulder.

The ejaculation had a veiled significance; for our quest of Dr. Fu-Manchu had come to an abrupt termination by reason of the fact that all trace of that malignant genius, and of the group surrounding him, had vanished with the destruction of Cragmire Tower.

"The house is called the Gables," continued the Scotland Yard man, "and I knew I was on a wild goose chase from the first—"

"Why?" snapped Smith.

"Because I was there before, six months ago or so—just before your present return to England—and I knew what to expect."

Smith looked up with some faint dawning of interest perceptible in his manner.

"I was unaware," he said with a slight smile, "that the cleaning-up of haunted houses came within the jurisdiction of Scotland Yard. I am learning something."

"In the ordinary way," replied the big man good-humoredly, "it doesn't. But a sudden death always excites suspicion, and—"

"A sudden death?" I said, glancing up; "you didn't explain that the ghost had killed any one!"

"I'm afraid I'm a poor hand at yarn-spinning, Doctor," said Weymouth, turning his blue, twinkling eyes in my direction. "Two people have died at the Gables within the last six months."

"You begin to interest me," declared Smith, and there came something of the old, eager look into his gaunt face, as, having lighted his pipe, he tossed the match-end into the hearth.

"I had hoped for some little excitement, myself," confessed the inspector. "This dead-end, with not a ghost of a clue to the whereabouts of the yellow fiend, has been getting on my nerves—"

Nayland Smith grunted sympathetically.

"Although Dr. Fu-Manchu has been in England for some months, now," continued Weymouth, "I have never set eyes upon him; the house we raided in Museum Street proved to be empty; in a word, I am wasting my time. So that I volunteered to run up to Hampstead and look into the matter of the Gables, principally as a distraction. It's a queer business, but more in the Psychical Research Society's line than mine, I'm afraid. Still, if there were no Dr. Fu-Manchu it might be of interest to you—and to you, Dr. Petrie, because it illustrates the fact, that, given the right sort of subject, death can be brought about without any elaborate mechanism—such as our Chinese friends employ."

"You interest me more and more," declared Smith, stretching himself in the long, white cane rest-chair.

"Two men, both fairly sound, except that the first one had an asthmatic heart, have died at the Gables without any one laying a little finger upon them. Oh! there was no jugglery! They weren't poisoned, or bitten by venomous insects, or suffocated, or anything like that. They just died of fear—stark fear."

With my elbows resting upon the table cover, and my chin in my hands, I was listening attentively, now, and Nayland Smith, a big cushion behind his head, was watching the speaker with a keen and speculative look in those steely eyes of his.

"You imply that Dr. Fu-Manchu has something to learn from the Gables?" he jerked.

Weymouth nodded stolidly.

"I can't work up anything like amazement in these days," continued the latter; "every other case seems stale and hackneyed alongside the case. But I must confess that when the Gables came on the books of the Yard the second time, I began to wonder. I thought there might be some tangible clue, some link connecting the two victims; perhaps some evidence of robbery or of revenge—of some sort of motive. In short, I hoped to find evidence of human agency at work, but, as before, I was disappointed."

"It's a legitimate case of a haunted house, then?" said Smith.

"Yes; we find them occasionally, these uninhabitable places, where there is something, something malignant and harmful to human life, but something that you cannot arrest, that you cannot hope to bring into court."

"Ah," replied Smith slowly; "I suppose you are right. There are historic instances, of course: Glamys Castle and Spedlins Tower in Scotland, Peel Castle, Isle of Man, with its Maudhe Dhug, the gray lady of Rainham Hall, the headless horses of Caistor, the Wesley ghost of Epworth Rectory, and others. But I have never come in personal contact with such a case, and if I did I should feel very humiliated to have to confess that there was any agency which could produce a physical result—death—but which was immune from physical retaliation."

Weymouth nodded his head again.

"I might feel a bit sour about it, too," he replied, "if it were not that I haven't much pride left in these days, considering the show of physical retaliation I have made against Dr. Fu-Manchu."

"A home thrust, Weymouth!" snapped Nayland Smith, with one of those rare, boyish laughs of his. "We're children to that Chinese doctor, Inspector, to that weird product of a weird people who are as old in evil as the pyramids are old in mystery. But about the Gables?"

"Well, it's an uncanny place. You mentioned Glamys Castle a moment ago, and it's possible to understand an old stronghold like that being haunted, but the Gables was only built about 1870; it's quite a modern house. It was built for a wealthy Quaker family, and they occupied it, uninterruptedly and apparently without anything unusual occurring, for over forty years. Then it was sold to a Mr. Maddison—and Mr. Maddison died there six months ago."

"Maddison?" said Smith sharply, staring across at Weymouth. "What was he? Where did he come from?"

"He was a retired tea-planter from Colombo," replied the inspector.

"Colombo?"

"There was a link with the East, certainly, if that's what you are thinking; and it was this fact which interested me at the time, and which led me to waste precious days and nights on the case. But there was no mortal connection between this liverish individual and the schemes of Dr. Fu-Manchu. I'm certain of that."

"And how did he die?" I asked, interestedly.

"He just died in his chair one evening, in the room which he used as a library. It was his custom to sit there every night, when there were no visitors, reading, until twelve o'clock—or later. He was a bachelor, and his household consisted of a cook, a housemaid, and a man who had been with him for thirty years, I believe. At the time of Mr. Maddison's death, his household had recently been deprived of two of its members. The cook and housemaid both resigned one morning, giving as their reason the fact that the place was haunted."

"In what way?"

"I interviewed the precious pair at the time, and they told me absurd and various tales about dark figures wandering along the corridors and bending over them in bed at night, whispering; but their chief trouble was a continuous ringing of bells about the house."

"Bells?"

"They said that it became unbearable. Night and day there were bells ringing all over the house. At any rate, they went, and for three or four days the Gables was occupied only by Mr. Maddison and his man, whose name was Stevens. I interviewed the latter also, and he was an altogether more reliable witness; a decent, steady sort of man whose story impressed me very much at the time."

"Did he confirm the ringing?"

"He swore to it—a sort of jangle, sometimes up in the air, near the ceilings, and sometimes under the floor, like the shaking of silver bells."

Nayland Smith stood up abruptly and began to pace the room, leaving great trails of blue-gray smoke behind him.

"Your story is sufficiently interesting, Inspector," he declared, "even to divert my mind from the eternal contemplation of the Fu-Manchu problem. This would appear to be distinctly a case of an 'astral bell' such as we sometimes hear of in India."

"It was Stevens," continued Weymouth, "who found Mr. Maddison. He (Stevens) had been out on business connected with the household arrangements, and at about eleven o'clock he returned, letting himself in with a key. There was a light in the library, and getting no response to his knocking, Stevens entered. He found his master sitting bolt upright in a chair, clutching the arms with rigid fingers and staring straight before him with a look of such frightful horror on his face, that Stevens positively ran from the room and out of the house. Mr. Maddison was stone dead. When a doctor, who lives at no great distance away, came and examined him, he could find no trace of violence whatever; he had apparently died of fright, to judge from the expression on his face."

"Anything else?"

"Only this: I learnt, indirectly, that the last member of the Quaker family to occupy the house had apparently witnessed the apparition, which had led to his vacating the place. I got the story from the wife of a man who had been employed as gardener there at that time. The apparition—which he witnessed in the hallway, if I remember rightly—took the form of a sort of luminous hand clutching a long, curved knife."

"Oh, Heavens!" cried Smith, and laughed shortly; "that's quite in order!"

"This gentleman told no one of the occurrence until after he had left the house, no doubt in order that the place should not acquire an evil reputation. Most of the original furniture remained, and Mr. Maddison took the house furnished. I don't think there can be any doubt that what killed him was fear at seeing a repetition—"

"Of the fiery hand?" concluded Smith.

"Quite so. Well, I examined the Gables pretty closely, and, with another Scotland Yard man, spent a night in the empty house. We saw nothing; but once, very faintly, we heard the ringing of bells."

Smith spun around upon him rapidly.

"You can swear to that?" he snapped.

"I can swear to it," declared Weymouth stolidly. "It seemed to be over our heads. We were sitting in the dining-room. Then it was gone, and we heard nothing more whatever of an unusual nature. Following the death of Mr. Maddison, the Gables remained empty until a while ago, when a French gentleman, name Lejay, leased it—"

"Furnished?"

"Yes; nothing was removed—"

"Who kept the place in order?"

"A married couple living in the neighborhood undertook to do so. The man attended to the lawn and so forth, and the woman came once a week, I believe, to clean up the house."

"And Lejay?"

"He came in only last week, having leased the house for six months. His family were to have joined him in a day or two, and he, with the aid of the pair I have just mentioned, and assisted by a French servant he brought over with him, was putting the place in order. At about twelve o'clock on Friday night this servant ran into a neighboring house screaming 'the fiery hand!' and when at last a constable arrived and a frightened group went up the avenue of the Gables, they found M. Lejay, dead in the avenue, near the steps just outside the hall door! He had the same face of horror..."

"What a tale for the press!" snapped Smith.

"The owner has managed to keep it quiet so far, but this time I think it will leak into the press—yes."

There was a short silence; then:

"And you have been down to the Gables again?"

"I was there on Saturday, but there's not a scrap of evidence. The man undoubtedly died of fright in the same way as Maddison. The place ought to be pulled down; it's unholy."

"Unholy is the word," I said. "I never heard anything like it. This M. Lejay had no enemies?—there could be no possible motive?"

"None whatever. He was a business man from Marseilles, and his affairs necessitated his remaining in or near London for some considerable time; therefore, he decided to make his headquarters here, temporarily, and leased the Gables with that intention."

Nayland Smith was pacing the floor with increasing rapidity; he was tugging at the lobe of his left ear and his pipe had long since gone out.

◆

CHAPTER XXV.

THE BELLS

I started to my feet as a tall, bearded man swung open the door and hurled himself impetuously into the room. He wore a silk hat, which fitted him very ill, and a black frock coat which did not fit him at all.

"It's all right, Petrie!" cried the apparition; "I've leased the Gables!"

It was Nayland Smith! I stared at him in amazement

"The first time I have employed a disguise," continued my friend rapidly, "since the memorable episode of the false pigtail." He threw a small brown leather grip upon the floor. "In case you should care to visit the house, Petrie, I have brought these things. My tenancy commences to-night!"

Two days had elapsed, and I had entirely forgotten the strange story of the Gables which Inspector Weymouth had related to us; evidently it was otherwise with my friend, and utterly at a loss for an explanation of his singular behavior, I stooped mechanically and opened the grip. It contained an odd assortment of garments, and amongst other things several gray wigs and a pair of gold-rimmed spectacles.

Kneeling there with this strange litter about me, I looked up amazedly. Nayland Smith, with the unsuitable silk hat set right upon the back of his head, was pacing the room excitedly, his fuming pipe protruding from the tangle of factitious beard.

"You see, Petrie," he began again, rapidly, "I did not entirely trust the agent. I've leased the house in the name of Professor Maxton..."

"But, Smith," I cried, "what possible reason can there be for disguise?"

"There's every reason," he snapped.

"Why should you interest yourself in the Gables?"

"Does no explanation occur to you?"

"None whatever; to me the whole thing smacks of stark lunacy."

"Then you won't come?"

"I've never stuck at anything, Smith," I replied, "however undignified, when it has seemed that my presence could be of the slightest use."

As I rose to my feet, Smith stepped in front of me, and the steely gray eyes shone out strangely from the altered face. He clapped his hands upon my shoulders.

"If I assure you that your presence is necessary to my safety," he said—"that if you fail me I must seek another companion—will you come?"

Intuitively, I knew that he was keeping something back, and I was conscious of some resentment, but nevertheless my reply was a foregone conclusion, and—with the borrowed appearance of an extremely untidy old man—I crept guiltily out of my house that evening and into the cab which Smith had waiting.

The Gables was a roomy and rambling place lying back a considerable distance from the road. A semicircular drive gave access to the door, and so densely wooded was the ground, that for the most part the drive was practically a tunnel—a verdant tunnel. A high brick wall concealed the building from the point of view of any one on the roadway, but either horn of the crescent drive terminated at a heavy, wrought-iron gateway.

Smith discharged the cab at the corner of the narrow and winding road upon which the Gables fronted. It was walled in on both sides; on the left the wall being broken by tradesmen's entrances to the houses fronting upon another street, and on the right following, uninterruptedly, the grounds of the Gables. As we came to the gate:

"Nothing now," said Smith, pointing into the darkness of the road before us, "except a couple of studios, until one comes to the Heath."

He inserted the key in the lock of the gate and swung it creakingly open. I looked into the black arch of the avenue, thought of the haunted residence that lay hidden somewhere beyond, of those who had died in it—especially of the one who had died there under the trees—and found myself out of love with the business of the night.

"Come on!" said Nayland Smith briskly, holding the gate open; "there should be a fire in the library and refreshments, if the charwoman has followed instructions."

I heard the great gate clang to behind us. Even had there been any moon (and there was none) I doubted if more than a patch or two of light could have penetrated there. The darkness was extraordinary. Nothing broke it, and I think Smith must have found his way by the aid of some sixth sense. At any rate, I saw nothing of the house until I stood some five paces from the steps leading up to the porch. A light was burning in the hallway, but dimly and inhospitably; of the facade of the building I could perceive little.

When we entered the hall and the door was closed behind us, I began wondering anew what purpose my friend hoped to serve by a vigil in this haunted place. There was a light in the library, the door of which was ajar, and on the large table were decanters, a siphon, and some biscuits and sandwiches. A large grip stood upon the floor, also. For some reason which was a mystery to me, Smith had decided that we must assume false names whilst under the roof of the Gables; and:

"Now, Pearce," he said, "a whisky-and-soda before we look around?"

The proposal was welcome enough, for I felt strangely dispirited, and, to tell the truth, in my strange disguise, not a little ridiculous.

All my nerves, no doubt, were highly strung, and my sense of hearing unusually acute, for I went in momentary expectation of some uncanny happening. I had not long to wait. As I raised the glass to my lips and glanced across the table at my friend, I heard the first faint sound heralding the coming of the bells.

It did not seem to proceed from anywhere within the library, but from some distant room, far away overhead. A musical sound it was, but breaking in upon the silence of that ill-omened house, its music was the music of terror. In a faint and very sweet cascade it rippled; a ringing as of tiny silver bells.

I set down my glass upon the table, and rising slowly from the chair in which I had been seated, stared fixedly at my companion, who was staring with equal fixity at me. I could see that I had not been deluded; Nayland Smith had heard the ringing, too.

"The ghosts waste no time!" he said softly. "This is not new to me; I spent an hour here last night and heard the same sound..."

I glanced hastily around the room. It was furnished as a library, and contained a considerable collection of works, principally novels. I was unable to judge of the outlook, for the two lofty windows were draped with heavy purple curtains which were drawn close. A silk shaded lamp swung from the center of the ceiling, and immediately over the table by which I stood. There was much shadow about the room; and now I glanced apprehensively about me, but especially toward the open door.

In that breathless suspense of listening we stood awhile; then:

"There it is again!" whispered Smith, tensely.

The ringing of bells was repeated, and seemingly much nearer to us; in fact it appeared to come from somewhere above, up near the ceiling of the room in which we stood. Simultaneously, we looked up, then Smith laughed, shortly.

"Instinctive, I suppose," he snapped; "but what do we expect to see in the air?"

The musical sound now grew in volume; the first tiny peal seemed to be reinforced by others and by others again, until the air around about us was filled with the pealings of these invisible bell-ringers.

Although, as I have said, the sound was rather musical than horrible, it was, on the other hand, so utterly unaccountable as to touch the supreme heights of the uncanny. I could not doubt that our presence had attracted these unseen ringers to the room in which we stood, and I knew quite well that I was growing pale. This was the room in which at least one unhappy occupant of the Gables had died of fear. I recognized the fact that if this mere overture were going to affect my nerves to such an extent, I could not hope to survive the ordeal of the night; a great effort was called for. I emptied my glass at a gulp, and stared across the table at Nayland Smith with a sort of defiance. He was standing very upright and motionless, but his eyes were turning right and left, searching every visible corner of the big room.

"Good!" he said in a very low voice. "The terrorizing power of the Unknown is boundless, but we must not get in the grip of panic, or we could not hope to remain in this house ten minutes."

I nodded without speaking. Then Smith, to my amazement, suddenly began to speak in a loud voice, a marked contrast to that, almost a whisper, in which he had spoken formerly.

"My dear Pearce," he cried, "do you hear the ringing of bells?"

Clearly the latter words were spoken for the benefit of the unseen intelligence controlling these manifestations; and although I regarded such finesse as somewhat wasted, I followed my friend's lead and replied in a voice as loud as his own:

"Distinctly, Professor!"

Silence followed my words, a silence in which both stood watchful and listening. Then, very faintly, I seemed to detect the silvern ringing receding away through distant rooms. Finally it became inaudible, and in the stillness of the Gables I could distinctly hear my companion breathing. For fully ten minutes we two remained thus, each momentarily expecting a repetition of the ringing, or the coming of some new and more sinister manifestation. But we heard nothing and saw nothing.

"Hand me that grip, and don't stir until I come back!" hissed Smith in my ear.

He turned and walked out of the library, his boots creaking very loudly in that awe-inspiring silence.

Standing beside the table, I watched the open door for his return, crushing down a dread that another form than his might suddenly appear there.

I could hear him moving from room to room, and presently, as I waited in hushed, tense watchfulness, he came in, depositing the grip upon the table. His eyes were gleaming feverishly.

"The house is haunted, Pearce!" he cried. "But no ghost ever frightened me! Come, I will show you your room."

✦✦✦✦◆✦✦✦✦

CHAPTER XXVI.

THE FIERY HAND

Smith walked ahead of me upstairs; he had snapped up the light in the hallway, and now he turned and cried back loudly:

"I fear we should never get servants to stay here."

Again I detected the appeal to a hidden Audience; and there was something very uncanny in the idea. The house now was deathly still; the ringing had entirely subsided. In the upper corridor my companion, who seemed to be well acquainted with the position of the switches, again turned up all the lights, and in pursuit of the strange comedy which he saw fit to enact, addressed me continuously in the loud and unnatural voice which he had adopted as part of his disguise.

We looked into a number of rooms all well and comfortably furnished, but although my imagination may have been responsible for the idea, they all seemed to possess a chilly and repellent atmosphere. I felt that to essay sleep in any one of them would be the merest farce, that the place to all intents and purposes was uninhabitable, that something incalculably evil presided over the house.

And through it all, so obtuse was I, that no glimmer of the truth entered my mind. Outside again in the long, brightly lighted corridor, we stood for a moment as if a mutual anticipation of some new event pending had come to us. It was curious that sudden pulling up and silent questioning of one another; because, although we acted thus, no sound had reached us. A few seconds later our anticipation was realized. From the direction of the stairs it came—a low wailing in a woman's voice; and the sweetness of the tones added to the terror of the sound. I clutched at Smith's arm convulsively whilst that uncanny cry rose and fell—rose and fell—and died away.

Neither of us moved immediately. My mind was working with feverish rapidity and seeking to run down a memory which the sound had stirred into faint quickness. My heart was still leaping wildly when the wailing began again, rising and falling in regular cadence. At that instant I identified it.

During the time Smith and I had spent together in Egypt, two years before, searching for Karamaneh, I had found myself on one occasion in the neighborhood of a native cemetery near to Bedrasheen. Now, the scene which I had witnessed there rose up again vividly before me, and I seemed to see a little group of black-robed women clustered together about a native grave; for the wailing which now was dying away again in the Gables was the same, or almost the same, as the wailing of those Egyptian mourners.

The house was very silent again, now. My forehead was damp with perspiration, and I became more and more convinced that the uncanny ordeal must prove too much for my nerves. Hitherto, I had accorded little credence to tales of the supernatural, but face to face with such manifestations as these, I realized that I would have faced rather a group of armed dacoits, nay! Dr. Fu-Manchu himself, than have remained another hour in that ill-omened house.

My companion must have read as much in my face. But he kept up the strange, and to me, purposeless comedy, when presently he spoke.

"I feel it to be incumbent upon me to suggest," he said, "that we spend the night at a hotel after all."

He walked rapidly downstairs and into the library and began to strap up the grip.

"After all," he said, "there may be a natural explanation of what we've heard; for it is noteworthy that we have actually seen nothing. It might even be possible to get used to the ringing and the wailing after a time. Frankly, I am loath to go back on my bargain!"

Whilst I stared at him in amazement, he stood there indeterminate as it seemed, Then:

"Come, Pearce!" he cried loudly, "I can see that you do not share my views; but for my own part I shall return to-morrow and devote further attention to the phenomena."

Extinguishing the light, he walked out into the hallway, carrying the grip in his hand. I was not far behind him. We walked toward the door together, and:

"Turn the light out, Pearce," directed Smith; "the switch is at your elbow. We can see our way to the door well enough, now."

In order to carry out these instructions, it became necessary for me to remain a few paces in the rear of my companion, and I think I have never experienced such a pang of nameless terror as pierced me at the moment of extinguishing the light; for Smith had not yet opened the door, and the utter darkness of the Gables was horrible beyond expression. Surely darkness is the most potent weapon of the Unknown. I know that at the moment my hand left the switch, I made for the door as though the hosts of hell pursued me. I collided violently with Smith. He was evidently facing toward me in the darkness, for at the moment of our collision, he grasped my shoulder as in a vise.

"My God, Petrie! look behind you!" he whispered.

I was enabled to judge of the extent and reality of his fear by the fact that the strange subterfuge of addressing me always as Pearce was forgotten. I turned, in a flash....

Never can I forget what I saw. Many strange and terrible memories are mine, memories stranger and more terrible than those of the average man; but this thing which now moved slowly down upon us through the impenetrable gloom of that haunted place, was (if the term be understood) almost absurdly horrible. It was a medieval legend come to life in modern London; it was as though some horrible chimera of the black and ignorant past was become create and potent in the present.

A luminous hand—a hand in the veins of which fire seemed to run so that the texture of the skin and the shape of the bones within were perceptible—in short a hand of glowing, fiery flesh clutching a short knife or dagger which also glowed with the same hellish, internal luminance, was advancing upon us where we stood—was not three paces removed!

What I did or how I came to do it, I can never recall. In all my years I have experienced nothing to equal the stark panic which seized upon me then. I know that I uttered a loud and frenzied cry; I know that I tore myself like a madman from Smith's restraining grip...

"Don't touch it! Keep away, for your life!" I heard...

But, dimly I recollect that, finding the thing approaching yet nearer, I lashed out with my fists—madly, blindly—and struck something palpable...

What was the result, I cannot say. At that point my recollections merge into confusion. Something or some one (Smith, as I afterwards discovered) was hauling me by main force through the darkness; I fell a considerable distance onto gravel which lacerated my hands and gashed my knees. Then, with the cool night air fanning my brow, I was running, running—my breath coming in hysterical sobs. Beside me fled another figure.... And my definite recollections commence again at that point. For this companion of my flight from the Gables threw himself roughly against me to alter my course.

"Not that way! not that way!" came pantingly.

"Not on to the Heath... we must keep to the roads..."

It was Nayland Smith. That healing realization came to me, bringing such a gladness as no words of mine can express nor convey. Still we ran on.

"There's a policeman's lantern," panted my companion. "They'll attempt nothing, now!

I gulped down the stiff brandy-and-soda, then glanced across to where Nayland Smith lay extended in the long, cane chair.

"Perhaps you will explain," I said, "for what purpose you submitted me to that ordeal. If you proposed to correct my skepticism concerning supernatural manifestations, you have succeeded."

"Yes," said my companion, musingly, "they are devilishly clever; but we knew that already."

I stared at him, fatuously.

"Have you ever known me to waste my time when there was important work to do?" he continued. "Do you seriously believe that my ghost-hunting was undertaken for amusement? Really, Petrie, although you are very fond of assuring me that I need a holiday, I think the shoe is on the other foot!"

From the pocket of his dressing-gown, he took out a piece of silk fringe which had apparently been torn from a scarf, and rolling it into a ball, tossed it across to me.

"Smell!" he snapped.

I did as he directed—and gave a great start. The silk exhaled a faint perfume, but its effect upon me was as though some one had cried aloud:—

"Karamaneh!"

Beyond doubt the silken fragment had belonged to the beautiful servant of Dr. Fu-Manchu, to the dark-eyed, seductive Karamaneh. Nayland Smith was watching me keenly.

"You recognize it—yes?"

I placed the piece of silk upon the table, slightly shrugging my shoulders.

"It was sufficient evidence in itself," continued my friend, "but I thought it better to seek confirmation, and the obvious way was to pose as a new lessee of the Gables..."

"But, Smith," I began...

"Let me explain, Petrie. The history of the Gables seemed to be susceptible of only one explanation; in short it was fairly evident to me that the object of the manifestations was to insure the place being kept empty. This idea suggested another, and with them both in mind, I set out to make my inquiries, first taking the precaution to disguise my identity, to which end Weymouth gave me the freedom of Scotland Yard's fancy wardrobe. I did not take the agent into my confidence, but posed as a stranger who had heard that the house was to let furnished and thought it might suit his purpose. My inquiries were directed to a particular end, but I failed to achieve it at the time. I had theories, as I have said, and when, having paid the deposit and secured possession of the keys, I was enabled to visit the place alone, I was fortunate enough to obtain evidence to show that my imagination had not misled me.

"You were very curious the other morning, I recall, respecting my object in borrowing a large brace and bit. My object, Petrie, was to bore a series of holes in the wainscoating of various rooms at the Gables—in inconspicuous positions, of course..."

"But, my dear Smith!" I cried, "you are merely adding to my mystification."

He stood up and began to pace the room in his restless fashion.

"I had cross-examined Weymouth closely regarding the phenomenon of the bell-ringing, and an exhaustive search of the premises led to the discovery that the house was in such excellent condition that, from ground-floor to attic, there was not a solitary crevice large enough to admit of the passage of a mouse."

I suppose I must have been staring very foolishly indeed, for Nayland Smith burst into one of his sudden laughs.

"A mouse, I said, Petrie!" he cried. "With the brace-and-bit I rectified that matter. I made the holes I have mentioned, and before each set a trap baited with a piece of succulent, toasted cheese. Just open that grip!"

The light at last was dawning upon my mental darkness, and I pounced upon the grip, which stood upon a chair near the window, and opened it. A sickly smell of cooked cheese assailed my nostrils.

"Mind your fingers!" cried Smith; "some of them are still set, possibly."

Out from the grip I began to take mouse-traps! Two or three of them were still set but in the case of the greater number the catches had slipped. Nine I took out and placed upon the table, and all were empty. In the tenth there crouched, panting, its soft furry body dank with perspiration, a little white mouse!

"Only one capture!" cried my companion, "showing how well-fed the creatures were. Examine his tail!"

But already I had perceived that to which Smith would draw my attention, and the mystery of the "astral bells" was a mystery no longer. Bound to the little creature's tail, close to the root, with fine soft wire such as is used for making up bouquets, were three tiny silver bells. I looked across at my companion in speechless surprise.

"Almost childish, is it not?" he said; "yet by means of this simple device the Gables has been emptied of occupant after occupant. There was small chance of the trick being detected, for, as I have said, there was absolutely no aperture from roof to basement by means of which one of them could have escaped into the building."

"Then..."

"They were admitted into the wall cavities and the rafters, from some cellar underneath, Petrie, to which, after a brief scamper under the floors and over the ceilings, they instinctively returned for the food they were accustomed to receive, and for which, even had it been possible (which it was not) they had no occasion to forage."

I, too, stood up; for excitement was growing within me. I took up the piece of silk from the table.

"Where did you find this?" I asked, my eyes upon Smith's keen face.

"In a sort of wine cellar, Petrie," he replied, "under the stair. There is no cellar proper to the Gables—at least no such cellar appears in the plans."

"But..."

"But there is one beyond doubt—yes! It must be part of some older building which occupied the site before the Gables was built. One can only surmise that it exists, although such a surmise is a fairly safe one, and the entrance to the subterranean portion of the building is situated beyond doubt in the wine cellar. Of this we have at least two evidences:—the finding of the fragment of silk there, and the fact that in one case at least—as I learned—the light was extinguished in the library unaccountably. This could only have been done in one way: by manipulating the main switch, which is also in the wine cellar."

"But Smith!" I cried, "do you mean that Fu-Manchu..."

Nayland Smith turned in his promenade of the floor, and stared into my eyes.

"I mean that Dr. Fu-Manchu has had a hiding-place under the Gables for an indefinite period!" he replied. "I always suspected that a man of his genius would have a second retreat prepared for him, anticipating the event of the first being discovered. Oh! I don't doubt it! The place probably is extensive, and I am almost certain—though the point has to be confirmed—that there is another entrance from the studio further along the road. We know, now, why our recent searchings in the East End have proved futile; why the house in Museum Street was deserted; he has been lying low in this burrow at Hampstead!"

"But the hand, Smith, the luminous hand..."

Nayland Smith laughed shortly.

"Your superstitious fears overcame you to such an extent, Petrie—and I don't wonder at it; the sight was a ghastly one—that probably you don't remember what occurred when you struck out at that same ghostly hand?"

"I seemed to hit something."

"That was why we ran. But I think our retreat had all the appearance of a rout, as I intended that it should. Pardon my playing upon your very natural fears, old man, but you could not have simulated panic half so naturally! And if they had suspected that the device was discovered, we might never have quitted the Gables alive. It was touch-and-go for a moment."

"But..."

"Turn out the light!" snapped my companion.

Wondering greatly, I did as he desired. I turned out the light... and in the darkness of my own study I saw a fiery fist being shaken at me threateningly!... The bones were distinctly visible, and the luminosity of the flesh was truly ghastly.

"Turn on the light, again!" cried Smith.

Deeply mystified, I did so... and my friend tossed a little electric pocket-lamp on to the writing-table.

"They used merely a small electric lamp fitted into the handle of a glass dagger," he said with a sort of contempt. "It was very effective, but the luminous hand is a phenomenon producible by any one who possesses an electric torch."

"The Gables—will be watched?"

"At last, Petrie, I think we have Fu-Manchu—in his own trap!"

CHAPTER XXVII.

THE NIGHT OF THE RAID

"Dash it all, Petrie!" cried Smith, "this is most annoying!"

The bell was ringing furiously, although midnight was long past. Whom could my late visitor be? Almost certainly this ringing portended an urgent case. In other words, I was not fated to take part in what I anticipated would prove to be the closing scene of the Fu-Manchu drama.

"Every one is in bed," I said, ruefully; "and how can I possibly see a patient—in this costume?"

Smith and I were both arrayed in rough tweeds, and anticipating the labors before us, had dispensed with collars and wore soft mufflers. It was hard to be called upon to face a professional interview dressed thus, and having a big tweed cap pulled down over my eyes.

Across the writing-table we confronted one another in dismayed silence, whilst, below, the bell sent up its ceaseless clangor.

"It has to be done, Smith," I said, regretfully. "Almost certainly it means a journey and probably an absence of some hours."

I threw my cap upon the table, turned up my coat to hide the absence of collar, and started for the door. My last sight of Smith showed him standing looking after me, tugging at the lobe of his ear and clicking his teeth together with suppressed irritability. I stumbled down the dark stairs, along the hall, and opened the front door. Vaguely visible in the light of a street lamp which stood at no great distance away, I saw a slender man of medium height confronting me. From the shadowed face two large and luminous eyes looked out into mine. My visitor, who, despite the warmth of the evening, wore a heavy greatcoat, was an Oriental!

I drew back, apprehensively; then:

"Ah! Dr. Petrie!" he said in a softly musical voice which made me start again, "to God be all praise that I have found you!"

Some emotion, which at present I could not define, was stirring within me. Where had I seen this graceful Eastern youth before? Where had I heard that soft voice?

"Do you wish to see me professionally?" I asked—yet even as I put the question, I seemed to know it unnecessary.

"So you know me no more?" said the stranger—and his teeth gleamed in a slight smile.

Heavens! I knew now what had struck that vibrant chord within me! The voice, though infinitely deeper, yet had an unmistakable resemblance to the dulcet tones of Karamaneh—of Karamaneh whose eyes haunted my dreams, whose beauty had done much to embitter my years.

The Oriental youth stepped forward, with outstretched hand.

"So you know me no more?" he repeated; "but I know you, and give praise to Allah that I have found you!"

I stepped back, pressed the electric switch, and turned, with leaping heart, to look into the face of my visitor. It was a face of the purest Greek beauty, a face that might have served as a model for Praxiteles; the skin had a golden pallor, which, with the crisp black hair and magnetic yet velvety eyes, suggested to my fancy that this was the young Antinious risen from the Nile, whose wraith now appeared to me out of the night. I stifled a cry of surprise, not unmingled with gladness.

It was Aziz—the brother of Karamaneh!

Never could the entrance of a figure upon the stage of a drama have been more dramatic than the coming of Aziz upon this night of all nights. I seized the outstretched hand and drew him forward, then reclosed the door and stood before him a moment in doubt.

A vaguely troubled look momentarily crossed the handsome face; with the Oriental's unerring instinct, he had detected the reserve of my greeting. Yet, when I thought of the treachery of Karamaneh, when I remember how she, whom we had befriended, whom we had rescued from the house of Fu-Manchu, now had turned like the beautiful viper that she was to strike at the hand that caressed her; when I thought how to-night we were set upon raiding the place where the evil Chinese doctor lurked in hiding, were set upon the arrest of that malignant genius and of all his creatures, Karamaneh amongst them, is it strange that I hesitated? Yet, again, when I thought of my last meeting with her, and of how, twice, she had risked her life to save me...

So, avoiding the gaze of the lad, I took his arm, and in silence we two ascended the stairs and entered my study... where Nayland Smith stood bolt upright beside the table, his steely eyes fixed upon the face of the new arrival.

No look of recognition crossed the bronzed features, and Aziz who had started forward with outstretched hands, fell back a step and looked pathetically from me to Nayland Smith, and from the grim commissioner back again to me. The appeal in the velvet eyes was more than I could tolerate, unmoved.

"Smith," I said shortly, "you remember Aziz?"

Not a muscle visibly moved in Smith's face, as he snapped back:

"I remember him perfectly."

"He has come, I think, to seek our assistance."

"Yes, yes!" cried Aziz laying his hand upon my arm with a gesture painfully reminiscent of Karamaneh—"I came only to-night to London. Oh, my gentlemen! I have searched, and searched, and searched, until I am weary. Often I have wished to die. And then at last I come to Rangoon..."

"To Rangoon!" snapped Smith, still with the gray eyes fixed almost fiercely upon the lad's face.

"To Rangoon—yes; and there I heard news at last. I hear that you have seen her—have seen Karamaneh—that you are back in London." He was not entirely at home with his English. "I know then that she must be here, too. I ask them everywhere, and they answer 'yes.' Oh,

Smith Pasha!"—he stepped forward and impulsively seized both Smith's hands—"You know where she is—take me to her!"

Smith's face was a study in perplexity, now. In the past we had befriended the young Aziz, and it was hard to look upon him in the light of an enemy. Yet had we not equally befriended his sister?—and she...

At last Smith glanced across at me where I stood just within the doorway.

"What do you make of it, Petrie?" he said harshly. "Personally I take it to mean that our plans have leaked out." He sprang suddenly back from Aziz and I saw his glance traveling rapidly over the slight figure as if in quest of concealed arms. "I take it to be a trap!"

A moment he stood so, regarding him, and despite my well-grounded distrust of the Oriental character, I could have sworn that the expression of pained surprise upon the youth's face was not simulated but real. Even Smith, I think, began to share my view; for suddenly he threw himself into the white cane rest-chair, and, still fixedly regarding Aziz:

"Perhaps I have wronged you," he said. "If I have, you shall know the reason presently. Tell your own story!"

There was a pathetic humidity in the velvet eyes of Aziz—eyes so like those others that were ever looking into mine in dreams—as glancing from Smith to me he began, hands outstretched, characteristically, palms upward and fingers curling, to tell in broken English the story of his search for Karamaneh...

"It was Fu-Manchu, my kind gentlemen—it was the hakim who is really not a man at all, but an efreet. He found us again less than four days after you had left us, Smith Pasha!... He found us in Cairo, and to Karamaneh he made the forgetting of all things—even of me—even of me..."

Nayland Smith snapped his teeth together sharply; then:

"What do you mean by that?" he demanded.

For my own part I understood well enough, remembering how the brilliant Chinese doctor once had performed such an operation as this upon poor Inspector Weymouth; how, by means of an injection of some serum prepared (as Karamaneh afterwards told us) from the venom of a swamp adder or similar reptile, he had induced amnesia, or complete loss of memory. I felt every drop of blood recede from my cheeks.

"Smith!" I began...

"Let him speak for himself," interrupted my friend sharply.

"They tried to take us both," continued Aziz still speaking in that soft, melodious manner, but with deep seriousness. "I escaped, I, who am swift of foot, hoping to bring help."—He shook his head sadly—"But, except the All Powerful, who is so powerful as the Hakim Fu-Manchu? I hid, my gentlemen, and watched and waited, one—two—three weeks. At last I saw her again, my sister, Karamaneh; but ah! she did not know me, did not know me, Aziz her brother! She was in an arabeeyeh, and passed me quickly along the Sharia en-Nahhasin. I ran, and ran, and ran, crying her name, but although she looked back, she did not know me—she did not know me! I felt that I was dying, and presently I fell—upon the steps of the Mosque of Abu."

He dropped the expressive hands wearily to his sides and sank his chin upon his breast.

"And then?" I said, huskily—for my heart was fluttering like a captive bird.

"Alas! from that day to this I see her no more, my gentlemen. I travel, not only in Egypt, but near and far, and still I see her no more until in Rangoon I hear that which brings me to England again"—he extended his palms naively—"and here I am—Smith Pasha."

Smith sprang upright again and turned to me.

"Either I am growing over-credulous," he said, "or Aziz speaks the truth. But"—he held up his hand—"you can tell me all that at some other time, Petrie! We must take no chances. Sergeant Carter is downstairs with the cab; you might ask him to step up. He and Aziz can remain here until our return."

◆

CHAPTER XXVIII.

THE SAMURAI'S SWORD

The muffled drumming of sleepless London seemed very remote from us, as side by side we crept up the narrow path to the studio. This was a starry but moonless night, and the little dingy white building with a solitary tree peeping, in silhouette, above the glazed roof, bore an odd resemblance to one of those tombs which form a city of the dead so near to the city of feverish life on the slopes of the Mokattam Hills. This line of reflection proved unpleasant, and I dismissed it sternly from my mind.

The shriek of a train-whistle reached me, a sound which breaks the stillness of the most silent London night, telling of the ceaseless, febrile life of the great world-capital whose activity ceases not with the coming of darkness. Around and about us a very great stillness reigned, however, and the velvet dusk which, with the star-jeweled sky, was strongly suggestive of an Eastern night—gave up no sign to show that it masked the presence of more than twenty men. Some distance away on our right was the Gables, that sinister and deserted mansion which we assumed, and with good reason, to be nothing less than the gateway to the subterranean abode of Dr. Fu-Manchu; before us was the studio, which, if Nayland Smith's deductions were accurate, concealed a second entrance to the same mysterious dwelling.

As my friend, glancing cautiously all about him, inserted the key in the lock, an owl hooted dismally almost immediately above our heads. I caught my breath sharply, for it might be a signal; but, looking upward, I saw a great black shape float slantingly from the tree beyond the studio into the coppice on the right which hemmed in the Gables. Silently the owl winged its uncanny flight into the greater darkness of the trees, and was gone. Smith opened the door and we stepped into the studio. Our plans had been well considered, and in accordance with these, I now moved up beside my friend, who was dimly perceptible to me in the starlight which found access through the glass roof, and pressed the catch of my electric pocket-lamp...

I suppose that by virtue of my self-imposed duty as chronicler of the deeds of Dr. Fu-Manchu—the greatest and most evil genius whom the later centuries have produced, the man who dreamt of an universal Yellow Empire—I should have acquired a certain facility in describing bizarre happenings. But I confess that it fails me now as I attempt in cold English to portray my emotions when the white beam from the little lamp cut through the darkness of the studio, and shone fully upon the beautiful face of Karamaneh!

Less than six feet away from me she stood, arrayed in the gauzy dress of the harem, her fingers and slim white arms laden with barbaric jewelry! The light wavered in my suddenly nerveless hand, gleaming momentarily upon bare ankles and golden anklets, upon little red leather shoes.

I spoke no word, and Smith was as silent as I; both of us, I think, were speechless rather from amazement than in obedience to the evident wishes of Fu-Manchu's slave-girl. Yet I have only to close my eyes at this moment to see her as she stood, one finger raised to her lips, enjoining us to silence. She looked ghastly pale in the light of the lamp, but so lovely that my rebellious heart threatened already, to make a fool of me.

So we stood in that untidy studio, with canvases and easels heaped against the wall and with all sorts of litter about us, a trio strangely met, and one to have amused the high gods watching through the windows of the stars.

"Go back!" came in a whisper from Karamaneh.

I saw the red lips moving and read a dreadful horror in the widely opened eyes, in those eyes like pools of mystery to taunt the thirsty soul. The world of realities was slipping past me; I seemed to be losing my hold on things actual; I had built up an Eastern palace about myself and Karamaneh wherein, the world shut out, I might pass the hours in reading the mystery of those dark eyes. Nayland Smith brought me sharply to my senses.

"Steady with the light, Petrie!" he hissed in my ear. "My skepticism has been shaken, to-night, but I am taking no chances."

He moved from my side and forward toward that lovely, unreal figure which stood immediately before the model's throne and its background of plush curtains. Karamaneh started forward to meet him, suppressing a little cry, whose real anguish could not have been simulated.

"Go back! go back!" she whispered urgently, and thrust out her hands against Smith's breast. "For God's sake, go back! I have risked my life to come here to-night. He knows, and is ready!"...

The words were spoken with passionate intensity, and Nayland Smith hesitated. To my nostrils was wafted that faint, delightful perfume which, since one night, two years ago, it had come to disturb my senses, had taunted me many times as the mirage taunts the parched Sahara traveler. I took a step forward.

"Don't move!" snapped Smith.

Karamaneh clutched frenziedly at the lapels of his coat.

"Listen to me!" she said, beseechingly and stamped one little foot upon the floor—"listen to me! You are a clever man, but you know nothing of a woman's heart—nothing—nothing—if seeing me, hearing me, knowing, as you do know, I risk, you can doubt that I speak the truth. And I tell you that it is death to go behind those curtains—that he..."

"That's what I wanted to know!" snapped Smith. His voice quivered with excitement.

Suddenly grasping Karamaneh by the waist, he lifted her and set her aside; then in three bounds he was on to the model's throne and had torn the Plush curtains bodily from their fastenings.

How it occurred I cannot hope to make dear, for here my recollections merge into a chaos. I know that Smith seemed to topple forward amid the purple billows of velvet, and his muffled cry came to me:

"Petrie! My God, Petrie!"...

The pale face of Karamaneh looked up into mine and her hands were clutching me, but the glamour of her personality had lost its hold, for I knew—heavens, how poignantly it struck home to me!—that Nayland Smith was gone to his death. What I hoped to achieve, I know not, but hurling the trembling girl aside, I snatched the Browning pistol from my coat pocket, and with the ray of the lamp directed upon the purple mound of velvet, I leaped forward.

I think I realized that the curtains had masked a collapsible trap, a sheer pit of blackness, an instant before I was precipitated into it, but certainly the knowledge came too late. With the sound of a soft, shuddering cry in my ears, I fell, dropping lamp and pistol, and clutching at the fallen hangings. But they offered me no support. My head seemed to be bursting; I could utter only a hoarse groan, as I fell—fell—fell...

When my mind began to work again, in returning consciousness, I found it to be laden with reproach. How often in the past had we blindly hurled ourselves into just such a trap as this? Should we never learn that where Fu-Manchu was, impetuosity must prove fatal? On two distinct occasions in the past we had been made the victims of this device, yet even although we had had practically conclusive evidence that this studio was used by Dr. Fu-Manchu, we had relied upon its floor being as secure as that of any other studio, we had failed to sound every foot of it ere trusting our weight to its support....

"There is such a divine simplicity in the English mind that one may lay one's plans with mathematical precision, and rely upon the Nayland Smiths and Dr. Petries to play their allotted parts. Excepting two faithful followers, my friends are long since departed. But here, in these vaults which time has overlooked and which are as secret and as serviceable to-day as they were two hundred years ago, I wait patiently, with my trap set, like the spider for the fly!..."

To the sound of that taunting voice, I opened my eyes. As I did so I strove to spring upright—only to realize that I was tied fast to a heavy ebony chair inlaid with ivory, and attached by means of two iron brackets to the floor.

"Even children learn from experience," continued the unforgettable voice, alternately guttural and sibilant, but always as deliberate as though the speaker were choosing with care words which should perfectly clothe his thoughts. "For 'a burnt child fears the fire,' says your English adage. But Mr. Commissioner Nayland Smith, who enjoys the confidence of the India Office, and who is empowered to control the movements of the Criminal Investigation Department, learns nothing from experience. He is less than a child, since he has twice rashly precipitated himself into a chamber charged with an anesthetic prepared, by a process of my own, from the lycoperdon or Common Puff-ball."

I became fully master of my senses, and I became fully alive to a stupendous fact. At last it was ended; we were utterly in the power of Dr. Fu-Manchu; our race was run.

I sat in a low vaulted room. The roof was of ancient brickwork, but the walls were draped with exquisite Chinese fabric having a green ground whereon was a design representing a grotesque procession of white peacocks. A green carpet covered the floor, and the whole of the furniture was of the same material as the chair to which I was strapped, viz:—ebony inlaid with ivory. This furniture was scanty. There was a heavy table in one corner of the dungeonesque place, on which were a number of books and papers. Before this table was a high-backed, heavily carven chair. A smaller table stood upon the right of the only visible opening, a low door partially draped with bead work curtains, above which hung a silver lamp. On this smaller table, a stick of incense, in a silver holder, sent up a pencil of vapor into the air, and the chamber was loaded with the sickly sweet fumes. A faint haze from the incense-stick hovered up under the roof.

In the high-backed chair sat Dr. Fu-Manchu, wearing a green robe upon which was embroidered a design, the subject of which at first glance was not perceptible, but which presently I made out to be a huge white peacock. He wore a little cap perched upon the dome of his amazing skull, and with one clawish hand resting upon the ebony of the table, he sat slightly turned toward me, his emotionless face a mask of incredible evil. In spite of, or because of, the high intellect written upon it, the face of Dr. Fu-Manchu was more utterly repellent than any I have ever known, and the green eyes, eyes green as those of a cat in the darkness, which sometimes burned like witch lamps, and sometimes were horribly filmed like nothing human or imaginable, might have mirrored not a soul, but an emanation of hell, incarnate in this gaunt, high-shouldered body.

Stretched flat upon the floor lay Nayland Smith, partially stripped, his arms thrown back over his head and his wrists chained to a stout iron staple attached to the wall; he was fully conscious and staring intently at the Chinese doctor. His bare ankles also were manacled, and fixed to a second chain, which quivered tautly across the green carpet and passed out through the doorway, being attached to something beyond the curtain, and invisible to me from where I sat.

Fu-Manchu was now silent. I could hear Smith's heavy breathing and hear my watch ticking in my pocket. I suddenly realized that although my body was lashed to the ebony chair, my hands and arms were free. Next, looking dazedly about me, my attention was drawn to a heavy sword which stood hilt upward against the wall within reach of my hand. It was a magnificent piece, of Japanese workmanship; a long, curved Damascened blade having a double-handed hilt of steel, inlaid with gold, and resembling fine Kuft work. A host of possibilities swept through my mind. Then I perceived that the sword was attached to the wall by a thin steel chain some five feet in length.

"Even if you had the dexterity of a Mexican knife-thrower," came the guttural voice of Fu-Manchu, "you would be unable to reach me, dear Dr. Petrie."

The Chinaman had read my thoughts.

Smith turned his eyes upon me momentarily, only to look away again in the direction of Fu-Manchu. My friend's face was slightly pale beneath the tan, and his jaw muscles stood out with unusual prominence. By this fact alone did he reveal his knowledge that he lay at the mercy of this enemy of the white race, of this inhuman being who himself knew no mercy, of this man whose very genius was inspired by the cool, calculated cruelty of his race, of that race which to this day disposes of hundreds, nay! thousands, of its unwanted girl-children by the simple measure of throwing them down a well specially dedicated to the purpose.

"The weapon near your hand," continued the Chinaman, imperturbably, "is a product of the civilization of our near neighbors, the Japanese, a race to whose courage I prostrate myself in meekness. It is the sword of a samurai, Dr. Petrie. It is of very great age, and was, until an unfortunate misunderstanding with myself led to the extinction of the family, a treasured possession of a noble Japanese house..."

The soft voice, into which an occasional sibilance crept, but which never rose above a cool monotone, gradually was lashing me into fury, and I could see the muscles moving in Smith's jaws as he convulsively clenched his teeth; whereby I knew that, impotent, he burned with a rage at least as great as mine. But I did not speak, and did not move.

"The ancient tradition of seppuku," continued the Chinaman, "or hara-kiri, still rules, as you know, in the great families of Japan. There is a sacred ritual, and the samurai who dedicates himself to this honorable end, must follow strictly the ritual. As a physician, the exact nature of the ceremony might possibly interest you, Dr. Petrie, but a technical account of the two incisions which the sacrificant employs in his self-dismissal, might, on the other hand, bore Mr. Nayland Smith. Therefore I will merely enlighten you upon one little point, a minor one, but interesting to the student of human nature. In short, even a samurai—and no braver race has ever honored the world—sometimes hesitates to complete the operation. The weapon near to your hand, my dear Dr. Petrie, is known as the Friend's Sword. On such occasions as we are discussing, a trusty friend is given the post—an honored one of standing behind the brave man who offers himself to his gods, and should the latter's courage momentarily fail him, the friend with the trusty blade (to which now I especially direct your attention) diverts the hierophant's mind from his digression, and rectifies his temporary breach of etiquette by severing the cervical vertebrae of the spinal column with the friendly blade—which you can reach quite easily, Dr. Petrie, if you care to extend your hand."

Some dim perceptions of the truth was beginning to creep into my mind. When I say a perception of the truth, I mean rather of some part of the purpose of Dr. Fu-Manchu; of the whole horrible truth, of the scheme which had been conceived by that mighty, evil man, I had no glimmering, but I foresaw that a frightful ordeal was before us both.

"That I hold you in high esteem," continued Fu-Manchu, "is a fact which must be apparent to you by this time, but in regard to your companion, I entertain very different sentiments...."

Always underlying the deliberate calm of the speaker, sometimes showing itself in an unusually deep guttural, sometimes in an unusually serpentine sibilance, lurked the frenzy of hatred which in the past had revealed itself occasionally in wild outbursts. Momentarily I expected such an outburst now, but it did not come.

"One quality possessed by Mr. Nayland Smith," resumed the Chinaman, "I admire; I refer to his courage. I would wish that so courageous a man should seek his own end, should voluntarily efface himself from the path of that world-movement which he is powerless to check. In short, I would have him show himself a samurai. Always his friend, you shall remain so to the end, Dr. Petrie. I have arranged for this."

He struck lightly a little silver gong, dependent from the corner of the table, whereupon, from the curtained doorway, there entered a short, thickly built Burman whom I recognized for a dacoit. He wore a shoddy blue suit, which had been made for a much larger man; but these things claimed little of my attention, which automatically was directed to the load beneath which the Burman labored.

Upon his back he carried a sort of wire box rather less than six feet long, some two feet high, and about two feet wide. In short, it was a stout framework covered with fine wire-netting on the top, sides and ends, but being open at the bottom. It seemed to be made in five sections or to contain four sliding partitions which could be raised or lowered at will. These were of wood, and in the bottom of each was cut a little arch. The arches in the four partitions varied in size, so that whereas the first was not more than five inches high, the fourth opened almost to the wire roof of the box or cage; and a fifth, which was but little higher than the first, was cut in the actual end of the contrivance.

So intent was I upon this device, the purpose of which I was wholly unable to divine, that I directed the whole of my attention upon it. Then, as the Burman paused in the doorway, resting a corner of the cage upon the brilliant carpet, I glanced toward Fu-Manchu. He was watching Nayland Smith, and revealing his irregular yellow teeth—the teeth of an opium smoker—in the awful mirthless smile which I knew.

"God!" whispered Smith—"the Six Gates!"

"The knowledge of my beautiful country serves you well," replied Fu-Manchu gently.

Instantly I looked to my friend... and every drop of blood seemed to recede from my heart, leaving it cold in my breast. If I did not know the purpose of the cage, obviously Smith knew it all too well. His pallor had grown more marked, and although his gray eyes stared defiantly at the Chinaman, I, who knew him, could read a deathly horror in their depths.

The dacoit, in obedience to a guttural order from Dr. Fu-Manchu, placed the cage upon the carpet, completely covering Smith's body, but leaving his neck and head exposed. The seared and pock-marked face set in a sort of placid leer, the dacoit adjusted the sliding partitions to Smith's recumbent form, and I saw the purpose of the graduated arches. They were intended to divide a human body in just such fashion, and, as I realized, were most cunningly shaped to that end. The whole of Smith's body lay now in the wire cage, each of the five compartments whereof was shut off from its neighbor.

The Burman stepped back and stood waiting in the doorway. Dr. Fu-Manchu, removing his gaze from the face of my friend, directed it now upon me.

"Mr. Commissioner Nayland Smith shall have the honor of acting as hierophant, admitting himself to the Mysteries," said Fu-Manchu softly, "and you, Dr. Petrie, shall be the Friend."

✦ ··· ◆ ··· ✦

CHAPTER XXIX.

THE SIX GATES

He glanced toward the Burman, who retired immediately, to reenter a moment later carrying a curious leather sack, in shape not unlike that of a sakka or Arab water-carrier. Opening a little trap in the top of the first compartment of the cage (that is, the compartment which covered Smith's bare feet and ankles) he inserted the neck of the sack, then suddenly seized it by the bottom and shook it vigorously. Before my horrified gaze four huge rats came tumbling out from the bag into the cage! The dacoit snatched away the sack and snapped the shutter fast. A moving mist obscured my sight, a mist through which I saw the green eyes of Dr. Fu-Manchu fixed upon me, and through which, as from a great distance, his voice, sunk to a snake-like hiss, came to my ears.

"Cantonese rats, Dr. Petrie, the most ravenous in the world... they have eaten nothing for nearly a week!"

Then all became blurred as though a painter with a brush steeped in red had smudged out the details of the picture. For an indefinite period, which seemed like many minutes yet probably was only a few seconds, I saw nothing and heard nothing; my sensory nerves were dulled entirely. From this state I was awakened and brought back to the realities by a sound which ever afterward I was doomed to associate with that ghastly scene.

This was the squealing of the rats.

The red mist seemed to disperse at that, and with frightfully intense interest, I began to study the awful torture to which Nayland Smith was being subjected. The dacoit had disappeared, and Fu-Manchu placidly was watching the four lean and hideous animals in the cage. As I also turned my eyes in that direction, the rats overcame their temporary fear, and began...

"You have been good enough to notice," said the Chinaman, his voice still sunk in that sibilant whisper, "my partiality for dumb allies. You have met my scorpions, my death-adders, my baboon-man. The uses of such a playful little animal as a marmoset have never been fully appreciated before, I think, but to an indiscretion of this last-named pet of mine, I seem to remember that you owed something in the past, Dr. Petrie..."

Nayland Smith stifled a deep groan. One rapid glance I ventured at his face. It was a grayish hue, now, and dank with perspiration. His gaze met mine.

The rats had almost ceased squealing.

"Much depends upon yourself, Doctor," continued Fu-Manchu, slightly raising his voice. "I credit Mr. Commissioner Nayland Smith with courage high enough to sustain the raising of all the gates; but I estimate the strength of your friendship highly, also, and predict that you will use the sword of the samurai certainly not later than the time when I shall raise the third gate...."

A low shuddering sound, which I cannot hope to describe, but alas I can never forget, broke from the lips of the tortured man.

"In China," resumed Fu-Manchu, "we call this quaint fancy the Six Gates of Joyful Wisdom. The first gate, by which the rats are admitted, is called the Gate of Joyous Hope; the second, the Gate of Mirthful Doubt. The third gate is poetically named, the Gate of True Rapture, and the fourth, the Gate of Gentle Sorrow. I once was honored in the friendship of an exalted mandarin who sustained the course of Joyful Wisdom to the raising of the Fifth Gate (called the Gate of Sweet Desires) and the admission of the twentieth rat. I esteem him almost equally with my ancestors. The Sixth, or Gate Celestial—whereby a man enters into the joy of Complete Understanding—I have dispensed with, here, substituting a Japanese fancy of an antiquity nearly as great and honorable. The introduction of this element of speculation, I count a happy thought, and accordingly take pride to myself."

"The sword, Petrie!" whispered Smith. I should not have recognized his voice, but he spoke quite evenly and steadily. "I rely upon you, old man, to spare me the humiliation of asking mercy from that yellow fiend!"

My mind throughout this time had been gaining a sort of dreadful clarity. I had avoided looking at the sword of hara-kiri, but my thoughts had been leading me mercilessly up to the point at which we were now arrived. No vestige of anger, of condemnation of the inhuman being seated in the ebony chair, remained; that was past. Of all that had gone before, and of what was to come in the future, I thought nothing, knew nothing. Our long fight against the yellow group, our encounters with the numberless creatures of Fu-Manchu, the dacoits—even Karamaneh—were forgotten, blotted out. I saw nothing of the strange appointments of that subterranean chamber; but face to face with the supreme moment of a lifetime, I was alone with my poor friend—and God.

The rats began squealing again. They were fighting...

"Quick, Petrie! Quick, man! I am weakening...."

I turned and took up the samurai sword. My hands were very hot and dry, but perfectly steady, and I tested the edge of the heavy weapon upon my left thumb-nail as quietly as one might test a razor blade. It was as keen, this blade of ghastly history, as any razor ever wrought in Sheffield. I seized the graven hilt, bent forward in my chair, and raised the Friend's Sword high above my head. With the heavy weapon poised there, I looked into my friend's eyes. They were feverishly bright, but never in all my days, nor upon the many beds of suffering which it had been my lot to visit, had I seen an expression like that within them.

"The raising of the First Gate is always a crucial moment," came the guttural voice of the Chinaman. Although I did not see him, and barely heard his words, I was aware that he had stood up and was bending forward over the lower end of the cage.

"Now, Petrie! now! God bless you... and good-by..."

From somewhere—somewhere remote—I heard a hoarse and animal-like cry, followed by the sound of a heavy fall. I can scarcely bear to write of that moment, for I had actually begun the downward sweep of the great sword when that sound came—a faint Hope, speaking of aid where I had thought no aid possible.

How I contrived to divert the blade, I do not know to this day; but I do know that its mighty sweep sheared a lock from Smith's head and laid bare the scalp. With the hilt in my quivering hands I saw the blade bite deeply through the carpet and floor above Nayland Smith's skull. There, buried fully two inches in the woodwork, it stuck, and still clutching the hilt, I looked to the right and across the room—I looked to the curtained doorway.

Fu-Manchu, with one long, claw-like hand upon the top of the First Gate, was bending over the trap, but his brilliant green eyes were turned in the same direction as my own—upon the curtained doorway.

Upright within it, her beautiful face as pale as death, but her great eyes blazing with a sort of splendid madness, stood Karamaneh!

She looked, not at the tortured man, not at me, but fully at Dr. Fu-Manchu. One hand clutched the trembling draperies; now she suddenly raised the other, so that the jewels on her white arm glittered in the light of the lamp above the door. She held my Browning pistol! Fu-Manchu sprang upright, inhaling sibilantly, as Karamaneh pointed the pistol point blank at his high skull and fired....

I saw a little red streak appear, up by the neutral colored hair, under the black cap. I became as a detached intelligence, unlinked with the corporeal, looking down upon a thing which for some reason I had never thought to witness.

Fu-Manchu threw up both arms, so that the sleeves of the green robe fell back to the elbows. He clutched at his head, and the black cap fell behind him. He began to utter short, guttural cries; he swayed backward—to the right—to the left then lurched forward right across the cage. There he lay, writhing, for a moment, his baneful eyes turned up, revealing the whites; and the great gray rats, released, began leaping about the room. Two shot like gray streaks past the slim figure in the doorway, one darted behind the chair to which I was lashed, and the fourth ran all around against the wall... Fu-Manchu, prostrate across the overturned cage, lay still, his massive head sagging downward.

I experienced a mental repetition of my adventure in the earlier evening—I was dropping, dropping, dropping into some bottomless pit ... warm arms were about my neck; and burning kisses upon my lips.

•••◆•••

CHAPTER XXX.

THE CALL OF THE EAST

I seemed to haul myself back out of the pit of unconsciousness by the aid of two little hands which clasped my own. I uttered a sigh that was almost a sob, and opened my eyes.

I was sitting in the big red-leathern armchair in my own study... and a lovely but truly bizarre figure, in a harem dress, was kneeling on the carpet at my feet; so that my first sight of the world was the sweetest sight that the world had to offer me, the dark eyes of Karamaneh, with tears trembling like jewels upon her lashes!

I looked no further than that, heeded not if there were others in the room beside we two, but, gripping the jewel-laden fingers in what must have been a cruel clasp, I searched the depths of the glorious eyes in ever growing wonder. What change had taken place in those limpid, mysterious pools? Why was a wild madness growing up within me like a flame? Why was the old longing returned, ten-thousandfold, to snatch that pliant, exquisite shape to my breast?

No word was spoken, but the spoken words of a thousand ages could not have expressed one tithe of what was held in that silent communion. A hand was laid hesitatingly on my shoulder. I tore my gaze away from the lovely face so near to mine, and glanced up.

Aziz stood at the back of my chair.

"God is all merciful," he said. "My sister is restored to us" (I loved him for the plural); "and she remembers."

Those few words were enough; I understood now that this lovely girl, who half knelt, half lay, at my feet, was not the evil, perverted creature of Fu-Manchu whom we had gone out to arrest with the other vile servants of the Chinese doctor, but was the old, beloved companion of two years ago, the Karamaneh for whom I had sought long and wearily in Egypt, who had been swallowed up and lost to me in that land of mystery.

The loss of memory which Fu-Manchu had artificially induced was subject to the same inexplicable laws which ordinarily rule in cases of amnesia. The shock of her brave action that night had begun to effect a cure; the sight of Aziz had completed it.

Inspector Weymouth was standing by the writing-table. My mind cleared rapidly now, and standing up, but without releasing the girl's hands, so that I drew her up beside me, I said:

"Weymouth—where is—?"

"He's waiting to see you, Doctor," replied the inspector.

A pang, almost physical, struck at my heart.

"Poor, dear old Smith!" I cried, with a break in my voice.

Dr. Gray, a neighboring practitioner, appeared in the doorway at the moment that I spoke the words.

"It's all right, Petrie," he said, reassuringly; "I think we took it in time. I have thoroughly cauterized the wounds, and granted that no complication sets in, he'll be on his feet again in a week or two."

I suppose I was in a condition closely bordering upon the hysterical. At any rate, my behavior was extraordinary. I raised both my hands above my head.

"Thank God!" I cried at the top of my voice, "thank God!—thank God!"

"Thank Him, indeed," responded the musical voice of Aziz. He spoke with all the passionate devoutness of the true Moslem.

Everything, even Karamaneh was forgotten, and I started for the door as though my life depended upon my speed. With one foot upon the landing, I turned, looked back, and met the glance of Inspector Weymouth.

"What have you done with—the body?" I asked.

"We haven't been able to get to it. That end of the vault collapsed two minutes after we hauled you out!"

As I write, now, of those strange days, already they seem remote and unreal. But, where other and more dreadful memories already are grown misty, the memory of that evening in my rooms remains clear-cut and intimate. It marked a crisis in my life.

During the days that immediately followed, whilst Smith was slowly recovering from his hurts, I made my plans deliberately; I prepared to cut myself off from old associations—prepared to exile myself, gladly; how gladly I cannot hope to express in mere cold words.

That my friend approved of my projects, I cannot truthfully state, but his disapproval at least was not openly expressed. To Karamaneh I said nothing of my plans, but her complete reliance in my powers to protect her, now, from all harm, was at once pathetic and exquisite.

Since, always, I have sought in these chronicles to confine myself to the facts directly relating to the malignant activity of Dr. Fu-Manchu, I shall abstain from burdening you with details of my private affairs. As an instrument of the Chinese doctor, it has sometimes been my duty to write of the beautiful Eastern girl; I cannot suppose that my readers have any further curiosity respecting her from the moment that Fate freed her from that awful servitude. Therefore, when I shall have dealt with the episodes which marked our voyage to Egypt—I had opened negotiations in regard to a practice in Cairo—I may honorably lay down my pen.

These episodes opened, dramatically, upon the second night of the voyage from Marseilles.

CHAPTER XXXI.

"MY SHADOW LIES UPON YOU"

I suppose I did not awake very readily. Following the nervous vigilance of the past six months, my tired nerves, in the enjoyment of this relaxation, were rapidly recuperating. I no longer feared to awake to find a knife at my throat, no longer dreaded the darkness as a foe.

So that the voice may have been calling (indeed, had been calling) for some time, and of this I had been hazily conscious before finally I awoke. Then, ere the new sense of security came to reassure me, the old sense of impending harm set my heart leaping nervously. There is always a certain physical panic attendant upon such awakening in the still of night, especially in novel surroundings. Now, I sat up abruptly, clutching at the rail of my berth and listening.

There was a soft thudding on my cabin door, and a voice, low and urgent, was crying my name.

Through the open porthole the moonlight streamed into my room, and save for a remote and soothing throb, inseparable from the progress of a great steamship, nothing else disturbed the stillness; I might have floated lonely upon the bosom of the Mediterranean. But there was the drumming on the door again, and the urgent appeal:

"Dr. Petrie! Dr. Petrie!"

I threw off the bedclothes and stepped on to the floor of the cabin, fumbling hastily for my slippers. A fear that something was amiss, that some aftermath, some wraith of the dread Chinaman, was yet to come to disturb our premature peace, began to haunt me. I threw open the door.

Upon the gleaming deck, blackly outlined against a wondrous sky, stood a man who wore a blue greatcoat over his pyjamas, and whose unstockinged feet were thrust into red slippers. It was Platts, the Marconi operator.

"I'm awfully sorry to disturb you, Dr. Petrie," he said, "and I was even less anxious to arouse your neighbor; but somebody seems to be trying to get a message, presumably urgent, through to you."

"To me!" I cried.

"I cannot make it out," admitted Platts, running his fingers through disheveled hair, "but I thought it better to arouse you. Will you come up?"

I turned without a word, slipped into my dressing-gown, and with Platts passed aft along the deserted deck. The sea was as calm as a great lake. Ahead, on the port bow, an angry flambeau burned redly beneath the peaceful vault of the heavens. Platts nodded absently in the direction of the weird flames.

"Stromboli," he said; "we shall be nearly through the Straits by breakfast-time."

We mounted the narrow stair to the Marconi deck. At the table sat Platts' assistant with the Marconi attachment upon his head—an apparatus which always set me thinking of the electric chair.

"Have you got it?" demanded my companion as we entered the room.

"It's still coming through," replied the other without moving, "but in the same jerky fashion. Every time I get it, it seems to have gone back to the beginning—just Dr. Petrie—Dr. Petrie."

He began to listen again for the elusive message. I turned to Platts.

"Where is it being sent from?" I asked.

Platts shook his head.

"That's the mystery," he declared. "Look!"—and he pointed to the table; "according to the Marconi chart, there's a Messagerie boat due west between us and Marseilles, and the homeward-bound P. & O.

which we passed this morning must be getting on that way also, by now. The Isis is somewhere ahead, but I've spoken to all these, and the message comes from none of them."

"Then it may come from Messina."

"It doesn't come from Messina," replied the man at the table, beginning to write rapidly.

Platts stepped forward and bent over the message which the other was writing.

"Here it is!" he cried, excitedly; "we're getting it."

Stepping in turn to the table, I leaned over between the two and read these words as the operator wrote them down:

Dr. Petrie—my shadow...

I drew a quick breath and gripped Platts' shoulder harshly. His assistant began fingering the instrument with irritation.

"Lost it again!" he muttered.

"This message," I began...

But again the pencil was traveling over the paper:—lies upon you all... end of message.

The operator stood up and unclasped the receivers from his ears. There, high above the sleeping ship's company, with the carpet of the blue Mediterranean stretched indefinitely about us, we three stood looking at one another. By virtue of a miracle of modern science, some one, divided from me by mile upon mile of boundless ocean, had spoken—and had been heard.

"Is there no means of learning," I said, "from whence this message emanated?"

Platts shook his head, perplexedly.

"They gave no code word," he said. "God knows who they were. It's a strange business and a strange message. Have you any sort of idea, Dr. Petrie, respecting the identity of the sender?"

I stared him hard in the face; an idea had mechanically entered my mind, but one of which I did not choose to speak, since it was opposed to human possibility.

But, had I not seen with my own eyes the bloody streak across his forehead as the shot fired by Karamaneh entered his high skull, had I not known, so certainly as it is given to man to know, that the giant intellect was no more, the mighty will impotent, I should have replied:

"The message is from Dr. Fu-Manchu!"

My reflections were rudely terminated and my sinister thoughts given new stimulus, by a loud though muffled cry which reached me from somewhere in the ship, below. Both my companions started as violently as I, whereby I knew that the mystery of the wireless message had not been without its effect upon their minds also. But whereas they paused in doubt, I leaped from the room and almost threw myself down the ladder.

It was Karamaneh who had uttered that cry of fear and horror!

Although I could perceive no connection betwixt the strange message and the cry in the night, intuitively I linked them, intuitively I knew that my fears had been well-grounded; that the shadow of Fu-Manchu still lay upon us.

Karamaneh occupied a large stateroom aft on the main deck; so that I had to descend from the upper deck on which my own room was situated to the promenade deck, again to the main deck and thence proceed nearly the whole length of the alleyway.

Karamaneh and her brother, Aziz, who occupied a neighboring room, met me, near the library. Karamaneh's eyes were wide with fear; her peerless coloring had fled, and she was white to the lips. Aziz, who wore a dressing-gown thrown hastily over his night attire, had his arm protectively about the girl's shoulders.

"The mummy!" she whispered tremulously—"the mummy!"

There came a sound of opening doors, and several passengers, whom Karamaneh cries had alarmed, appeared in various stages of undress. A stewardess came running from the far end of the alleyway, and I found time to wonder at my own speed; for, starting from the distant Marconi deck, yet I had been the first to arrive upon the scene.

Stacey, the ship's doctor, was quartered at no great distance from the spot, and he now joined the group. Anticipating the question which trembled upon the lips of several of those about me:

"Come to Dr. Stacey's room," I said, taking Karamaneh arm; "we will give you something to enable you to sleep." I turned to the group. "My patient has had severe nerve trouble," I explained, "and has developed somnambulistic tendencies."

I declined the stewardess' offer of assistance, with a slight shake of the head, and shortly the four of us entered the doctor's cabin, on the deck above. Stacey carefully closed the door. He was an old fellow student of mine, and already he knew much of the history of the beautiful Eastern girl and her brother Aziz.

"I fear there's mischief afoot, Petrie," he said.

"Thanks to your presence of mind, the ship's gossips need know nothing of it."

I glanced at Karamaneh who, since the moment of my arrival had never once removed her gaze from me; she remained in that state of passive fear in which I had found her, the lovely face pallid; and she stared at me fixedly in a childish, expressionless way which made me fear that the shock to which she had been subjected, whatever its nature, had caused a relapse into that strange condition of forgetfulness from which a previous shock had aroused her. I could see that Stacey shared my view, for:

"Something has frightened you," he said gently, seating himself on the arm of Karamaneh's chair and patting her hand as if to reassure her. "Tell us all about it."

For the first time since our meeting that night, the girl turned her eyes from me and glanced up at Stacey, a sudden warm blush stealing over her face and throat and as quickly departing, to leave her even more pale than before. She grasped Stacey's hand in both her own—and looked again at me.

"Send for Mr. Nayland Smith without delay!" she said, and her sweet voice was slightly tremulous. "He must be put on his guard!"

I started up.

"Why?" I said. "For God's sake tell us what has happened!"

Aziz who evidently was as anxious as myself for information, and who now knelt at his sister's feet looking at her with that strange love, which was almost adoration, in his eyes, glanced back at me and nodded his head rapidly.

"Something"—Karamaneh paused, shuddering violently—"some dreadful thing, like a mummy escaped from its tomb, came into my room to-night through the porthole..."

"Through the porthole?" echoed Stacey, amazedly.

"Yes, yes, through the porthole! A creature tall and very, very thin. He wore wrappings—yellow wrappings—swathed about his head, so that only his eyes, his evil gleaming eyes, were visible.... From waist to knees he was covered, also, but his body, his feet, and his legs were bare..."

"Was he—?" I began...

"He was a brown man, yes,"—Karamaneh divining my question, nodded, and the shimmering cloud of her wonderful hair, hastily confined, burst free and rippled about her shoulders. "A gaunt, fleshless brown man, who bent, and writhed bony fingers—so!"

"A thug!" I cried.

"He—it—the mummy thing—would have strangled me if I had slept, for he crouched over the berth—seeking—seeking..."

I clenched my teeth convulsively.

"But I was sitting up—"

"With the light on?" interrupted Stacey in surprise.

"No," added Karamaneh; "the light was out." She turned her eyes toward me, as the wonderful blush overspread her face once more. "I was sitting thinking. It all happened within a few seconds, and quite silently. As the mummy crouched over the berth, I unlocked the door and leaped out into the passage. I think I screamed; I did not mean to. Oh, Dr. Stacey, there is not a moment to spare! Mr. Nayland Smith must be warned immediately. Some horrible servant of Dr. Fu-Manchu is on the ship!"

◆

CHAPTER XXXII.

THE TRAGEDY

Nayland Smith leaned against the edge of the dressing-table, attired in pyjamas. The little stateroom was hazy with smoke, and my friend gripped the charred briar between his teeth and watched the blue-gray clouds arising from the bowl, in an abstracted way. I knew that he was thinking hard, and from the fact that he had exhibited no surprise when I had related to him the particular's of the attack upon Karamaneh I judged that he had half anticipated something of the kind. Suddenly he stood up, staring at me fixedly.

"Your tact has saved the situation, Petrie," he snapped. "It failed you momentarily, though, when you proposed to me just now that we should muster the lascars for inspection. Our game is to pretend that we know nothing—that we believe Karamaneh to have had a bad dream."

"But, Smith," I began—

"It would be useless, Petrie," he interrupted me. "You cannot suppose that I overlooked the possibility of some creature of the doctor's being among the lascars. I can assure you that not one of them answers to the description of the midnight assailant. From the girl's account we have to look (discarding the idea of a revivified mummy) for a man of unusual height—and there's no lascar of unusual height on board; and from the visible evidence, that he entered the stateroom through the porthole, we have to look for a man more than normally thin. In a word, the servant of Dr. Fu-Manchu who attempted the life of Karamaneh is either in hiding on the ship, or, if visible, is disguised."

With his usual clarity of vision, Nayland Smith had visualized the facts of the case; I passed in mental survey each one of the passengers, and those of the crew whose appearances were familiar to me, with the result that I had to admit the justice of my friend's conclusions. Smith began to pace the narrow strip of carpet between the dressing-table and the door. Suddenly he began again. "From our knowledge of Fu-Manchu and of the group surrounding him (and, don't forget, surviving him)—we may further assume that the wireless message was no gratuitous piece of melodrama, but that it was directed to a definite end. Let us endeavor to link up the chain a little. You occupy an upper deck berth; so do I. Experience of the Chinaman has formed a habit in both of us; that of sleeping with closed windows. Your port was fastened and so was my own. Karamaneh is quartered on the main deck, and her brother's stateroom opens into the same alleyway. Since the ship is in the Straits of Messina, and the glass set fair, the stewards have not closed the portholes nightly at present. We know that that of Karamaneh's stateroom was open. Therefore, in any attempt upon our quartet, Karamaneh would automatically be selected for the victim, since failing you or myself she may be regarded as being the most obnoxious to Dr. Fu-Manchu."

I nodded comprehendingly. Smith's capacity for throwing the white light of reason into the darkest places often amazed me.

"You may have noticed," he continued, "that Karamaneh's room is directly below your own. In the event of any outcry, you would be sooner upon the scene than I should, for instance, because I sleep on the opposite side of the ship. This circumstance I take to be the explanation of the wireless message, which, because of its hesitancy (a piece of ingenuity very characteristic of the group), led to your being awakened and invited up to the Marconi deck; in short, it gave the would-be assassin a better chance of escaping before your arrival."

I watched my friend in growing wonder. The strange events, seemingly having no link, took their places in the drama, and became well-ordered episodes in a plot that only a criminal genius could have devised. As I studied the keen, bronzed face, I realized to the full the stupendous mental power of Dr. Fu-Manchu, measuring it by the criterion of Nayland Smith's. For the cunning Chinaman, in a sense, had foiled this brilliant man before me, whereby, if by nought else, I might know him a master of his evil art.

"I regard the episode," continued Smith, "as a posthumous attempt of the doctor's; a legacy of hate which may prove more disastrous than any attempt made upon us by Fu-Manchu in life. Some fiendish member of the murder group is on board the ship. We must, as always, meet guile with guile. There must be no appeal to the captain, no public examination of passengers and crew. One attempt has failed; I do not doubt that others will be made. At present, you will enact the role of physician-in-attendance upon Karamaneh, and will put it about for whom it may interest that a slight return of her nervous trouble is causing her to pass uneasy nights. I can safely leave this part of the case to you, I think?"

I nodded rapidly.

"I haven't troubled to make inquiries," added Smith, "but I think it probable that the regulation respecting closed ports will come into operation immediately we have passed the Straits, or at any rate immediately there is any likelihood of bad weather."

"You mean—"

"I mean that no alteration should be made in our habits. A second attempt along similar lines is to be apprehended—to-night. After that we may begin to look out for a new danger."

"I pray we may avoid it," I said fervently.

As I entered the saloon for breakfast in the morning, I was subjected to solicitous inquiries from Mrs. Prior, the gossip of the ship. Her room adjoined Karamaneh's and she had been one of the passengers aroused by the girl's cries in the night. Strictly adhering to my role, I explained that my patient was threatened with a second nervous breakdown, and was subject to vivid and disturbing dreams. One or two other inquiries I met in the same way, ere escaping to the corner table reserved to us.

That iron-bound code of conduct which rules the Anglo-Indian, in the first days of the voyage had threatened to ostracize Karamaneh and Aziz, by reason of the Eastern blood to which their brilliant but peculiar type of beauty bore witness. Smith's attitude, however—and, in a Burmese commissioner, it constituted something of a law—had done much to break down the barriers; the extraordinary beauty of the girl had done the rest. So that now, far from finding themselves shunned, the society of Karamaneh and her romantic-looking brother was universally courted. The last inquiry that morning, respecting my interesting patient, came from the bishop of Damascus, a benevolent old gentleman whose ancestry was not wholly innocent of Oriental strains, and who sat at a table immediately behind me. As I settled down to my porridge, he turned his chair slightly and bent to my ear.

"Mrs. Prior tells me that your charming friend was disturbed last night," he whispered. "She seems rather pale this morning; I sincerely trust that she is suffering no ill-effect."

I swung around, with a smile. Owing to my carelessness, there was a slight collision, and the poor bishop, who had been invalided to England after typhoid, in order to undergo special treatment, suppressed an exclamation of pain, although his fine dark eyes gleamed kindly upon me through the pebbles of his gold-rimmed pince-nez.

Indeed, despite his Eastern blood, he might have posed for a Sadler picture, his small and refined features seeming out of place above the bulky body.

"Can you forgive my clumsiness," I began—

But the bishop raised his small, slim fingered hand of old ivory hue, deprecatingly.

His system was supercharged with typhoid bacilli, and, as sometimes occurs, the superfluous "bugs" had sought exit. He could only walk with the aid of two stout sticks, and bent very much at that. His left leg had been surgically scraped to the bone, and I appreciated the exquisite torture to which my awkwardness had subjected him. But he would entertain no apologies, pressing his inquiry respecting Karamaneh in the kindly manner which had made him so deservedly popular on board.

"Many thanks for your solicitude," I said; "I have promised her sound repose to-night, and since my professional reputation is at stake, I shall see that she secures it."

In short, we were in pleasant company, and the day passed happily enough and without notable event. Smith spent some considerable time with the chief officer, wandering about unfrequented parts of the ship. I learned later that he had explored the lascars' quarters, the forecastle, the engine-room, and had even descended to the stokehold; but this was done so unostentatiously that it occasioned no comment.

With the approach of evening, in place of that physical contentment which usually heralds the dinner-hour, at sea, I experienced a fit of the seemingly causeless apprehension which too often in the past had harbingered the coming of grim events; which I had learnt to associate with the nearing presence of one of Fu-Manchu's death-agents. In view of the facts, as I afterwards knew them to be, I cannot account for this.

Yet, in an unexpected manner, my forebodings were realized. That night I was destined to meet a sorrow surpassing any which my troubled life had known. Even now I experience great difficulty in relating the matters which befell, in speaking of the sense of irrevocable loss which came to me. Briefly, then, at about ten minutes before the dining hour, whilst all the passengers, myself included, were below, dressing, a faint cry arose from somewhere aft on the upper deck—a cry which was swiftly taken up by other voices, so that presently a deck steward echoed it immediately outside my own stateroom:

"Man overboard! Man overboard!"

All my premonitions rallying in that one sickening moment, I sprang out on the deck, half dressed as I was, and leaping past the boat which swung nearly opposite my door, craned over the rail, looking astern.

For a long time I could detect nothing unusual. The engine-room telegraph was ringing—and the motion of the screws momentarily ceased; then, in response to further ringing, recommenced, but so as to jar the whole structure of the vessel; whereby I knew that the engines were reversed. Peering intently into the wake of the ship, I was but dimly aware of the ever growing turmoil around me, of the swift mustering of a boat's crew, of the shouted orders of the third-officer. Suddenly I saw it—the sight which was to haunt me for succeeding days and nights.

Half in the streak of the wake and half out of it, I perceived the sleeve of a white jacket, and, near to it, a soft felt hat. The sleeve rose up once into clear view, seemed to describe a half-circle in the air then sink back again into the glassy swell of the water. Only the hat remained floating upon the surface.

By the evidence of the white sleeve alone I might have remained unconvinced, although upon the voyage I had become familiar enough with the drill shooting-jacket, but the presence of the gray felt hat was almost conclusive.

The man overboard was Nayland Smith!

I cannot hope, writing now, to convey in any words at my command, a sense, even remote, of the utter loneliness which in that dreadful moment closed coldly down upon me.

To spring overboard to the rescue was a natural impulse, but to have obeyed it would have been worse than quixotic. In the first place, the drowning man was close upon half a mile astern; in the second place, others had seen the hat and the white coat as clearly as I; among them the third-officer, standing upright in the stern of the boat—which, with commendable promptitude had already been swung into the water. The steamer was being put about, describing a wide arc around the little boat dancing on the deep blue rollers....

Of the next hour, I cannot bear to write at all. Long as I had known him, I was ignorant of my friend's powers as a swimmer, but I judged that he must have been a poor one from the fact that he had sunk so rapidly in a calm sea. Except the hat, no trace of Nayland Smith remained when the boat got to the spot.

CHAPTER XXXIII.

THE MUMMY

Dinner was out of the question that night for all of us. Karamaneh who had spoken no word, but, grasping my hands, had looked into my eyes—her own glassy with unshed tears—and then stolen away to her cabin, had not since reappeared. Seated upon my berth, I stared unseeingly before me, upon a changed ship, a changed sea and sky upon another world. The poor old bishop, my neighbor, had glanced in several times, as he hobbled by, and his spectacles were unmistakably humid; but even he had vouchsafed no word, realizing that my sorrow was too deep for such consolation.

When at last I became capable of connected thought, I found myself faced by a big problem. Should I place the facts of the matter, as I knew them to be, before the captain? or could I hope to apprehend Fu-Manchu's servant by the methods suggested by my poor friend? That Smith's death was an accident, I did not believe for a moment; it was impossible not to link it with the attempt upon Karamaneh. In my misery and doubt, I determined to take counsel with Dr. Stacey. I stood up, and passed out on to the deck.

Those passengers whom I met on my way to his room regarded me in respectful silence. By contrast, Stacey's attitude surprised and even annoyed me.

"I'd be prepared to stake all I possess—although it's not much," he said, "that this was not the work of your hidden enemy."

He blankly refused to give me his reasons for the statement and strongly advised me to watch and wait but to make no communication to the captain.

At this hour I can look back and savor again something of the profound dejection of that time. I could not face the passengers; I even avoided Karamaneh and Aziz. I shut myself in my cabin and sat staring aimlessly into the growing darkness. The steward knocked, once, inquiring if I needed anything, but I dismissed him abruptly. So I passed the evening and the greater part of the night.

Those groups of promenaders who passed my door, invariably were discussing my poor friend's tragic end; but as the night wore on, the deck grew empty, and I sat amid a silence that in my miserable state I welcomed more than the presence of any friend, saving only the one whom I should never welcome again.

Since I had not counted the bells, to this day I have only the vaguest idea respecting the time whereat the next incident occurred which it is my duty to chronicle. Perhaps I was on the verge of falling asleep, seated there as I was; at any rate, I could scarcely believe myself awake, when, unheralded by any footsteps to indicate his coming, some one who seemed to be crouching outside my stateroom, slightly raised himself and peered in through the porthole—which I had not troubled to close.

He must have been a fairly tall man to have looked in at all, and although his features were indistinguishable in the darkness, his outline, which was clearly perceptible against the white boat beyond, was unfamiliar to me. He seemed to have a small, and oddly swathed head, and what I could make out of the gaunt neck and square shoulders in some way suggested an unnatural thinness; in short, the smudgy silhouette in the porthole was weirdly like that of a mummy!

For some moments I stared at the apparition; then, rousing myself from the apathy into which I had sunk, I stood up very quickly and stepped across the room. As I did so the figure vanished, and when I threw open the door and looked out upon the deck... the deck was wholly untenanted!

I realized at once that it would be useless, even had I chosen the course, to seek confirmation of what I had seen from the officer on the bridge: my own berth, together with the one adjoining—that of the bishop—was not visible from the bridge.

For some time I stood in my doorway, wondering in a disinterested fashion which now I cannot explain, if the hidden enemy had revealed himself to me, or if disordered imagination had played me a trick. Later, I was destined to know the truth of the matter, but when at last I fell into a troubled sleep, that night, I was still in some doubt upon the point.

My state of mind when I awakened on the following day was indescribable; I found it difficult to doubt that Nayland Smith would meet me on the way to the bathroom as usual, with the cracked briar fuming between his teeth. I felt myself almost compelled to pass around to his stateroom in order to convince myself that he was not really there. The catastrophe was still unreal to me, and the world a dream-world. Indeed I retain scarcely any recollections of the traffic of that day, or of the days that followed it until we reached Port Said.

Two things only made any striking appeal to my dulled intelligence at that time. These were: the aloof attitude of Dr. Stacey, who seemed carefully to avoid me; and a curious circumstance which the second officer mentioned in conversation one evening as we strolled up and down the main deck together.

"Either I was fast asleep at my post, Dr. Petrie," he said, "or last night, in the middle watch, some one or something came over the side of the ship just aft the bridge, slipped across the deck, and disappeared."

I stared at him wonderingly.

"Do you mean something that came up out of the sea?" I said.

"Nothing could very well have come up out of the sea," he replied, smiling slightly, "so that it must have come up from the deck below."

"Was it a man?"

"It looked like a man, and a fairly tall one, but he came and was gone like a flash, and I saw no more of him up to the time I was relieved. To tell you the truth, I did not report it because I thought I must have been dozing; it's a dead slow watch, and the navigation on this part of the run is child's play."

I was on the point of telling him what I had seen myself, two evenings before, but for some reason I refrained from doing so, although I think had I confided in him he would have abandoned the idea that what he had seen was phantasmal; for the pair of us could not very well have been dreaming. Some malignant presence haunted the ship; I could not doubt this; yet I remained passive, sunk in a lethargy of sorrow.

We were scheduled to reach Port Said at about eight o'clock in the evening, but by reason of the delay occasioned so tragically, I learned that in all probability we should not arrive earlier than midnight, whilst passengers would not go ashore until the following morning. Karamaneh who had been staring ahead all day, seeking a first glimpse of her native land, was determined to remain up until the hour of our arrival, but after dinner a notice was posted up that we should not be in before two A.M. Even those passengers who were the most enthusiastic thereupon determined to postpone, for a few hours, their first glimpse of the land of the Pharaohs and even to forego the sight— one of the strangest and most interesting in the world—of Port Said by night.

For my own part, I confess that all the interest and hope with which I had looked forward to our arrival, had left me, and often I detected tears in the eyes of Karamaneh whereby I knew that the coldness in my heart had manifested itself even to her. I had sustained the greatest blow of my life, and not even the presence of so lovely a companion could entirely recompense me for the loss of my dearest friend.

The lights on the Egyptian shore were faintly visible when the last group of stragglers on deck broke up. I had long since prevailed upon Karamaneh to retire, and now, utterly sick at heart, I sought my own stateroom, mechanically undressed, and turned in.

It may, or may not be singular that I had neglected all precautions since the night of the tragedy; I was not even conscious of a desire to visit retribution upon our hidden enemy; in some strange fashion I took it for granted that there would be no further attempts upon Karamaneh, Aziz, or myself. I had not troubled to confirm Smith's surmise respecting the closing of the portholes; but I know now for a fact that, whereas they had been closed from the time of our leaving the Straits of Messina, to-night, in sight of the Egyptian coast, the regulation was relaxed again. I cannot say if this is usual, but that it occurred on this ship is a fact to which I can testify—a fact to which my attention was to be drawn dramatically.

The night was steamingly hot, and because I welcomed the circumstance that my own port was widely opened, I reflected that those on the lower decks might be open also. A faint sense of danger stirred within me; indeed, I sat upright and was about to spring out of my berth when that occurred which induced me to change my mind.

All passengers had long since retired, and a midnight silence descended upon the ship, for we were not yet close enough to port for any unusual activities to have commenced.

Clearly outlined in the open porthole there suddenly arose that same grotesque silhouette which I had seen once before.

Prompted by I know not what, I lay still and simulated heavy breathing; for it was evident to me that I must be partly visible to the watcher, so bright was the night. For ten—twenty—thirty seconds he studied me in absolute silence, that gaunt thing so like a mummy; and, with my eyes partly closed, I watched him, breathing heavily all the time. Then, making no more noise than a cat, he moved away across the deck, and I could judge of his height by the fact that his small, swathed head remained visible almost to the time that he passed to the end of the white boat which swung opposite my stateroom.

In a moment I slipped quietly to the floor, crossed, and peered out of the porthole; so that at last I had a clear view of the sinister mummy-man. He was crouching under the bow of the boat, and attaching to the white rails, below, a contrivance of a kind with which I was not entirely unfamiliar. This was a thin ladder of silken rope, having bamboo rungs, with two metal hooks for attaching it to any suitable object.

The one thus engaged was, as Karamaneh had declared, almost superhumanly thin. His loins were swathed in a sort of linen garment, and his head so bound about, turban fashion, that only his gleaming eyes remained visible. The bare limbs and body were of a dusky yellow color, and, at sight of him, I experienced a sudden nausea.

My pistol was in my cabin-trunk, and to have found it in the dark, without making a good deal of noise, would have been impossible. Doubting how I should act, I stood watching the man with the swathed head whilst he threw the end of the ladder over the side, crept past the bow of the boat, and swung his gaunt body over the rail, exhibiting the agility of an ape. One quick glance fore and aft he gave, then began to swarm down the ladder: in which instant I knew his mission.

With a choking cry, which forced itself unwilled from my lips, I tore at the door, threw it open, and sprang across the deck. Plans, I had none, and since I carried no instrument wherewith to sever the ladder, the murderer might indeed have carried out his design for all that I could have done to prevent him, were it not that another took a hand in the game....

At the moment that the mummy-man—his head now on a level with the deck—perceived me, he stopped dead. Coincident with his stopping, the crack of a pistol shot sounded—from immediately beyond the boat.

Uttering a sort of sobbing sound, the creature fell—then clutched, with straining yellow fingers, at the rails, and, seemingly by dint of a great effort, swarmed along aft some twenty feet, with incredible swiftness and agility, and clambered onto the deck.

A second shot cracked sharply; and a voice (God! was I mad!) cried: "Hold him, Petrie!"

Rigid with fearful astonishment I stood, as out from the boat above me leaped a figure attired solely in shirt and trousers. The newcomer leaped away in the wake of the mummy-man—who had vanished around the corner by the smoke-room. Over his shoulder he cried back at me:

"The bishop's stateroom! See that no one enters!"

I clutched at my head—which seemed to be fiery hot; I realized in my own person the sensation of one who knows himself mad.

For the man who pursued the mummy was Nayland Smith!

I stood in the bishop's state-room, Nayland Smith, his gaunt face wet with perspiration, beside me, handling certain odd looking objects which littered the place, and lay about amid the discarded garments of the absent cleric.

"Pneumatic pads!" he snapped. "The man was a walking air-cushion!" He gingerly fingered two strange rubber appliances. "For distending the cheeks," he muttered, dropping them disgustedly on the floor. "His hands and wrists betrayed him, Petrie. He wore his cuff unusually long but he could not entirely hide his bony wrists. To have watched him, whilst remaining myself unseen, was next to impossible; hence my device of tossing a dummy overboard, calculated to float for less than ten minutes! It actually floated nearly fifteen, as a matter of fact, and I had some horrible moments!"

"Smith!" I said—"how could you submit me..."

He clapped his hands on my shoulders.

"My dear old chap—there was no other way, believe me. From that boat I could see right into his stateroom, but, once in, I dare not leave it—except late at night, stealthily! The second spotted me one night and I thought the game was up, but evidently he didn't report it."

"But you might have confided..."

"Impossible! I'll admit I nearly fell to the temptation that first night; for I could see into your room as well as into his!" He slapped me boisterously on the back, but his gray eyes were suspiciously moist. "Dear old Petrie! Thank God for our friends! But you'd be the first to admit, old man, that you're a dead rotten actor! Your portrayal of grief for the loss of a valued chum would not have convinced a soul on board!

"Therefore I made use of Stacey, whose callous attitude was less remarkable. Gad, Petrie! I nearly bagged our man the first night! The elaborate plan—Marconi message to get you out of the way, and so forth—had miscarried, and he knew the porthole trick would be useless once we got into the open sea. He took a big chance. He discarded his clerical guise and peeped into your room—you remember?—but you were awake, and I made no move when he slipped back to his own cabin; I wanted to take him red-handed."

"Have you any idea..."

"Who he is? No more than where he is! Probably some creature of Dr. Fu-Manchu specially chosen for the purpose; obviously a man of culture, and probably of thug ancestry. I hit him—in the shoulder; but even then he ran like a hare. We've searched the ship, without result. He may have gone overboard and chanced the swim to shore..."

We stepped out onto the deck. Around us was that unforgettable scene—Port Said by night. The ship was barely moving through the glassy water, now. Smith took my arm and we walked forward. Above us was the mighty peace of Egypt's sky ablaze with splendor; around and about us moved the unique turmoil of the clearing-house of the Near East.

"I would give much to know the real identity of the bishop of Damascus," muttered Smith.

He stopped abruptly, snapping his teeth together and grasping my arm as in a vise. Hard upon his words had followed the rattling clangor as the great anchor was let go; but horribly intermingled with the metallic roar there came to us such a fearful, inarticulate shrieking as to chill one's heart.

The anchor plunged into the water of the harbor; the shrieking ceased. Smith turned to me, and his face was tragic in the light of the arc lamp swung hard by.

"We shall never know," he whispered. "God forgive him—he must be in bloody tatters now. Petrie, the poor fool was hiding in the chainlocker!"

A little hand stole into mine. I turned quickly. Karamaneh stood beside me. I placed my arm about her shoulders, drawing her close; and I blush to relate that all else was forgotten.

For a moment, heedless of the fearful turmoil forward, Nayland Smith stood looking at us. Then he turned, with his rare smile, and walked aft.

"Perhaps you're right, Petrie!" he said.